Salki

T0151553

Salki

Wojciech Nowicki

Translated from the Polish
by Jan Pytalski

OPEN LETTER

LITERARY TRANSLATIONS FROM THE UNIVERSITY OF ROCHESTER

Copyright © by Wojciech Nowicki, 2013. All rights reserved.
Published by arrangement with Wydawnictwo Czarne, Poland
Translation copyright © by Jan Pytalski, 2017
Originally published in Poland as *Salki*

First edition, 2017
All rights reserved

Library of Congress Cataloging-in-Publication Data: Available.
ISBN-13: 978-1-940953-58-8 | ISBN-10: 1-940953-58-8

Printed on acid-free paper in the United States of America.

Text set in Baskerville, a serif typeface originally designed in 1757 by
John Baskerville in Birmingham, England.

Design by N. J. Furl

Open Letter is the University of Rochester's nonprofit, literary translation press:
Lattimore Hall 411, Box 270082, Rochester, NY 14627

www.openletterbooks.org

During our trip we didn't see anything particularly interesting.
The landscape was flat.
—Anna Dostoyevskaya

Salki

Salki

The sea was barging in through the window and tree branches were scratching the walls of the hotel. It sounded as if workers were outside, high up on their scaffolds, chiseling off old plaster, but in fact it was the raging tempest. Earlier in the afternoon, I saw boats rocking in the harbor and the sun setting earlier than usual. The evening ferry was late for the first time in a month, and when it finally emerged from behind the trees along the shore, it looked as if it were plowing through each wave against a great force. The streets were deserted.

Back then, I'd already been in Gotland for a month. The next morning I was supposed to begin my journey back home, and someone promised to give me a ride to the harbor at seven in the morning. My bed was too short, too narrow, but I stayed up late and went to sleep early in the morning anyway, so I quickly stopped caring. I would collapse exhausted and wake up late. That last night I lay awake, trying to tame my wildly beating heart, cursing and guessing that it must've been out of sheer frugality that they built this bed so small. It's like they built it for a midget, just like this whole island with its one town and dwarf houses. Even their sheep were smallish, with a hint of black in their fleece. Their forests were stunted. I went to the bathroom to get some water. I consciously avoided looking at the clock.

3

This is how I am. It's called *reisefieber*—a measly ride across town and I start to feel uncomfortable, much less any longer journeys. I suffer from vertigo and insomnia, just like that time in Gotland. I throw fits of anger, targeting everybody in sight. I make lists of essentials and I become extremely methodical with packing. I stockpile unnecessary things, as if no stores exist wherever I'm going. I lie in bed and go through all those lists one more time, according to their priority: one, medication, I never leave without it; two, credit cards; three, documents; four, tickets. I could easily forget about the rest, I know that perfectly well, but I simply can't. It's stronger than me. I name objects one by one with malice: sweater, pair of pants, and another pair, shoes, batteries, on and on, until I'm done. For me, *reisefieber* is not merely a foreign word, smuggled into my own language, like *nachkastlik*—full of melody, but redundant and outdated. No, *reisefieber* is a condition impossible to overcome, a stab in the heart, pain that goes away only after I commence my journey. The only medicine for the fear of travel is travel itself. It's enough for me to stand in a line of passengers waiting to board—not for check-in, not for security screening, but boarding. I need the landing strip under my feet and a plane within hand's reach. It's enough for me to board a train, feel it slowly start, and a joyful pang of excitement takes the place of fear.

That night I finally went out into the corridor. As usual, it was brightly lit because in this Swedish abode everything was safe and comfortable. The lights were on even during the night, so that no guest would ever trip, even if coming back drunk. I went downstairs quietly, trying not to wake anyone. The wind howled all around us and all my efforts to stay quiet were pointless anyway, since every room was equally filled with noises from the storm. I went outside to smoke, to occupy my hands. I had to do something. So I smoked and wrestled with the wind, wondering if the ferry would leave as scheduled, if I'd make it to the airport on time. And fear was growing in me. I went to the other side of the street to take a closer look at a neighboring building. A lonely man lived in the basement. He had an aquarium and a TV set. He either played action video games, or watched porn. And if he ever got bored, he just changed the channel. He was currently in the middle of a movie—two women and a man. It looks comical when you have no sound on and the TV is in a basement turned into an apartment. It took them a while, then he switched the channel to a car race. I went back to my room.

"I stayed in bed for ample enough time to grant myself much desired rest" is what I should've written about that night, just like one diarist from the seventeenth century who will make an appearance on the following pages. But instead, I kept turning over, thinking about all the places I continually depart to but never reach, all my previous journeys, trips both long and short. Truth be told, it's when I travel that I feel at peace the most, and *reisefieber* has nothing to do with it. I thought how in the morning I would board the ferry. Even the seemingly dreadful thought of sailing the Baltic Sea during the storm—drowned in the smell of bar food which everyone will greedily assault the minute the lines are cast away—didn't cause me concern. For whatever reason, Swedes love food served on the ferries. None of my grandparents, or my parents, has ever set foot on a ferry. In the back of my mind, I keep comparing myself to them. It's only my generation, only me who goes back and forth like this. The striking difference between our lives has always made me lightheaded—as if we'd lived in two completely different worlds, separated by a hard membrane. That's what I was thinking about, while covering my head with a pillow, warding off the light, muting the howling wind.

"Why is that, anyway?" I kept thinking to myself. "Why do they sit in the same place all the time?" I guess they must be afraid of travel, and the act of departure must be seen as a betrayal of one's nature. It's almost as if it was every reasonable man's destiny to sit in one place, to never leave your permanent residence. They acted as if they expected the Last Judgment to occur any moment. And if it occurred while they were in transit, the angel—because it had to be a legitimate angel and not some minor celestial being—would not find them at home. They inhabited dull houses filled with furniture too big to fit in it, brought from God knows where, from their exile paradise, or inherited from old tenants. If there was even the smallest garden to go along with the house, there could be nothing else, no other pleasures, or foreign countries. It was always too far away anyway—too far even to the closest city, an hour away by train. They would never go by car. Cars were a sign of debauchery. It was far better to send letters and endlessly wait for responses. And if they never arrived, you'd curse the post office, or communism, so that everybody knew that the world, even here, right where you were, was a dreadful challenge. That's how I always thought of my family.

They were like mountains, fixed elements of the landscape, always there on the horizon. They would rarely visit the city and only for a very limited time, always forced by some official errands or necessary shopping. All of them indulged in housekeeping and cleaning. They tended their gardens. They sat on their porches and watched trees, watched TV, played cards, and knew each other's tricks by heart. Always at dawn, Grandma and Grandpa Kopiec would retreat to their marital bed and lie down under the painting of the Holy Family: Saint Joseph, an ax resting on his shoulder, and a plate of fruits in the other hand, little Jesus in a white baby gown standing on Mary's knees, holding an apple in one hand and reaching for more. In the background you could see cypresses, morning glories, and all was dark so that you could easily spot three distinct halos. There was one more painting in the room. It showed Mary Magdalene in a cave, with a skull, a book, and a naked breast. The painting was a copy of a work by Anton Raphael Mengs, although, looking at it for so many years, I wasn't even aware of said painter's existence; neither was the faithful copyist, I'm sure. He probably didn't know, just like I didn't, that the German painter Mengs, father of twenty, was born in

Aussig, or Uść, by the Elbe River. He was the son of Ismael Mengs, a painter from Denmark. All those years I slept in my grandparents' bed, I was blissfully unaware of being guarded by the painting of the Holy Family. The last work of art in their bedroom was a wooden sculpture of an eagle on a rock. It was a gift from our Ukrainian side of the family, and stood on an old wardrobe, a German leftover, that still gave off the scent of mothballs. You prayed to the Holy Family, Mary Magdalene was mysterious, and the eagle scared you—there was no escaping it, you don't choose your family.

Turning on the radio that resided in this very bedroom was Grandpa's best trick. The radio was mounted at the head of the bed, on its left-hand side. He would start turning a knob and the scale would gradually illuminate. The radio had to warm up. On the scale you could find names of different cities, and every day my grandparents would embark on an expedition from city to city, until they found their Holy Land again—the radio station to which they listened as if it were prophecy. The radio itself would crackle and when it finally spoke, the voice was forcible and it pronounced: "This is a Polish broadcast of Radio Free Europe!" The voice was otherworldly, extremely solemn, and I've never known anybody to speak in a voice like that. My grandparents lay next to each other, one shushing the other, since you could hardly hear anything, Grandpa always with his right hand by the knob, ready to act. The voice came in waves, it fluctuated, only to suddenly disappear among the whizz and cracks of jamming, as if swallowed by a swamp. Whenever that happened, Grandpa's hand turned the knob patiently, until the voice was recovered. "Air waves," to us, meant tidal patterns of the coming and going voice, uneasy matter, rowdy and hard to tame.

I lay in this midget Swedish bed, pondering the marital bed of my grandparents in their bedroom with windows facing one short and quiet street; their bedroom filled with the smell of freshly pressed sheets and covers. I lay there, trembling, reminding myself that it was time to finally fall asleep, to rest, even though I knew there was no chance for sleep that very night. And then, out of nowhere, it suddenly dawned on me. I realized that there's no chance for redemption, that this peculiar sickness, anxiety triggered by travel, was with me to stay. There's no point in asking for salvation. This is how it was and this is how it will be. Amen. As if in a chain reaction of epiphanies, I also understood what happened to my family: my grandparents, uncles and aunts, all the members of my clan frozen in their houses and gardens, under the frozen image of the Holy Family and in Mary Magdalene's cave, or in Munich, from where the news of the real world came. Listening to the sounds of gardens, the voices of the city—they sat calcified and the world kept spinning around them. In order to observe these perpetual movements, this unstoppable rush, you had to sit motionless in your own cage, calibrate yourself to receive. They were afraid, I realized, afraid of leaving. And leaving was the last thing they wanted. Cowered in my Swedish bed, my temporary safe haven, inundated by the rumble coming from outside, the whistling of the wind through the crack—probably the only crack on the entire island—in the window pane, I thought for a brief moment that I wanted to be just like them. I wished to become an active member of my tribe again, comply with its sacred laws, understand its fears. Because they were my fears as well.

I understood in an instant, just like that, why my great grandfather—whom I've never seen in entire my life, except in pictures (but I can't even remember them now)—never visited even once. For years, as a child, I was upset with Grandma Kopiec for not going to meet him in London. After all, she knew where he lived, knew his address, that he was still alive. Instead, they wrote letters to each other. She would share them over and over again, crying in the kitchen, or her room, and then wiping her nose with a kerchief in a dignified manner. After she calmed herself down, she would put the letter back in its neatly cut envelope and place it with the others, right where it belonged. In my family's houses, everything had its own place and order was to be observed. I had a quiet grudge against my grandma about her father, my great grandfather. I tried to convince her to travel, I asked why won't he visit us. "He can't," she would reply, communism being the excuse. But I was angry with her, not him somehow, even though he never budged his old ass, even though he never gave a shit about her.

This curious not-seeing between daughter and father had lasted since the war. I didn't know back then that it was his second escape; the escape of a rich farmer who mounted his horse and fled from his family the minute the war broke out. There was no news of Great Grandpa and suddenly, after many years, they found each other. In a time when everything seemed hopeless, it all turned out to be quite ordinary. Apparently, there was a misspelling in his last name and the Red Cross lost track of him in their registers. But who knows, maybe it was just another lie. They all used lies as a smoke screen, from behind which you could see only a blurred outline of a model family. Never mind. Grandma never left and there's no mystery to it—she was afraid. And he never really pressed too hard, either. He offered money for tickets, but never insisted too much. Maybe he didn't want to buy her the ticket, after all. He had his own life and its random fragments reached as far as my grandparent's garden in this post-German town of theirs. Pieces of life somehow ordered anew, and a daughter not seen for decades would be, after all, and maybe even particularly so, a nuisance.

My family sat firm in their garden chairs or ugly sofas all their lives. I couldn't figure it out until that night spent in my Swedish bed of the wrong size. All of them were parked in those chairs, on those sofas, by war, against their will. They wanted to live right where they were born, some at the outskirts of Ternopil, others in the Vilnius region. "Back there, everything was simpler, more beautiful, one's own," was how they would go on for hours among themselves, and to us, too, who never saw any of those places, who didn't care to listen and couldn't make heads or tails of what they were saying. They talked on about their misfortunes, full of rancor or simply boring with their mantra about cities cordoned off, cities lost, about cousins, aunts, friends who had been killed and buried in a ditch. "Shanked," my grandma would say—and nobody used words like she did. Their former lives were shanked to death, lost forever. They boarded cattle wagons, loaded with anything worth carting, and headed west. What they took, they lost along the way. They traveled for weeks, fearing for their lives, and they got off the train where the war had exiled others and where houses were there for the taking.

Grandpa was blue-eyed and resourceful. One of my aunts used to talk maliciously about his sexual excesses. She held the sins of his youth, his love conquests, against him. The stories she kept reviving were her revenge, but he paid her tit for tat. It was particularly easy, since she never stopped enjoying her life to the fullest, drinking vodka with great pleasure. They're both dead now, and it's awkward to ask my own mother how it really was; she probably wouldn't know herself. What I would really like is for this one story in particular to be true—the one of my grandpa running away, naked, on some dirt road, from a betrayed husband. So I proclaim its truth. My grandpa had an appetite for women, so chances are this chase could've happened. He was also the greatest "make-doer" in the family. He was the one who got paintings and sculptures for bread and vodka from the Ruskies. He got himself and Grandma a house, only God knows how. He was the one to run a little grocery store right outside the house, until you couldn't do that anymore, and then he switched to a government-owned operation. Dark like a gypsy, Grandmother despised her skin color, her brown, almost black eyes, she hated her aquiline nose with its little mole. She used to apply the lightest Yardley's face powder available, which my great grandpa would send her from England. It was one of the very few things she ever asked him for: always the same face powder, always the lightest, the brightest one, to hide the mark of her exotic beauty. With all this face powder, sitting in the church, she looked like a black actress playing a white woman in a silent film. But she smelled fabulous. Their faces, histories, misfortunes—it all came from out there, from their previous life, which I had no idea about because it was of no interest to me. I didn't listen to them for years, I was bored with their monologues, consistently, until they all died. Now, everyone is gone and there's no one left to ask. I lived immersed in my own life, which was anchored neither here nor there. That's what occupied my thoughts as I was lying in my midget's bed, scared to death God knows how many times over.

The heavy rain came down, streets were wet, and girls stuck to their soaked skirts just like a quarter of a century ago. It smelled the same back then, I remembered, although it was a different city and so long ago. That day, I was sitting on a bench and a barefoot girl walked by. She asked if I had a cigarette. Shivering, she smoked, cried, and soon left.

This time around, we were sitting in some restaurant's garden patio, in the back of a tenement house. From where we were, you could simultaneously see how magnificent and murky Krakow is. You could see how the city's facade is supported by the shapeless mass of concrete hidden in the back. The facade is beautiful, behind it—mold. In the skies, there was a bright star shining and nothing had prophesied the upcoming winter yet. There was very little light, an ashtray, a glass, a tablecloth, the glimpse of a passing hand. We were in high spirits, since the conversation was about diseases and that's always a good topic, an uplifting one. "Write it down," I heard S. saying at one point, "at least you'll have something to do, at least you'll get it off your chest."

I was telling him how, back in school, I lost consciousness in the gym once. I woke up in the hospital, surrounded by pregnant women and elderly people, waiting patiently like only they can wait. Not much time passed and soon I woke up again, above me were the basketball hoop and my P.E. teacher, telling the paramedics to hurry, screaming that he's here, right here, and why won't they fucking move?! At the hospital, they said people faint sometimes, but to make sure they ordered some additional tests. I remember how the doctor said "Well, unfortunately, our suspicions turned out to be correct," and when I heard that, everything came crashing down.

There were ups and downs. The tedious run to catch a morning train, too much or too little of something, and I'm already gone. I open my eyes, but I can't see anything. Someone talks to me, and I go "Eh, eh." I begin to understand that there are pipes and fluorescent lamps running above my head and someone says "Hold it," and something cold lands on my forehead. I lay on the ground, under the blanket, still in my winter jacket and boots, terrazzo tiles pressed against my cheek. White dots, black dots, gray. I can see somebody's hand hanging off the stretcher. A lady leans over me and says "Don't cry, what's your name, tell me your name," and I can't remember. Later, my father shows up, "You blacked out on the bus, they found your ID and called home." He helps me get out of bed and I'm like jam from a broken jar pouring out of my backpack onto the floor. This is how it was, more or less. This is how I kept trying to run away, tripping all the time, from my first city.

Where I live now, everyone knows everybody else, and when people pass each other on the street, they say "Hello," because they are either related or at least went to school together. This is my town, historical, built on bones. This town will always be praised because it praises itself. And in the city I come from there's almost no history left, just a few sandstone tombs and one tower. The rest was either destroyed, flooded, or the wood rotted and didn't last. Two sandstone tombs and a tower, a few decrepit cars in the museum's basement, "and the rest is German leftovers" people whispered. People from Opole talked about the history as if only bits and pieces were preserved, only little islands of memory, as if only the Piast dynasty ever reigned there.

And if it was a Piast ruler it must've been a Pole. Apart from that, only a few moments in history are worth one's attention: a German, who by definition is an invader, later the Red Army—always victorious—and back to us-ness and to *our* Poland. That was the official version of history at the time of my escape.

Back in school, we used to go out with our P.E. teacher to wash the monument commemorating Soviet soldiers, to wash their gravestones in return for their saving this hyper-Polish city of Oppeln from the German invaders. Whenever I go to visit Ukraine, to immerse myself in me, when in truth I immerse myself in mendacity, I look at it with a peculiar kind of calmness. I know all the lies by heart, straight from the cement-mill city, the capital of bullshit, where all was of Piast decent and Polish. That's what they taught us. But in the Silesian plebiscite, and it's worthwhile to take a closer look at the numbers, over ninety percent of my city said they stood by the Germans, with a little less in the countryside—over seventy percent. No wonder they had to push this bullshit in the schools and newspapers. And so, when I travel to Ukraine and I hear: "Poles, the masters," "Poles, the butchers" and I see heirs of Stepan Bandera in their black uniforms, marching in the streets, raising their banners with the trident, I know that my grandmother, all my aunts, my grandfather, and his family shudder in their graves, whispering curses. And with them, all of their children and their siblings murdered in Gaje Wielkie shudder and curse too. There are young men in boots, marching with banners bearing something resembling a swastika, always more menacing when speaking in an alien tongue. I see them and I feel ill, but I know that this is how it has to be. To form a nation they have to obliterate all other nations, they have to tell the same, simplified version of history, where you have room only for your own people. They march with their banners and tell the story of a nation that went from rags to riches.

I feel calm when I see this, because I myself used to go with a scrubbing brush to clean bird shit from the monument with the red star. With a circular motion, I soaped the gravestones in the only cemetery in the city that no one in a right mind ever visited. Only the party members paid visits, always on a particular day of a particular anniversary; the anniversary of the liberation of the city, or the Great October Socialist Revolution. And we had to scrub those gravestones and throw away last year's wreaths, so they wouldn't be celebrating in a pigsty. "Let's pay tribute . . . for tomorrow, bring cleaning supplies, detergent, a scrubbing brush, and a bucket." But in reality, the party chose us because the labor was free, and our school was the closest one.

We washed other monuments, symbols of the Polish Spirit, too. For punishment, or as a reward, they would send me to the park in front of the post-German church. Back then, people said things like that openly, everything was post-something, only lately has language become so impossibly polished, so oily. I was sent there for misdemeanors never proven, so technically, nonexistent—for some vulgar writing on the wall with a crayon. I was sent to scrub Adam Mickiewicz. It was a little bust, but what a shit-magnet. I went there with the same brush, the same bucket I took to tackle the Ruskies. The janitor lady handed out the equipment from her house by the school soccer field. I remember the layout of the place, but I check Google Earth anyway. In a picture taken from space, there's no janitor's house anymore, but I can see the windows of the classrooms where I took Polish, chemistry, physics, and geography classes—the last three without success.

And so I get hooked on spying from space, obviously, and I look at Mickiewicz's bust from above and can see that he is still bothered by the birds. Guano runs from the tip of his head, leaving a white trail that meanders by his nose, turns under his eye and freezes on

15

his cheek. But compared to the old days, he's relatively clean. "In the memory of the nation's bard" is what it says on the pedestal. This bard was placed facing the street, with a church in the background. And it's no coincidence at all as he was supposed to separate the city from the temple.

This was supposed to be my city, because I was born here. But my folks claimed otherwise. They worked, they labored to make ends meet, but neither of them was born here. Every member of my family came from somewhere else, was uprooted and planted again. Post-German hospital, post-German church—I remember the mute rage of our people—people from the East—when *they* started having church services in German. For many, even several dozen years after the great carnage, it was outrageous. And we're not talking about masses dedicated to the Waffen-SS, but to our neighbors from around the corner. My people—people from nowhere—settled on the bones of another nation, on the streets and squares named after the heroes of a class warfare that was meaningless to them. There was a street named after Rosa Luxemburg, and other small and quiet streets filled with tenement houses and courtyards—before the war named Damaschkestrasse, and now Lviv Eaglets street, or Lenin's Square. There were streets named after Julian Marchlewski, Lucjan Szenwald, and the favorite of the masses—Felix Dzerzhinsky. There was a street dedicated to the Red Army, which they cleverly renamed to praise the Home Army. Liebknecht stepped down and Eichendorff stepped in. And Michurin's street changed to I don't even know what.

For them, it was a great orbiting of the planets, an endless universe. They left their little patch of land, stepped off the cattle-train cars and stepped onto the streets with German plaques, with houses still filled with Germans, or Silesians, whom they equally disregarded. And then again, once more, everything had to be renamed. There came a parade of Lenins, Michurins, lasting for almost all of their adult lives.

Our people's attics were spacious and clean—empty spaces without a past. You only entered the attic with good reason. It's where you'd find coffers reminding of unsuccessful travels, and laundry was dried there on the rainy days. Silesians' attics were full, goods were stored in woven baskets, objects spilled over the rims. I could list them for hours, items like the *Brockhaus Encyclopedia*—mint condition—a sign that things used to be different around here. And it wasn't about the Germans, but about the era in which the household of C, in whose attic I leafed through the encyclopedia, was a household where people read. Even more, it was a household that felt the need to possess artifacts of the printed word. Multiple prayer books, all in German, useless now, all in different states of decomposition. But you don't throw things like that away. You can burn them, but it seems like C's family didn't dare. No one made use of them since the grandmother died—the last one in the family to speak German and to the very end furious with her grandsons who, even when encouraged by beating, never learned even a few sentences in the language. The posthumous victory of the grandmother, however, was colossal. All thanks to the younger, less talented, grandson. That was the same boy who, two years after a slightly delayed graduation from primary school, came to the school soccer field on his motorcycle and, in an act of revenge for all his humiliations, took a brick and smashed the window of the physics classroom. Both the window and the soccer field I can still see from space. That's how Waldek was—stubborn. He was the one who would soon present his late grandmother with eternal satisfaction. In the end, he immigrated to Germany and learned to stutter a few sentences in their alien tongue. He didn't need much more, his work required more muscle than linguistic proficiency.

I look at his old house from space, I glare from above. Waldek himself wouldn't recognize the place. The old house has evolved into a monstrous manor a couple times larger than what we explored together while lost in the attic, staring at the Bible written in German

Gothic, discovering (me—with astonishment, him—with laughter) Hitler's portrait and his family's military uniforms, neatly folded: souvenirs of service in the Wehrmacht; discovering old photographs, tired Silesian headscarves—this whole massive collection that clearly stated it was me and all of my people who were alien to the place. And once the time is right, we would be thrown out again.

I remember the soil. It seems a little strange to remember soil, but what can I do? All around the house, the ground would keep exuding scraps, already digested and no longer disgusting. Although peeled of all their meaty pulp after being buried for so long, you still could tell our house was built on top of *something*. "I brought over so much good, dark soil," my father kept saying, "and just look what's going on here!" And so we would pick up whatever it was, or poke it with a stick—the *thing* found under the apple tree. Among the things we found were bones of farm animals, which I thought was normal, because we always found them, but my father was perpetually surprised, always shaking his head, uneasy and fearing that it would never end. Rags, pieces of clothing bleached colorless, parts of—I don't know—furniture, wood and metal shrapnel polished by the subterranean undertows—it was all expelled from the organism, as if underground frictions pushed everything up to the surface. We stood by my neighbors' fence, right where the compost box used to be in this not yet perfect, empty garden. It was a garden that years later would become exuberant with artificial ponds, covered with little rocky, flowery hills. It would spread and would be constantly limited from spreading too much. We stood there and before us was a bone, cleaned by something of all its meat. Sometimes, the edge of something buried would stick out, and later a larger part of what it was would be revealed, some handle maybe, a part of a washbasin, the metal bucket's bottom with a crown of rust. Glass was the worst because you could get cut. There was no grassy carpet yet to protect your feet from broken bottles the color of pale green or dirty brown, camouflaged and hidden between lumps of soil. Father kept bending over, always bending over, to collect those objects spat out by the earth. "Look" he said, counting all the horse-carts of soil he traded for vodka or money. "Here, I dumped half a meter, or maybe even a meter, I don't remember, there was so much of it. And look! Things still come out."

Our house is built on what used to be a dump, right behind the last garden of German houses in the new town. Those who came afterward, as if to be ridiculed, had to live on a dump, in the Oder River floodplain, or right by the cemetery. The city expanded, devouring villages and fields. And beneath our house all was busy, buzzing, and I kept imagining what richness had gathered, over time, under the concrete slab of our foundations. I thought about the day when all of it would finally flex its muscle, the surge would rise and rip the concrete, barging inside the basement; a wave of trash on which my parents built their lives, or rather had their lives built by a collective of drunks, thieves, and sons of bitches. I imagined these tensions, pressures under the thin skin of the earth, effects of which I've seen every day in the garden. "Why on the dumpsite?" I kept asking, "Wasn't there any better place?" They mumbled some excuses. I didn't understand yet, that it was all there was, that any other choices were only in my head. That was all they had. And they were happy with it, my father, my mother—children of the displaced, the displaced themselves. That was their journey, from dreams about the better future, commenced back in the East, through the bloody harvest in Aunt Janka's room, through cattle cars filled with belongings lost along the way, to the slow growth of the roots in the ground, which wasn't even ground, but a landfill mix of rotting particles covered by a thin layer of soil. Other members of my clan ended up inhabiting the old apartments—shells—still warm from the exiled German snails. "Is it really surprising?" I thought to myself in my narrow bed on a narrow Swedish island, over the beating of the wind and rain on my not-so-tightly sealed window. "Can anyone really wonder about their calcification? Can I really be surprised they invest all the money they make in their houses on that dump; houses which they've turned into an oasis?"

We were driving through Budapest; somewhere past Kecskemét we started anxiously looking for a rest stop, for strong coffee. It seemed like it was going to be an all-night drive. At first the road was empty, but suddenly the surge of cars washed over us and we found ourselves in the middle of a giant shoal. You could spot plates from Germany, Netherlands, Switzerland, and Austria, but they were clearly traveling together. It felt like a reunion of people from the same village who happened to meet in the middle of a highway and decided to keep each other company—everyone with a car completely loaded up, with chairs and tables on their roofs. Three generations, sometimes four, traveled together in one car. All Turks. They were headed home, I guess, because it was hard to call it a holiday destination. Regardless of their passports, their home is always there and if my family would've lived in different times, modern ones, they would probably do the same: go back and forth between the new home and the old one. But now what? All they are left with is pacing sadly from wall to wall, from house to garden, trapped, as if in a jar stored at the bottom of an old wardrobe.

We tried stopping at different gas stations, but we couldn't stop at any of them because there was not a single empty spot, as if Hungary had become too small, as if they'd ran out of space for even one more car, as if that would take it over the limit. The Turks parked randomly, according to their liking, and usurped every parking space, every pit stop. Even the truck drivers couldn't fit, so they parked on the highway. They not only took over the parking lots, but parked right next to the gas tank, at the exits, on the lawns, everywhere: three, four, five rows of cars. They took over the cafe, restrooms, those lawns, and playgrounds. Collectively, they occupied the bathrooms, they shaved and brushed their teeth, they stood in their T-shirts in front of splashed mirrors. An old man raised his foot to the sink with both hands, his leg plowed thoroughly with varicose veins. You could tell he was on the cusp, that he wouldn't make it much longer. They prayed on their little carpets, between the restrooms and a dumpster. Two women wrapped in towels smoked cigarettes and scolded their children in German in the beer garden. The Turkish women of a new era, raised in German freedom, among dozens, hundreds of other Turkish women dressed all in black. Others gathered inside the bar, pulling out food from containers, pouring coffee from thermoses, and the service people had long ago given up. They stopped cleaning, stopped making remarks—there was no point. This Turkish deluge was like a wall. It was here and had no intention of moving anywhere else or assimilating. There were hundreds of bundled-up people, mostly elderly, resting on the lawns. The younger generation gathered around their cars. In the past they probably gathered around their horses, patted them on the side, praised their virtues, how they shined, their color, appreciated how well kept they were, how their teeth were still white and not yet abraded. Now they were sitting all together, puffing their pipes, a Turk from Germany helping a Turk from the Netherlands, and while according to the passports it's a German helping a Dutch, it's a sham and they know it. These are all Turks sitting around their cars, praising their own rides, checking the suspension, because something's dented and screeching. They are like neighbors from the same village, neighbors separated only by a short fence, even though in reality they are separated by a number of borders. Even when in Turkey they live on two different continents.

Those who were thrown among the Turks by accident kept warning one another. They would call each other from the border and say: "They're here, run, the customs officer said 30 kilometers up north it's still clean." Massive bird migrations, locusts, only these come to mind. Black, screaming flocks of birds hovering over cities when it's cold. They circle the city and have nowhere to land. These Turks look the same, freezing before dawn, exhausted, they push forward to their distant villages in cars that they prepped to look like new. But even in the dark of night you can tell they aren't. So they ride and when they stop to rest they pray for safe travels, and there is a lot to pray for. That's why they feel better as a group, as if they were afraid to be on their own. So they go, the Turkish court, the Turkish nation in exile. And they carry their mosque inside them, or maybe they've already forgotten about their mosque. They go till they can't go anymore. They build huge camps on the borders, and the closer they get to home, the more anxious and impatient they get. The customs of migratory species always evoke awe and astonishment. It's enough to say: "Sargasso Sea" and the *perpetum mobile* of imagination is unleashed. It's a peculiar sea anyway, always on the move, without concrete land borders, locked between currents. It is a prison on a vast open expanse, so naturally it invites myths like no other place. Here, similarly, the highway and its infrastructure are the sea and it's enough to step aside to see the kingdom on the move, the sultanate of outcasts loaded with tourist equipment and blue portable refrigerators. This is how Turkish eels swim back to their sea, to their nest.

In the morning you think it never happened. It couldn't have happened. An exodus of such magnitude simply never happens in our part of the world. Nobody is there, but the lawns have impressions in the shapes of men, and a guy whose car won't go any farther sits alone. He sits, smoking, the ground around him carpeted with wrappers, bottles. Where there were dumpsters the other day, there are now heaps, mountains of trash. The garbage collector hasn't made it from the city yet. It's a gutter after the Turkish aerial kingdom left, but it's always that way. Our knowledge of kingdoms of yore comes from places like this, it comes from their landfills and graves. From their crappers comes our knowledge. It's only a few hours, but it already feels like something that happened in a different life, or didn't happen at all. The Turkish cars will soon reach Nišu, from where they will turn east and head home through Bulgaria.

I tried to imagine how it would look with my own family, what a commotion would arise, how cautiously they would dial the phone numbers on their rotary telephones. They didn't have modern ones, because they refused to acknowledge them. They found buying such novelties to be extravagant and in bad taste. Their kingdom seemed to be truly otherworldly. And so they would dial their phone numbers, make arrangements for years on end to go and visit their old villages, their old neighborhoods. But they never went. With a cup of tea and a random hand of cards, with a little bit of vodka in their glasses, they discussed the beauty of their old country, which has now become a dumpsite and a grave, a treasury of useless knowledge about the past. They made use of this odd wealth willingly, sharing with others, convinced that it's a gesture of utmost generosity, worthy of praise. They schemed via letters with the family members who stayed, agreed on dates, planned on buying tickets. They polished their shoes and packed whatever they could pack. They went only once.

embarked on a great journey to Ternopil with them in 1975. It wasn't like a holiday trip; it was more of a homecoming to a place they'd had to run from thirty years earlier. We set out late in the evening. I shared the same fear, and theirs vibrated in unison with mine. When the train finally rolled into the Opole Główne station, we started to run from one end of the platform to the other, from car to car, finally realizing it was pointless. We stood looking up at the windows, and saw people crammed between the bags and suitcases. Finally, somebody managed to address the mercy of a train conductor and we got a place in a cargo car. There was a cargo car attached to the end of the train, as if only for the members of my clan to return home the same way their exile had been executed, to nourish and nurture the conviction they had deep inside: that travel cannot be pleasurable. It doesn't bring you closer to anything and there's nothing decent about it.

Someone grabbed me and pulled me up. The door shut and my eyes took a while to get used to the darkness. At first I sat and later I lay down on the roped stacks of newspapers that filled the entire cargo car. I could smell the ink and it stuck to my face a little. The door would open at every station and a railroad worker would grab some newspapers and unload them, until there were very few left, almost none. Only the grownups' suitcases and children's bags were left. Just enough to sit on. The door opened for the last time, the remaining newspapers made an arc in the air and slapped the concrete of the station. They told us to get off.

The border station was crowded. Men in uniforms cruised between passengers and their luggage. It was dawn.

I woke up in Lviv. We exited the train station. I saw a truck loaded with sand going through the gate of the church of St. Elizabeth. It had been turned into a building-supplies depot. In the streets you could see tank-trucks with "beer" and "kvass" written on their sides. They had to read it for me, since I didn't know the Cyrillic alphabet. Everything was different.

My aunt and her husband waited for us in Ternopil. "He's not our family," my grandmother told me about the uncle, "he only married your auntie." My aunt and the rest of my relatives, which I didn't take into consideration at that time, were Ukrainian. In the evenings, my uncle sat in the kitchen drinking pure spirits, smelling the whole-wheat bread and biting into a stick of butter. He was a pleasant man with glassy eyes visited by men similar to him—quiet and resigned alcoholics. We went to different households filled with different alcoholics, where my cousins lived with their hair braided in one long plait, tied with a bow and dressed in draped suspender skirts. House bathtubs were filled with cold water, bottles submerged, all of that ready for us, vodka for men and champagne and beer for women and children. Aunt Milasia's ducks were fed with duckweed from the pond and bread from the local store. By every block of flats was a bulletin board with descriptions of despicable crimes and a picture of the criminal, a name, a patronymic and a last name: "Fifteen years old, she smoked cigarettes and skipped classes." I spent time by the river with one of my younger uncles. We could communicate easily. He told me: "My brother drowned. He drove his car into the river, didn't see the bridge, it was a dark night and he was drunk." The wife of my fellow fisherman dried fish on a laundry line. I felt like I was a part of something big and momentous. Fish was a snack for when you drink, so you needed a lot of it. On Saturdays we bathed in the garden, one after another, in a tub by the wooden fence. My aunt heated the water in a large kettle. My grandmother cried openly and my grandfather tried to hide his tears. I didn't understand that this was what they were telling me about, that this was their paradise lost.

His name was Bednarski, Franciszek Bednarski, I think. They used to call him *wujcio*—a sweet diminutive for uncle—*wujcio* Bednarski. That was their speech, full of endearments. He was one of those who died years before I was born, the part of the family I have never met yet was always present. "Oh, *wujcio* this, oh *wujcio* that, oh . . . right, you've never met him." And they would keep on going, because the tempest of the past's description was their native element. Those stories weren't of great deeds because my family was never involved in greatness or grandeur, maybe except for the war, something they couldn't control anyway. Butter, for example, I remember clearly; stories about butter back there and then and here and today. Butter, a long time ago and way back when, was yellow and buttery, fat like butter should be, and always fresh. Or sugar. The sugar we have now was a symbol of humanity's fall and both grandmothers, otherwise cold toward one another, remained disturbingly unanimous. "Sugar is less sweet, it's bland," one would say, "you need much more of it than before." The other one was far more radical in her statements. "They put salt in our sugar," she would say, and my brother and I would knock on our foreheads. "Salt in sugar," she would say, "I can taste it!" That was her revenge. Salt in sugar was her slap in the face aimed at those above her, and, of course, a prologue of the upcoming fall—but hers this time. That was certain.

However, *wujcio* Bednarski. He belonged to this better, older generation. They would show me pictures of a bald elder with a thick mustache, or that's what I thought back then. I had no idea that mustaches used to be a thing, a fashion, because he wasn't that old after all. *Wujcio* was a principal in a local, rural primary school, they would tell me, and a school principal before the war—heavy stress on "before the war"—he was a somebody. "He was a very important person," my grandmother would say, and everyone nodded approvingly. Besides Bednarski, there was also Grandmother's cousin, a doctor. When he was in school, all the money went to him because he had certain demands. "Everything," Grandmother would repeat, "Absolutely everything had to be of the highest quality." The suit, the boots, the suede gloves. His winter coat—the best. Everything expensive. Once when his father saved up some money and bought a different kind of boots, "a little cheaper, but still very good," Grandmother assured us. "He took one look, took the shoes, and chopped them up with an ax in complete silence. So he had to get the new ones, there was no choice." You couldn't detect any scorn in her voice, even though she'd rather let you cut off her hand than destroy her clothes herself, not to mention shoes. But he was allowed, he was designated to do great things, he was supposed to become a doctor and start a new chapter in the family's history. He was different, better, a Golem made of a mediocre clay, of us—a Ukrainian of the new era, ambitious and well educated. Nothing came of it, of course. The war started and somebody shot him against a fence, after a mere two years of his medical practice.

Bednarski graduated from a teaching seminar. Ternopil didn't offer more, and that's the reason for such an abundance of educators in my family, almost no one managed to break away. There is one class picture left in the album. He's sitting in a chair under a tree, and you can immediately tell it's the countryside, thatched roofs all around. The bald dome of his head, as usual, and his mustache handsomely trimmed. There is a kind of, let me think, a kind of austerity in his pose, one leg over the other, hands flat on his thighs, trousers neatly pressed, you could cut steel with their creases. His tie violently seizes his neck and his head faces the camera. There are children on both sides. I count bare feet and shoes and attempt to reach some conclusions from the proportions of one to the other but it's pointless, since the entire picture is a farce. After all, these clothes aren't theirs, they were borrowed, or just passed on and will be passed on further—small suits worn for decades. Some lose their hands in sleeves too long, others wear pants too short. Girls are in dresses remade from their mothers' dresses; these are not children's patterns and designs. Little suits and bare feet, dirty all the way up above the ankle, and so they sit in the dirt of some backyard or road. Some of the kids wear ribbons and soon they will grow up a little and start killing one another. The ones with ribbons will start, those without them will fight back, if they survive. Among them *wujcio*, with a face of a god, a just tribune, deliverer of punishment and reward.

I don't even know what the name of the school was or where the picture was taken. About him and others I know very little; I've no idea where they were born or where they lived. All I know is what happened to some of them.

My aunt would come from far away. The Christmas tree was in the corner, and after midnight there was carp in jelly and vodka in small glasses. "*Zdrowie*," my grandfather would say, and they would clink glasses ceremoniously. All the ladies would gasp loudly to let everyone know how unused to drinking vodka they were, and Grandmother would even close her eyes and make faces. They would drink vodka and explain it helps digestion; my aunt would drink sitting all stiff in her chair. She barely swallowed and the story would begin and everyone knew that this is how it would be because it's how it had always been. She had only one story: it was in Gaje Wielkie, the troops of Stepan Bandera came into the house and murdered the entire family. "I was laying in bed, Mom was there, Father was there" she would talk about the rest of the family and I can't remember exactly what, and why there were so many people in the house. Maybe someone came to visit, like it happens in the countryside, like when there's a war? "When *they* came, I jumped behind the bed and lay quietly on the floor, quiet as a mouse, and they kept shooting at Mommy, at Daddy, until they'd murdered them all. Six people, six, all in front of me. And they kept killing our people all through the night. In the morning they dragged everyone out and buried them in a mass grave by the Orthodox Church. Only my family," she would tell us "was buried by the house, right where the trees were planted the other day." And she would start weeping, nothing could stop her now. She wept all the time anyway, waving her arms as if drunk, and then going back to peaceful weeping. Her eyes simply got wet, as if she suffered form chronic eye inflammation, and she delivered her story like a poorly trained actor. Bandera's soldiers, the bed, the floor, killing, running into the night. And again, trembling as if from Parkinson's disease, every tremble releasing an identical little cloud of history. I hated her. I begged my parents to never invite her again with her bloody story; a story that leads to madness. I didn't care about Bandera, about the Ukrainian Insurgent Army. For them, Bandera was as obvious as dirt, water, or air was for me—they were convinced you don't need to explain those things. Just like Gaje Wielkie, which was an empty sound, impossible to understand, full of grief over what was long lost. Their national identification cards claimed they were born in the USSR, and I couldn't understand it. My family used words that nobody knew, nobody used, that had nothing to do with our half of the house and garden in this post-German city. They would say: "*ryskal*" instead of shovel, "*banderowcy*" for the Bandera troops, "*upowcy*" for the Ukranian Insurgent Army, and they would say "*taskać*" instead of "carry"; I started talking like them and my brother would go berserk. "You talk like a Ukrainian!" he would shout, not sensing that, in part, he was one himself. My father's family, on the Nowicki side, would speak differently too. For example: "*salki*"—we didn't know this word. *Salki* are the rooms in an attic; they also used "*nyże*," for places where you can store your memories and memorabilia right above your head. Just like those stories here, the *salki* of my memory, which I open for everyone. They would even call to the hens differently, "*pul, pul, pul*" instead of "cheep, cheep, cheep," and even my Lithuanian grandparents differed in this regard; a difference according to which history established its own border—my grandfather came from Lithuania, my grandmother from Belarus. They would say "*przeżegrać*" instead of burn through, and describe a long-legged horse; when the skies were ripped open by a distant storm you could hear the silent *małanka*—silent lightning. It was where they lived that you could find *żagary*—brushwood—growing, they were the ones who would go out to get some *braha*—leftover home brew. Their language was otherworldly, from a beautiful yet grim fairytale that they nurtured within them, even though they seemed cheerful and pleasant. They would contract the disease through foul air, spoil other's minds, even though during the day you wanted to sit with them forever. Dividing lines went straight through the middle of the family, through the room, the table, the bed. Two brothers would face each other, one a Polish soldier, the other a Lithuanian policeman. Their children live in different countries and know very little about each other; and it can't be glued back together. On both sides of the border they would curse the enemy and praise the memory of their own people; it's hardly surprising they didn't want to remember the others. They were labeled themselves, oppressed, so they labeled and oppressed others, not even realizing that they did.

I feel better now," my Aunt would say, still crying. "There's no more suffering, no more of this constricting pain. It's been so many years, so many, I've cried enough. It's been going on since March 27, 1945. There's no more fear about how I'm going to keep on living. Back then, they took away everything, they stole everything with the murders in Gaje Wielkie. I didn't have a single shirt to put on my back after they murdered my parents. Nothing to wear, nothing to eat, no parents," she would tell us. "And this helplessness, horror . . . I didn't know how I was going to make it."

We had to calm her down because she would talk about everything at once, about her dreams and those of others, about the prophecies from the dreams becoming reality. She dreamt that it was 1942 and she was walking on an asphalt road, nothing around her, only the gray ground, gray ground. She kept walking and every time she reached the horizon there was just more road. But she kept walking because she wasn't carrying anything and it was an easy walk. She was wearing a dress, shoes, her hands were empty. And after the seventh horizon she reached a cliff: the asphalt ended and dropped into a giant canyon, a river at its bottom, and terrifying waves kept echoing, foaming in rage. On the other side was her family, and others, but she couldn't cross because the river was as wide as the Styx. And so she kept waiting for decades, she waited for the number of

35

the deceased in her family to match what was foretold, to match the number of those standing on the other side of that dream river.

And afterward, as if fulfilling some calling, she would begin to talk about the place she used to live in. She would say: "My father used to teach in Gaje Wielkie, next to Ternopil, even though he was already retired. There wasn't enough money because when the Russians came to Ternopil, we lost everything. Gaje was a village stretched along the road," she kept describing with passion, and she only had passion for things past. "It was situated almost inside the forest itself. It wasn't like any other village: house, house, house, garden, orchard." "We would say that every house was hidden in the bushes" my grandmother would add. "A beautiful village. A beautiful oak park. Before the war, the wealthy would drive in their *fiakry*—horse carriages—to vacation there, as they say. The school in Gaje was almost inside the forest, too, and my father was afraid to live there, even though they offered him an apartment. 'It's so grim out there,' he would say 'and those Ukrainians all around do nothing but watch us.' So we rented a house in the village." She would stop. And now I don't know, listening to the recording—because, thank God, my father recorded her for the radio—if they were really scared way back then, or if the fear imposed itself on her memories later.

And after that, with her unbearably high-pitched voice, a voice that was fast and rambling, she would tell the story of a murder—the most important moment of her life. For Easter the whole village took up a collection and every teacher was supposed to get some flour. "My father took the horse cart," she would tell us, "and went around to deliver this flour and when he came back it was already dark, maybe around eight at night. He was tired, he ate his dinner and went to bed." She would add that they must've sent him around with the flour on purpose, to wear him down, because otherwise he would never go by himself, he was lazy by nature. "We women, we stay up talking for a little longer," she'd report for the nth time. "We ate dinner," and she told us about the dinner because there were no parts to the story that were irrelevant, all of it had to be told, "and only then did we go to bed. We slept for maybe an hour, it was eleven at night when Bandera's men started knocking, waking everybody up, and we knew it was them, my father knew they were out there. A local farmer brought them to us. He told us they were coming, but he said we shouldn't be afraid, that they just wanted to talk."

"I had a friend named Jańcia," my aunt would digress again, "and half a year earlier she told me on the road in Gaje"—today I remember that road in Gaje Wielkie, I stood in the middle of it not so long ago, your average asphalt street in the middle of today's Ternopil, full of potholes and surrounded by uninteresting buildings—"so Jańcia, a friend whose parents were well off because they went to America once, she told me that Bandera's men came to them dressed in Polish uniforms. They came and asked for some hay for their horses, and spoke beautiful Polish." But my aunt, clever from the crib, would ask Jańcia: "And how did you know they were Bandera's?" "Because," Jańcia would answer, "at the end they asked us: 'Don't we speak beautiful Polish?'" And after forty something years my aunt would keep quoting them with the same spite in her voice. "Do you like us as Poles?" And Jańcia, this friend from Gaje, would reply, "Well, I like you as men," because she already knew what was going to happen. "Her father, Mr. Wagner, gave Bandera's men some hay, and about a half a year later," she would tell us, forgetting for a second about her own family's fate, "when this big murder happened they killed Jańcia's parents too, and they ripped open her belly, like that, into four flaps, and nestled her brother's head in her entrails."

"The killing itself was quick," she continued matter-of-factly about her own family.

"Three men came in, all very tall. All with long beards and machine guns. 'Documents!' Two of them came into the room and went straight to Tońcio's bed. 'Who are you?' 'I'm a Pole.' Tońcio was very sick and pale. Later they came to me, I was in bed with little Zdzisio. 'And you?' So I told them *'ya dochka'* because I didn't want to anger them. And they responded *'nie boysia, tiebia nitchevo nie budiet'*—'don't worry, you'll be all right.' When he said that, I felt a rush of panic, I didn't know what to do." She would say this, and her voice, already nauseating with its high pitch, would start drilling through the ceiling, trying to escape outside. "Then they went back to the kitchen. I stood on my bed and I didn't know what to do," she would recollect, breathing heavily. "At first, I wanted to climb the wardrobe, but I couldn't—it was too high. I looked at Tońcio and he had our mother's big black eyes, I looked at him and quickly, quickly jumped behind the bed. Then they shot Miecio, he was the son of our aunt from Canada, a cripple. They didn't let him into Canada with his mother, so he stayed in Gaje. He would help in the field, he would plow by hand, he was strong. They shot Miecio. When they came back into the room, I was already behind the bed, I couldn't see who went first, I only counted the shots. Father, Mother, Mrs. Skowrońska, or Mrs. Skowrońska and then my mother. Three. Footsteps to Tońcio's bed. A burst of shots. Later, footsteps to Zdzisio's bed, the one I was hiding behind. Another burst. Right by my ear, because his little head was right by mine, only on the other side of the board. And I was all tense, ready for them to pull me out because they can see there's no way for me to run. The door to the kitchen, the winter windows locked for good, where would I run? So I clutched the bed, my fingernails deep in the wood," and I see my own fingers clutching the table when she tells this story, I can't listen anymore; a story that I have erased from my memory completely and now have to recreate from the recording. "I thought," my aunt continued, "that if they started to pull me out by my hair, I would beg them to kill me right then and there, then and there! I would curse them, call them pigs and bandits to make them angry, so they'd kill me right there, behind the bed. Finally I heard, and the lights were out, how they opened and rummaged through all the wardrobes, how they ripped the old Singer sewing machine off its little wooden table. There was nothing else to steal, only my parents' furs, Genio's clothes and coat, and Tońcio's things, completely worn out. Right in the middle was my coat, and I kept praying because I had a picture of Our Lady of Perpetual Help in one of the pockets, I prayed for her sanctity to be safe, because the picture was sanctified in Rome by the Pope. I prayed so that they wouldn't take the picture and taint it with their murderous hands. Let them take the coat," she would say, "just let the picture fall out of the pocket." And I couldn't stand that nonsense about the holy picture and their coats, I thought she had no right, and I wanted her to stop.

"They took everything outside to the horse cart and then there was silence. Only the cows mooed. I went outside, through the barn into the field, and started to run. I kept losing my shoes. I saw something bright flash in the air, and only after I heard it whizzing by my ear did I realize that they were shooting at me. I fell down a few times. Past the tracks, I started walking against the plow pattern in the field, slowly, slowly toward our people. Right outside Gaje, behind the statue, I heard a horse approaching. And it was a full moon, bright as day. It was one of Bandera's men. We stood there, staring at each other, and he finally turned around and left. And I got to my aunt on 17 Ogrodowa Street, to my grandmother I mean, it was her Ternopil address," because they all had two addresses after all, one current—the bad one—and one from their paradise lost. "And I knocked. I thought I was knocking . . ." "But she banged on the door like crazy," Grandmother Kopiec adds from beyond the grave, recorded on the tape, "It almost fell out of the frame!"

And my aunt kept screaming like crazy, "Gaje! Gaje! Blood, Mrs. Skowrońska too, Mrs. Skowrońska too!" And Mrs. Skowrońska, it's about time to explain, was my great-grandmother, Grandmother Kopiec's mother. She was Ukrainian, and she had gone there to warn the other six; she was a relative of all those who remained citizens of Ukraine to this day, members of my family. "And Aunt Emma asked: 'And what about my Zdzisio?' and the same from Aunt Paulisia." Some of them I knew, and I didn't realize they'd all lost children in that mass murder because they never said a word. They all kept asking, terrified, and finally Aunt Walercia told them "Stop, don't ask her, can't you see she's gone crazy?"

"The next day we went to Gaje Wielkie, the four of us, down the road running through the middle of the village. We got there, everyone was on the ground and the sight was horrific. The bodies stiff, blood coagulated. No clothes to dress them in. Nothing to dress them in, none. We had to bury them the way they were. Aunt Aniela washed a little bit of blood off their faces because I couldn't," said my aunt. "Some Ukrainian women came and stood there for a while, said a little prayer, then one said, 'At least they decided to shoot, spared them suffering.' There were corpses on the floor and I asked the women: What did they shoot them for? What?"

This was Christmas with my aunt.

nother member of my family, Władysław Kopiec, also lamented over his paradise lost. He wrote: "Czahary! Village of my birth and of my youth! Village of beekeepers, flowing with milk and honey, rich with orchards. Village free of neighborly disputes because all the neighbors lived away from one another." I'm curious about this last sentence in particular because there's not a single word in there about people of Czahary being better, only about the world being better organized. People didn't fight because they were far away from each other.

Uncle continues in his *How it Used to Be in Podolia*, which came into existence only as a manuscript: "In all of Zbarski district, there was no other village as rich with fruit orchards and with apiaries so well tended. In conditions like that, the youth were happy growing up, full of life and eager to play pranks. Everyone talked about them, plotting their own benign pranks in return."

When I listen to them now, years after they've passed away, I can tell there is one voice speaking through all of them. They were dispersed all over the world, but it was as if they conspired to tell the same story, to add new verses to the same psalm. And when one psalm would end, another one would commence: "In order to be free, every other nation in the world went to the trenches with rifles ready to fire. Ukrainians were awful cowards in this regard. They would march at night and go wherever they thought there would be no resistance. They would outnumber the enemy ten to one. They would murder old men, toddlers, women. They would be cruel," Uncle Władysław would write, but it could've been written by Janka, or Grandfather, or Aunt Walercia just as well.

"They call themselves Ukrainians," we read, "but in their veins flows Tartar blood, too. That is where this drive to murder, burn, and destroy comes from. No other nation in Europe has this craving. The Ukrainians were Hitler's right hand in murdering, in torturing the prisoners of concentration camps as capos, in prisons. Their crimes were horrifying. There was no act of barbarity, no act of cruelty that Bandera's men wouldn't perform. They would terrify even Ukrainians themselves, the ones with a humane side."

My uncle's lecture on Ukrainians was conceived years before the Balkan massacre, but I don't believe that Serbian or Croatian blood thirst, or their ethnic cleansing, would impress him. His story, the story of my kin, had only two endings: paradise lost, butchered by the Ukrainian butchers; and a perpetual sadness and longing afterward. They couldn't see much beyond that, and not because they were evil or indifferent, but because their eyes had been gouged out and their bodies were burned out hollow.

When my grandmother was dying, I used to go and visit her on occasion. She was resting in bed, her marital bed under the painting of the Holy Family, usually silent. I preferred when she was silent anyway. The end was tough. With her clarity still intact, she told me: "You know I'm Ukrainian?" Just like her mother, Skowrońska, killed in Gaje, like her sister, like her cousin Kernyczny, the doctor killed right by the fence, just like her entire family. And since they killed her mother, she never spoke of Ukrainians other than as dogs, murderers, *huncwoty*—scamps—Russian scum. She hated her nation and put a curse on it, but at the very end she decided to take the burden on her back once again, the burden of her origin. After that she fell silent. If she ever spoke at all, she was usually delirious and rarely recognized the person visiting. In moments of lucidity she would call for my grandfather, long dead by then, and I recalled one Christmas after his passing when she sat quiet, stubborn, until she suddenly screamed—she, who never screamed and spent her entire life quiet, screamed: "I don't want to live, I have nothing to live for, take me away already!" So I would visit and she'd be resting in bed. I took a picture of her once, close to the end, but I never developed it because I felt like a thief. The white sheets, her dark face—she looked like an Arabian elder, like a Gypsy, like a Sephardic Jew. Her pantry was almost empty, only a stoneware bowl in which she used to keep butter was still there. Behind the cabinet was a pastry board, once perfectly flat and now full of hills and valleys—marks from years of kneading dough—with yellow rubber gloves hanging from it, tools of the trade of one of the nurses taking care of her. Her bathroom felt suddenly forsaken, as if nobody had entered it in decades. The smell of her apartment grew stronger and more hostile. It was obvious nothing would change there. In the smaller room, as usual, pears were ripening on some newspapers, spreading their sweet scent in the general fug of the apartment. It was quiet, all so quiet. The painting of the Holy Family was still hanging over the bed, Mary Magdalene exposing her milk-white breast inside the cave. The eagle on the wardrobe was still getting ready to take off.

"Hey gypsy, you fuckin' thief!" a beefed-up guy in a white tracksuit kept shouting at me on the train. "Whatcha lookin' at? Want me to fuck you up? Fuckin' Arab, dirty piece of shit, where did you crawl out from? No shame to walk among the whites? Get the fuck off the train, you cocksucker! Out! Piece of shit! They should've burned you, you fuckin' Jew, what you lookin' at? You never seen a Pole?"

This is my inheritance from Grandmother Kopiec. But she had it easy; she had her Yardley's face powder, scented flour to pretend she's local. I have nothing, I'm powerless, my skin color reveals my identity. That's her heritage. I keep bumming around the world carrying her basket, and in this basket there is something all too obvious for others: me, always darker than the rest, smiling awkwardly, always a little off.

or no apparent reason, my grandmother ripped out pictures from the family album. I'm not quite sure, but I suspect it was because back then she was full of anger and easily enraged. She must've been haunted by the past, too. Although, on the other hand, I'm not sure if she knew that it was her past that she was mad about. In this incomplete album there's a picture—a small one retouched in a country style, exaggerated, more of an original creation of the retoucher than a photo print. She's on the left, and on the right some man with a wide face and a single smug ringlet hanging on his forehead, probably curled with an iron. There's a gentle circle encompassing the photograph and a comment in the margin, written in the one-of-a-kind handwriting of my mother (interesting, by the way—where did she learn to write like that?). "Grandmother only." The commandment was for me—to scan only Grandmother and erase the simple-faced man from our family's history, this penulti-mate choice of my grandmother, a man from Ternopil who did not become my grandfather. But since he was already in the album, since he was pasted in and Grandfather didn't cut him out in all those years, since Grandmother didn't rip him out when the torpor fogged her world—let him stay. I won't sugar coat it. It's more interesting that way.

Another album—this one devoted to the family on my mother's side. I don't recognize too many faces. Places keep repeating. Mostly a house, a family room or a living room, at first not used that often, saved for guests, just like the best room in a country house. They would sit together, mostly in the kitchen, with this canary of theirs, they would sit in the garden, mostly eager to take pictures on the stairs leading to the house. The only pictures taken while traveling are of my grandfather on top of Mount Śnieżka, surrounded by a group of people unknown to me, probably friends from work, taken in 1949. My grandfather always traveled without his wife. In their older days they would go for holidays to the lake, but it wasn't the holidays—it was work. He was overseeing a campground with several summerhouses. For the whole summer they would stay in a damp house and go to the forest, picking whatever there was to pick. They didn't know how to swim, so they organized their time according to their routines and recreated their own home as best they could in this little box-house. They worked because to be right next to their house, to sit and work: that was their idea of a perfect life. The history of their travels is a history of failed excursions, or ones that never came to happen. I go through this ransacked album, page after page, and try to find pictures from their trips, but there are none. That's how they were. A few pictures, a short story.

They had this canary in a cage in the kitchen, I remember my grandmother lined it with fresh newspapers every day, changed the water, made sure there were plenty of fresh seeds, provided lime, which the canary pecked with a passion worthy of a greater cause. Grandma was, one could say, a breeder. The canary was not only company throughout her hours spent in the kitchen, or vacuuming; the canary was a responsibility. Just like everything was a responsibility: the garden, free time, news on the TV. She knew how to laugh, but life she approached with diligence, even if it was the life of a canary. She would let the canary out of the cage after the furnace plate cooled off. And it would fly out from his cage, yellow lightning, and circle the lamp, fly by the clock, which had the figure of a woman to indicate good weather and a male one for bad, or the other way around. But the clock was broken and showed whatever it wanted, regardless of air pressure or rainfall, and the canary flew by the window and sometimes it even tried to peck its way to freedom. It kept flying, resting on the dishes drying by the sink, resting on my head, where its little talons would scratch my scalp because they were always long and I kept laughing and she, this grandmother of mine, always so solemn and sullen all her life, would laugh her head off too.

Bedlam:
Your Salvation Is the Reason for My Journey

It was seventeen degrees below zero Celsius and the streets were empty. Water as green as tropical algae dripped across the street. It was coming from the gate of a house that had been rebuilt after the war, including its overall sense of narrowness required three or four hundred years earlier by property prices in this prosperous port city. The city was rebuilt to restore its previous look, sometimes down to exact details, following a naive belief that that would turn it back into what it used to be before the war. It was an exercise in fidelity without purpose, an empty gesture of men in love with history. The water kept flowing through the gate from this tenement house, from the laundry room, and froze in the square, creating a puddle the color of shower gel that smells of bergamot and verbena—or that was what it brought to mind because it was odorless. Women were evacuating the laundry room, grabbing whatever was at hand, some papers, packages. Nobody paid attention to the artificial Gardens of Eden congealing in the freezing cold, as if the parrot-green slick was an everyday occurrence in these parts. "The cold burst the pipes again," a woman who saw my amazement told me. "They color the water used in the central heating here like that."

I went to the almost-empty restaurant, just me and two other young men in suits, from whose table an avalanche of stories about money kept rolling my way. The owner's son played the role of waiter:

49

he would approach to ask if we needed anything, but we only wanted to sit for a little while with our tea. The cook watched a game on TV in the back, the waiter was bored and soon fell asleep behind the bar; he'd wanted to close for some time now. I was overcome with pain; I could barely sit. I kept counting: how many steps left to the hotel, how many floors to the room, how many hours till morning. Outside there were no cars, no pedestrians—there was just a great silence covered in snow, interrupted only by seagulls. The artificial city, rebuilt in its own image, and wherever men lost their zeal to rebuild they left deep holes looming in the ground. They had been looming like that since I can remember. The snow-covered city waited for its Huns, who come back every summer to take possession of the streets. To kill time, they listened to the radio, and on the radio the city felt alive, as if they were talking about a completely different place. Anyway, at least nobody was in the downtown area; it was silent and you could hear only those seagulls. Taxi drivers kept listening about the accidents, road blocks, about this complex organism, a wild termitary. In the meantime, from above, from a plane, you could see empty spaces, land turning into sea, both gray and under a layer of snow.

I had come here every year since I can remember. We would walk the same streets, as if only to see what had changed. From the train station, through the underpass, on the right a music store, past the store a right turn, a deli, a tower; in the market hall we looked in awe at the smoked eels and all the merchandise from forbidden worlds, and finally the city made of reinforced concrete, not Danzig, or Gdańsk anymore, but its fairly faithful copy created out of the need for continuity. A lie made of concrete and brick, half a hole in the ground and half houses almost identical with the original, but flat like modern apartment buildings, with crooked carpentry, a mix of local baroque and social realism. The old town in my own city was the same, leveled to the ground in 1945 and later rebuilt.

"Rebuilding" is a key word in my part of the world, similar to other words like "war," "besieged," "murder," like "liberation," "exile," "escape," like "cemetery" and "displacement," like "Regained Territories" and "post-German houses." Here, if you dig a little deeper, it turns out to be fake, not original, a couple dozen years old at the most. Gdańsk was one of those spots on the map, also Wrocław—a field of rubble, Warsaw, of course, and later Berlin and Dresden, also Nuremberg. Or the castle on the island in Troki, a masterpiece of forgery, taller with every passing year, and newer. The first time I was there it was merely a ruin among the bushes; the last time I visited it stood tall and brand new in the middle of Troki's frozen lake on which cars and horse-drawn carriages kept driving back and forth in the cold of March; so similar to Malbork and other places like that, rebuilt from scratch. These cities, those places need the cover of snow to hide their architectural absurdities. They came into being because of the belief in continuity, in a thread connecting then with now. That's where my distrust of other cities comes from—cities better equipped with souvenirs, cities spared by misfortune or simply indifferent to the Middle Ages, taking down their remains without a blink of an eye—my distrust of Paris with its mad builder and demolition expert, Count Haussmann, with its crazy mayors, or to a lesser extent, my distrust for nineteenth century Krakow, leveling its moats, taking down its city walls and towers. There was an obligation in me, in us, to sit in all the churches until the last painting was seen and immediately forgotten. There was a need to ride across the world along the thread unwound by the Baedeker.

I came back to the hotel and spent the rest of the night in a torpor. On our way to the airport we didn't see a single car. The taxi driver was listening to the blasting radio, and on the radio the city felt surprisingly alive again, completely different from what was outside our windows, impossible to recognize.

A thousand and a few odd years ago, precisely in the year 997 A.D., Christ's juggernaut, the bishop of Prague, Adalbert, also known as Wojciech, visited Gdańsk, the name of which in the first recorded account was "Gyddanyzc," and according to one of hagiographers of the nineteenth century, Father Piotr Pękalski, "doctor of the holy theology, canon, guardian of the holy tomb of Christ": "The merciful God had blessed his arrival because the people crowded for the baptism and he, while conducting the mass, made an offering of Christ to God the Father, to whom he was soon to offer himself. From here, he decided to set out to Eastern Prussia; that is why the next day after the mass, with tears in his eyes, he bid farewell to the converted and, giving them a blessing, he boarded a ship with his retinue and headed toward the mouth of the Vistula River, toward the open sea, and soon disappeared from their sight forever."

It's a beautiful story, a prequel to all the heart-wrenching movies, St. Wojciech—Adalbert—my namesake and my patron, I hope, departs on a boat in the company of Brother Radzim and Priest Benedict, in other sources known as Bogusz, never to come back again. It is well known what fate awaits him. He dreamt his fate and the dream foretells the future, the truth, because his hand can heal others and his dreams become reality. He keeps on going, and says about himself: "I am a Slav. My name is Wojciech. Once, a bishop, now a friar, and by God's inspiration your Apostle. Your salvation is the reason for my journey, so that you shall abandon your idols and know your Creator, who himself is the only God, and you shall have no gods before him; so that you believe in His name and live eternally and earn a reward in the eternal house of heaven."

Not everyone, however, has ears for a speech so sweet, since, as the hagiographer claims, "Once Wojciech exclaimed those very words, the rabid plebeians started to hurl profanities, cursing him and God alike; the very God whom he had come to herald. Greatly aggravated, they threatened him with death; baffled, they beat their clubs against the ground, swung them above their heads and in rage they screamed: 'You're lucky, you've come so far without punishment, but if you don't leave immediately you shall die here soon. Only one law and only one custom reigns over us and over this entire country, at the very end of which we live. You, who abide by a different law alien to us, if you don't leave this very night you shall die tomorrow.'" And they stayed, and Wojciech died.

"But the vile perpetrators," Thietmar, the unmatched Bishop of Merseburg notes, "committed a crime even greater, and earned a punishment from God of an even greater magnitude. Upon seeing Wojciech dead, they threw his holy corpse into the sea; his head they stuck on a pole to ridicule him and, cheering, returned to their abodes." A similar fate met Bruno of Querfurt, toward whom I feel an affinity because, like me ten centuries later, he traveled in the valley of the Tisa and Mureş Rivers and on top of that has recorded the life of St. Wojciech. Thietmar recounts: "In the twelfth year of his pious, eremite life he traveled to Prussia, and with the seed of God tried to fertilize its barren soil, but the thorns made his toil hard. When on the fourteenth of February [of 1009] he was preaching the gospel of God at the border of this country and the Kievan Rus, the villagers forbade him, and when he kept on preaching, they captured him and for loving Christ, who is the head of the Church, they cut off his head, the peaceful lamb, and the heads of his eighteen fellow travelers."

I came back to Gyddanyzc, a city I had remembered differently, which I thought was more blue collar and Eastern—after all, somebody had to fill in the gap left by the exiled, and who better for the job than my countrymen, always ready to squeeze into the void because they're deprived of their own space. I found myself back in the city after a few years of absence; this time I rebuilt it my own way. I wove history, not stone. I enrich my Gdańsk with St. Wojciech, the burning torch, my patron saint, and with his arrival on the boat, along with about thirty armed men on their way toward death.

Bishop Wojciech was a Czech misfit who abandoned his herd because they wouldn't listen. Thietmar notes in his chronicle that: "When toiling to make his sheep obey God's commandments, he could not avert them from the sins of past barbarity, and thus excommunicated them all." That's how he was, my namesake. He would abandon an idea for, as he thought, a better one. One minute a bishop and a townsman, a shepherd of his herd and its leader, although against his will, and the next minute a pilgrim on the way to Jerusalem, then a friar on Monte Cassino, and then a bishop again, then a pilgrim once more, and on and on. His life wasn't easy, although his biographers did everything to make it straightforward and snow-white pure.

Wojciech, later a martyr and a saint, came to Gdańsk by boat. He had to sail on the Vistula River, and I wonder what villages he passed by and how it looked back then. Water everywhere, everywhere I go, the Dnieper River, the Dniester and Ganges, the Cheremosh and Tisa, the Neman River and Oder, the Vistula, the După and Seine, the Neris and Vilnia, the Atlantic Ocean and Baltic Sea, a puddle and snow. Everything blends, waters run down. Travel by water, travel in the winter. We are sailing the same boat with the bishop, death awaiting us at the end.

The flood of 1997 robbed the Opole zoo of its animals. Even the hippopotamus drowned. I read about it in the newspaper and it was one of thousands of pieces on the great deluge and the losses, about the heroism and misery, all kitschy and in the same grim tone, to the point where even the world sports sections seemed to belong to a universe in the midst of a cataclysm; to the point where you wanted to wall yourself off and stop listening. This one hippopotamus seemed to me like an unnecessary casualty. All around you could hear people complaining, the people who built their houses in the areas known for flooding, residents of the blocks of flats built on floodplains, as if surprised that the river took that particular area. The hippopotamus was different, he drowned on the sidelines, just like that. He drowned even though he was an aquatic animal.

I imagine a different version: if the hippopotamus were to survive and keep swimming, freed from his enclosure by the water, his terrifying bulk—terrifying now since he'd no longer be sequestered behind a moat and iron bars, looking like the living dead, evoking pity and disgust—swimming and baring his yellow teeth, like he used to do in his outdoor enclosure, there would probably be a huge hunt for him—firemen, hunters, and veterinarians would board a ship, the same tour ship with a puppet show I used to go on as a child, on a mission to tranquilize him or kill him, depending on the circumstances. From the mourned-over hippopotamus, he would turn into a killer beast that needs to be immediately tracked down and shot for the sake of safety. TV stations, radio, and the newspapers would abandon their teary tone and report as if it was a safari. But that never happened. The hippopotamus drowned in his cage on Bolko Island, named that way for everybody to remember that these grounds are of Piast decent, and the hippopotamus's bloated body confirmed the zoo's downfall, just as the heaps of rags, furniture, and rotting plants releasing an asphyxiating stench confirmed the downfall of the city, its suffering and suicidal shortsightedness.

That trip completely washed away the menagerie of my childhood, the island of unhappiness that I liked to visit. I observed peacocks with their fan-like tails, strolling along the paths. I drew tapirs with their weird noses curled down like trunks, and monkeys in their concrete bunker with shelves and an old tire-swing on a chain, where there was always someone cleaning in vain because the stench was unrelenting. I watched the zookeepers moving from cage to cage, bringing in food, just a simple technical supervision over the matters of animals; that was their role and nothing more.

The flood was the second death of that zoo. The first—and total one—happened, unsurprisingly, during the war. (The zoo died once from the fire and once from the water—a fair balance). The first death never even crossed my mind; I simply didn't pause to think about the history of that real-life bestiary. I thought it was there forever. I know only some basic facts and I can only imagine the rest.

The year the flood came, the summer was hot and everything rotted exceptionally fast. The city was under the threat of plague, so the ground in front of houses was sprinkled with lime, and smoke rose everywhere from hastily burned belongings, from rotten furniture and wallpaper peeling off the walls. The fetor clogged the noses, stuck to bodies and wouldn't go away even after a bath. Strangers showed me their most intimate wounds: empty rooms, once filled with furniture, the water line sometimes close to the ceiling of the first floor and the void which filled them. Piled in front of the blocks of flats were jars with jam and compote, zealously gathered in basements, but now waiting for the garbage collectors. The entire city was rotting and rusting, useless boats stood on almost dried up streets; there was a camping trailer lying on its side at the evangelical cemetery. The Oder River and Ulga Canal were much broader than during even the rainiest summers; huge pieces of driftwood, roofs, and carcasses kept floating down. In the middle were two lines of trees. They looked like posts marking a mountain path when there's a heavy snowfall. Where the trees were, there used to be riverbanks.

It reminded me of a flood from years before which, back then, was called the flood of the century, but the next flood in the same century was soon to take over that boastful title. We were camping, it rained every day, and life grew limited to patching holes in the tents, and moving to the higher, semi-dry spots. We were awaiting the end of rain, which refused to come. Puddles grew into ponds with grass rotting at their edges. The kitchen stood right next to the creek that had momentarily turned into a river. The water took away a little bridge and there was no passage to town or anywhere else. Then the pond turned into a muddy sea and people wondered not how to find water, but how to escape it. Although there was an abundance of water, you couldn't use any of it. As a sign of ultimate defeat in the place of an old ford, where only a week earlier you could safely cross, was the carcass of a dead goat stuck in some tree branches, bloated to its limits like bagpipes mockingly overfilled with air.

While reading about the hippopotamus, I remembered that monstrously bloated goat and wondered how this hippo looked after a few days in the sun.

We were on our way to Zhytomyr, a convulsive ride on the back roads and then farther south, to Moldova. The town of Rivne was on our way, and was just like all the other towns there, filled with numb people standing at the bus stops with bouquets of flowers and bags of sunflower seeds for sale. Just outside town was a zoo, which is always good for entertainment if there's nothing interesting around for hundreds of kilometers and all there is to do is to make sure people coming back from the store at night won't suddenly jump in front of your car.

The path in the Rivne zoo immediately reminded me of how, many years earlier, somewhere in India, but I can't recall the name of the city now, I went to another zoo. It was one of those scorching hot days with no hope for rain, when rivers shrink to the size of creeks and you don't really know what to do with yourself. Sweat runs down your face and burns your eyes with salt. The only thought you have is to go back home, immediately, or at least to a hotel. I went to the zoo because I was bored and because in my mind crossing the country turned into a vast network of connections, rides on the train and bus, and a chain of cheap hotels. All the rest—landscapes, people—evaporated. I also went there because I was curious, because everything there was different from what I'd known, although what about their caged animals could be different from ours, what could be the difference between visitors here and there?

There, in India, I often felt as if I were the one on the other side of the bars because there would be an elephant crossing the street, or a rattlesnake stopping in the middle of the path in the park, or camels running in the south of the country; running on their thin, spidery legs with that bulge in their joints, their legs so different from any other legs—and so they would run, dragging a cart, climbing sand dunes, rising up and then coming down, as if riding on a wave. And I stood frozen on the train tracks and couldn't hear the train coming, so it had to whistle at me and brake. In their zoo the paths were flat, only beaten ground, not a single blade of grass, and many more people than animals. Everyone was smoking, eating, throwing trash and cigarette butts into the cages. Apathetic animals lay far away, as far away from humans as possible. Everyone wanted to take pictures, show the animal to a child, but there was no way because the cages were small, like a rabbit hutch, and only two or three people from the entire crowd could see anything. And the inside, even though there was so little space, appeared almost empty. Someone managed to find a broom and kept poking the puma to take a picture of if with a child—a live puma and not some dead one by the wall. The noise was penetrating. I didn't even want to watch, I remember, I wanted to sit on a bench, but there were no empty ones. I left. I kept telling myself that it was so completely different in my city. I found consolation in that. These sights are for somebody without experience, like the first visit to a slaughterhouse, when the mechanics of animal insides still seem dark and repulsive.

And yet, years later, in Rivne, so close to home, it looked exactly the same. Only the surroundings were more familiar, because the grass was green and there were hills instead of a desert-like landscape. But the small zoo was identical, and there were too many people, equally loud and throwing lumps of dirt at the animals to bring them back to life for their home movies, because back there it was the time of photographs and here it was already the time of video cameras. Teenagers were wearing knock-off Adidas sneakers, sweats, beige pants with a prominent crease; young boys left alone to run free made noise with their toy guns, but the raccoons and foxes ignored them. They were sprawled on the ground as if their spirit had abandoned them. Newlyweds paced the lawns for their wedding videos because there is nothing more interesting in all of Rivne; Rivne is the capital of provincial numbness, so they go and shoot their video at the zoo. They stop by the pines in their shiny suits and meringue-like dresses and kiss shyly, following the directions of the movie guy who shouts "One more, one more time, now to the left, not this way, that way, by the birch!" and behind them in cages, the animals. It's not about the animals anyway. I know because I've seen movies like that, there are plenty of them on the Internet: the movie is about the people and their costumes. Sometimes the cages in this zoo were peculiarly fragile, more like goat or sheep pens, but instead—they held a predator. And sometimes the cages were built as if for a rhinoceros, double walled, and a bear, clearly mad from the heat, from people, would pace in circles, not paying attention to anything, ready to crash against the wall, but always turning around at the last moment. The other bear would be sitting inert. It did not react to being sprayed with sodas, to cigarette butts thrown down from the path. It just sat, hostage to this bullshit correctional house for animals. And the more insane the animals acted, the better you could smell their near end on them, and the more vicious people got.

I often observe animals, I simply enjoy it. But the zoo is the worst of all options because it's a walk through a world that is more dead than that on the other side of the fence. The zoo is deprived of everything; nothing but plaques, descriptions, order. And even if the resemblance between the zoo and some natural habitat is striking, there is a bus waiting outside, home is right around the corner. Boredom and artificiality is the zoo's nature. There's no hope for a pang of fear; here, they remove dead bodies at night. The zoo comes to life after dark, when people finally leave, in the evening, or when there's a flood and you can no longer camouflage the cages. The water revealed, just like heat reveals a message written in invisible ink, the true nature of the zoo—iron bars, prison, and the hippopotamus's final resting place.

This is a journey through the cold, divided between all the seasons of the year; a journey through trouble, deep snow, and black waters. It's not really a journey, more an escape from my family's fate, from being anchored down. My legs get sucked in by the mud until a shoe or a galosh stays behind and I continue barefoot. With envy I think of my predecessors, tourists of the early days, true travelers who knew how to stay upbeat on the endlessly rough path. They had to sneak over borders, ask bankers for money every single time, exchange vouchers, present letters of recommendation. They had to visit the representatives' offices, spend days in the antechambers of consulates until someone made an appointment for them; until someone found mercy or the police decided they weren't bandits after all—and the police of all eras tend to be suspicious. And yet, I envy them. Although I'm not sure of what exactly, I guess I envy the fact that they were gambling with madness, with finality, while we are left with hygienic travels by car or a plane. There is nothing finite about those travels; coming back is always an option. Nobody awaits you with an ax, the journey doesn't last for too long, and it is for pleasure. I read about those who traveled before me, who like me were running away, hitting an actual road or one only in their heads, about those who didn't make it because they were sucked in by the swamps; about journeys without the promise of return.

"Hospitalization card. Holy Ghost Hospital—Mental Ward."
These are excerpts from papers found in attics, pulled out of the
trash, or bought at the flea market, my favorite shopping place in
my home city, which digests everything that the previous generation
had already chewed on. Nothing disappears here, and if it does, it's
only for a brief moment. This is my city, it takes pride in its excre-
ments, fossils straight from the dump site. "You want it? You got it!
My fellow citizens! If you kept those documents, take them back with
humility."

"Date of admission: 07/02/1875. Name of disease: [left blank,
maybe they were waiting for the nature of this madness to reveal
itself]." "Name of patient: Kazimierz Brykowski." The fields for
"age, religion, civil status" are empty. "Occupation: cook," farther
down something was crossed out. It used to say: "Count's cook," but
the source of the employer's embarrassment, his servant's mental illness, was quickly removed; and thank God the doctor didn't manage
to write down the Count's name. So, "cook" will have to do. The
subsequent fields, as is usually the case in this type of document,
have been omitted. Who would measure the "diameter of chest"
of a nutcase, who would decide on the "heredity" if the name of
the illness is not known? "Doctor's report—course of the disease—
current condition," these are transcribed from a different hospital,
from the Nervous Disease Ward at St. Lazarus in the same city, or
town, rather, if we were to measure it by today's standards, because
how many citizens could Krakow have back in those days? Merely
fifty thousand, but it needed at least two wards to accommodate its
patients; it was proud of and famous for its nuts, crazies, weirdoes,
and alcoholics and that's how it is today too, amen. "Well until 6/26,
led a proper life—extremely pious," that's how this description of life
and the beginnings of death starts, because we already know what
direction this patient card is headed. You don't omit the essentials,
you don't grant only a name, last name, and occupation to a patient,

just to have him released and taken back in again soon after. Many of them, as I was going to learn in the course of reading card after card, would return to the ward, go mad time after time, be sent back by the police or a family that was going through hell on earth with them. And so it would go until the very last trip back, when nothing could help anymore. Then they would drink themselves to death in some murky inn or apartment, or else would disappear for good. When there was hope for their return, the card had to be filled in thoroughly to remind everyone who the patient used to be.

There were two sides to the life of the Count's cook: first, immaculate sainthood and freedom from faults of character; he wasn't tempted by the bottle or the skirt, most likely didn't catch syphilis, and his access to the pantry key didn't ruin him either—he must've been a flawless man. It must've been the Count's testimony, the same Count who was quick enough to stop the doctor's fountain pen before it recorded his name, thus making him present in the psychiatric register only as a witness. Or maybe it was the cook's wife or his coworkers who spoke for him. Someone had to testify on his behalf because he didn't talk much back then, I imagine. "He was extremely pious—it was only later that he grew restless—he dressed and undressed over and over again and always kept to himself—he didn't answer questions; he would suddenly throw himself on the ground and lay with his arms splayed out to the sides, all strained, his pulse low." On the following pages, in the field titled "Course of disease, treatment, diet" are the following episodes of the cook's struggle with fate, parts of it hard to decipher, written shakily in an ink that turned brown, demanding a better reader than myself, a Benedictine monk trained in the calligraphy of a different era: "7/4, from time to time he arches his entire body and lies as if frozen—pulse 72—didn't sleep the whole night, hasn't eaten this entire time—he does not answer questions, forehead is hot. He sleeps in the morning—pulse 68 etc. etc." "Forehead hot, I let some blood from his right arm" (at this point I recall that, in his memoirs, Jakub Sobieski, father of the king, complained in the chapter about his own sickness that some medic, an Irish man, performed blood-letting on him some thirty odd times and wanted to do more, not really worried about the patient's condition, because "the Poles are temperamental people and have a lot of fluids."); and after treatment the cook-reject is "conscious, answers all questions and promises to stay in bed calmly and permit application of cold compresses," as if he was a scolded child promising to be better. What difference does it make, cook, if already the next morning "[he] was submitted to electroshock with a direct current for 5 minutes." That shows how interesting the days of the Count's cook's convalescence were for the world of medicine: they were still letting his blood, or practiced phlebotomy—which will become outdated very soon—and at the same time used shock therapy, just as ineffective, but more technologically advanced. A note appears under the date, July 7th, claiming that "the cook has not eaten for the last two days—was fed with a probe." Maybe he was disgusted by the hospital food, maybe they didn't consider that. I experience that same disgust today, because the hospital food is usually pig slop served as punishment. Where food is concerned, the modern hospital is identical with its nineteenth century predecessor. The history of hospitals is the history of shaming, of locking up, coercion at all times, deprivation of privacy, various and often confusing procedures: colon wash, electroshock, bloodletting, very often a straightjacket—for the safety of the patient himself, for the safety and convenience of others—and finally the food, like scraps for a dog. I wouldn't be surprised if the ex-cook couldn't handle the food. After all he could've been good at his job, possibly, before he went crazy, maybe he even liked his job a little bit. So he walked up and down the corridor, shuffling his feet in what, exactly? Slippers? Shoes? I bet on shoes. He wandered, ever more angry. From that point on it was straightforward: "the cook wants to go home . . ." (he must've sensed that nothing good would come of his treatment) ". . . in order to resume working." Another entry: "high pulse rate, pain in the chest, spit the color of rust,"—it doesn't look like a symptom of madness, so there's a quick examination: "wheezing sound in the right lung, stabbing pain during deep breaths." And so, on July 19th, 1875—"swallowing impeded, neck veins tense, pain in the side, quinine, short breath, bloated stomach," ". . . bulging eyes. He died with symptoms of pneumothorax at 10 P.M.—no post-mortem," and the doctor's signature, a Hancock, only partially legible, a self-assured confirmation of an undeniable fact: they were treating him for his head, he died because of his lungs.

I have a whole pile of stories like that, written on yellowish and damp paper smelling of mold; someone wanted to sell it so some of the pages are trimmed, so they don't turn away potential buyers with their crumbling edges. And yet, the efforts of a street vendor, a trash diver, possibly the most colorful person on the entire square, to make those papers more attractive were pointless. He always sits by the very entrance, from 4 to 5 A.M. in the summer, and a little later in the winter—always on a camping stool since he can barely walk. He used to smell of vodka and be surrounded by a cloud of smoke, but now, since the doctors threatened him with the possibility of leg amputation, and even sudden death, he's sober much more often and virtually a non-smoker; more often absent in thought and somewhat quieter. This merchant of mine, a member of the clan of my trusted first-rate liars, storytellers, bullshit pushers, calling his clients fuckers and dumbasses, on a first-name basis with everyone (and those youngsters reading glossy magazines about fashion call him "sir" and are afraid of him, and pay whatever he tells them to pay); he's covered in sagging tattoos, ones that you can't get in a tattoo parlor—they cost him a prison sentence. As he managed to add up one lazy Sunday, he spent over twelve years in different prisons. His skin was a work of a lifetime. He sits on his camping stool, all twisted from drinking and surgeries, deformed, practically useless, croaking dramatically as if ready to turn silent forever any moment now, but exposes his skin proudly; he has nothing else left. Because what else is there, anyway? Junk for sale ravaged from basements and garages, his woman, as drunk as himself, a life companion and vengeful servant, and this—his collection of tattoos like the Bayeux Tapestry—his own history inked into his skin by the bored hands of his cellmates. He was the one who trimmed the edges of the hospital records, who tried to give them some antique allure, tried to change trash into an object of desire. He didn't foresee, however, or maybe he did but didn't care in the end, that the stench of mold and the stories described in the papers themselves might be discouraging to buyers. That's how I intercepted them, and now I can't break free.

So I keep reading. Ferdynand Budryński, thirty years old, admitted to the hospital for the third time. According to his card, he was a citizen of Myślenice: "height 173 cm, weight 57 kg." This patient was described more thoroughly because it wasn't his first visit. "Occupation: ex-tutor. Name of disease: stupefaction of the mind." The year was 1880, and the disease common to a point where anyone could be admitted from time to time. "Face is swollen. Talks to himself. Holds his head. Restless." At the end of July, somebody from Myślenice takes him away, but in October the ex-tutor comes back. "Doesn't do anything. Calm," state the subsequent assessments. At the beginning of the 1881, nothing changes: "Sits, doesn't do anything, holds his head in his hands." Later again, "is sad—won't eat—tongue swollen—laxative prescribed. He continues to read—when asked about his reading, he doesn't answer." So they keep on going, "laxatives for the swollen tongue." After that, his appetite came back and the patient "asked for a cigar." This improvement doesn't last for long: "frowning again." In 1882, "is calm, reads books, eager to smoke a cigar—has good appetite." Finally, after years of entries made in shaky handwriting, there appear tiny, unsettlingly legible letters written in a violet ink. Only four entries, nothing special. "5/26, silent, keeps staring at the floor, sometimes will pinch or pull at the staff, sometimes paces down the corridor, most often sits solemnly, staring at the ground; 6/21, condition is the same; 7/14, provides short answers to questions, recognizes prof. Blumenstock and talks to him; So far: head low, eyes on the ground—sometimes he will lie down on the ground, arms spread out to the sides; 8/28, transferred to Kulparkowo as incurable, but harmful."

That's how I lose track of the ex-tutor forever.

But others replace him. "Wincenty Sleńdziński, age: 39, religion: catholic, marital status: bachelor, occupation: painter," who had lived temporarily in Krakow, and who had been admitted to the Holy Ghost Hospital in 1875 for "disease: delirium tremens"—and I wonder what back roads the disease took on its way. After severe epileptic seizures, he was "prescribed thirteen leeches: six on his temples; seven on the neck"—an alternative way of bloodletting, as opposed to the classic one. His seizures continued, however weakened. Six days after being admitted, Sleńdziński "is more lucid—he says that during his seizures he feels as if he is being bound by chains and led into the unknown"; and that's probably how it was, his body locked up there, his mind blown to pieces. Ten days after being admitted, on "6/20, patient leaves hospital cured," and the same signature, illegible, found earlier on the cook's card. Cured of madness, I imagine, because there are no other entries for Sleńdziński, and it's a shame, since he was probably the best-known patient who got lost among the stories of mental disease. It's even more interesting to me since he was an artist involved with photography, although indirectly, along with others in his family. So I'll stretch this story, a little to the sides; it's roomy, and will easily accommodate more details. Sleńdziński's father, Aleksander, who was a painter himself (Ludomir, Wincenty's son, will become a painter—and the most famous one among the three), painted in the Count Benedykt Tyszkiewicz's residence outside of Vilnius, a photographer whose magnitude we can judge only by the reprints published in the artistic periodicals of the era, some pictures preserved in the private album, and several individual photos that have survived. Not too many left for such a busy life, but there's a simple explanation for that: Count's Parisian atelier burned down, and after that he never went back to photography. Wincenty Sleńdziński, Aleksander's son, learned how to paint from his father, but later, when he was in exile in Moscow—Krakow seemed like one of many stops on his twisted way back. In the end, he went back to his home town of Vilnius. I'm not sure if he was finally at peace, or still tormented by demons, or maybe felt the cold of metal wrapped around his chest. I don't know and never will. Only one thing is certain: after he came back, he married Anna Czechowicz, the widow of Józef Czechowicz, a famous photographer whose pictures of Vilnius and surrounding areas—taken during the period when Sleńdziński was at the Holy Ghost Psychiatric Hospital in Krakow struggling against bed restraints—always take me far away whenever I take them out of the box. Anna, now Sleńdzińska, kept running the studio inherited from her first husband, who thus lived on in balance with her second husband, ever present by her side, ever reprinted from the salvaged negatives, because Józef Czechowicz's career (and he deserved it) was not impeded by his death.

Czechowicz's studio, later owned by his widow, was located in a wooden house in the park, under Castle Mountain, today known as Giedymin's Mountain. Behind it flows the Neris River. From the east, the park is enclosed by the Vilnia River, behind which the Three Crosses Mountain begins. That's where Wincenty and Anna used to work and now, both in the winter and in the summer, soldiers go walking there with girls, even though it's hard to find some privacy. Mothers push baby carriages, fathers take pictures, and on the other side of the black water, beyond the Vilnia River—a laughably narrow river with ducks on the ice pack; a river that will drop into the Neris River in a couple hundred meters and disappear forever—someone is just getting on the trail leading to the top of Three Crosses Mountain. There is no atelier for Mrs. Sleńdziński, only tennis courts covered with snow and girls with cigarettes. I was walking there one winter, talking to myself, "you wanted winter, now you've got one," wrapped in the thickest coat I had, and with only one glove, the left one, because I lost the right one somewhere in the countryside. The sensation of temporariness that I get when I travel, the feeling of being alien, is expressed even in those smallest gestures: I won't buy new gloves, I'm not even looking for a new pair. Instead, I'll keep freezing my right hand, an angry red from the cold, for the whole day, and then I'll just start freezing both my hands off, because it looks stupid to walk around with one glove on. You buy things when you're home.

I was walking around the park that day, others were walking too, but it's not the time to list them all; I was complaining about the cold and my lost piece of attire, I was looking at the same place the Sleńdziński family looked at over a hundred years earlier and, blinded, I couldn't see anything. I had just come back from a place, not so far away, where fields, a few trees, and a bush are all that there is. That bush marks the spot where the house was, one of the houses that belonged to my clan. There is only one bush like that in the entire neighborhood. It was planted by some great-aunt of mine; I know her name was Malwina. I felt as if I'd lost my senses when I got out of the car in that place that was not mine, because it felt as if I was going to visit a gravesite; as if somewhere under a meter of snow I wanted to find preserved traces of gravestone. My father found that stone by the bush when we visited a few years earlier. I should be the one locked up in the Holy Ghost Hospital, not Wincenty.

Delirium tremens not only brought the Vilnius native Sleńdziski to the Holy Ghost Hospital, but also many others, including Jan Bartoszka, "a vicar from Tyniec, marital status: bachelor." It happened in 1875, on March 29th. "Admitted with symptoms of violent madness," the book says in the doctor's arabesque writing, "throws himself around, beats everyone, when in a straightjacket, he kicks himself in the head." He must've been quite limber, or else kicked himself while seated. What's more, "he threatens and curses those who claim he is crazy." This vicar has so little description to his name, that our knowledge of him is reduced to those shakes, madness, to him soiling himself, his furious attacks and maladjustment. But I find something else fascinating about him. It's not his stay at Holy Ghost and the doctor's care, but what came before: his church career, solitary drinking (supposedly solitary, because if not, then with whom?), long winters, long summers—because there are no good seasons for a man who lives in suspended misery, almost alone, with a detestable old hag of a housekeeper by his side—and a lack of interest in the spiritual life. Or maybe I'm wrong, maybe it was different, maybe the vicar from Tyniec was a sociable person and basked himself, as if in sunlight, in the love of people, liked to have a drink with them and played some cards for little money, just to stay busy? I can't decide, but it's not important; there's a gap that could fit an entire lifetime between his alleged beginning and the end at the hospital, where they put him in a straightjacket and pronounced him crazy, and where he started kicking himself in the head. After a month of therapy, the vicar from Tyniec "is calmer—slept through the night without opiates." It is, however, only a temporary improvement because he remains restless, the drugs don't help, he suffers, cries, soils himself at night, screams, and won't let others sleep. Three months later he suffered from an "epileptic seizure," and is "restless—bites, screams that wolves are biting him." (It's interesting, by the way, what excites the minds of modern alcoholics, what images are brought on by a night of torment in a police station drunk-tank or a hospital, because the drunk visions of wolves and shackled ankles that people feared in the nineteenth century aren't relevant today). At the end of the year, without signs of any visible improvement to his condition, the vicar travels the same path that the ex-tutor and many after him took—the path to Kulparkowo. Because there were three paths I know of from the records: the first is when patients leave cured, or when someone bails them out once informed of their dire condition, and takes them away; either way, once they're outside the confines of the hospital walls: "Welcome freedom!" The second, and apparently very common path, was a journey to Kulparkowo, the brand new Lviv clinic— a dead-end path, it seems. The third path was a coffin—if there was pneumothorax involved, or if treatment lasted for too long.

I know how those who were released felt. It must've felt the same way as when I was walking back from Świeradów in the direction of Gierczyn to visit my uncle, the collector. And that's all I remember from that visit—a house and outbuildings filled with everything you could possibly collect: farm equipment, clocks, horse buggies, feeding troughs, coffers full of books and papers of unknown origin and mainly in German, so, for me, not interesting; etchings, rustic and bourgeois furniture, banners, sculptures, paintings by local and foreign painters that were preserved quite well or completely moldy. He had everything, and this massive collection would leave me in awe because I didn't yet know how a house could become buried under objects, how uncomfortable it can become, and I couldn't understand my family's complaints; that they would rather have room to park their cars in the barn instead of dealing with the objects amassed there, in that chaos comprehendible only to one person—my uncle. They wanted a bathroom, a garage, and a set of proper kitchen appliances. They would dream about spending holidays at Lake Balaton, or at least a nice Sunday road trip, but my uncle wanted to keep these things because that was how he would preserve his memory. He is convinced of that to this very day. My uncle presented me recently with a stack of nineteenth-century cooking magazines filled with etchings portraying mystical objects and tools long-forgotten and unused. The names of the presented dishes leave one in complete darkness as well; they read almost like a fairytale, a novella for young girls from a different century, where everything seems unreal. He attached a tiny old photo taken during the January Uprising, showing a group of dissenters with a caption the size of several scattered poppy seeds. He, an old man with a magnifying glass, part of a long family line of teachers, deciphered the description for me. He must've known I wouldn't be patient, or capable of doing it myself. He deciphered it and typed it out on his typewriter. This is how you preserve memory. I contracted this passion from my uncle, although I don't really know him at all.

On that day I was walking toward his house through the forest, technically not a forest anymore but a huge pit of fallen trees—not a single one was standing after the strong winds a few weeks before, and that calamity was all people talked about. A massive logging operation had started and the hills buzzed with chainsaws; workers stood in the mud of the forest paths, and the ground was squashed by trucks. The hills were shiny, bald, and it felt like walking through Mordor, all black and repulsive. Instead of a humming silence there was the thumping of axes and roaring of chainsaws, large trucks on the sides of the road, filled with lifeless trees that had been felled overnight, or just few moments ago, and had stopped being a forest. I went down into the valley and there was nothing there, just green up the brim, a valley filled with sun and echoing with the Eurythmics song. When I think back on it now, it echoed for miles. But songs can last for that long only in my memory, and I know it's my inner storyteller, suggesting a prettier version of that walk. The saws became quiet. I walked, and the crystal clear air carried "Sweet Dreams." I entered the valley of light. This is how those who, after months of treatment, were proclaimed cured and saw the world again must've felt.

The vicar from Tyniec was not the only priest recorded on the hospital cards. Another was Benedictine Krawczyk, a capuchin from Goszyce where Miłosz lived during the war; a capuchin suffering

from violent madness (I should mention that I don't always understand why it's mild at times and why violent at others). He arrives at
the hospital in January and is released after a short stay, but his condition doesn't improve, so he comes back. "According to those closest
to the patient, it was only recently—two weeks since his ordination,
after his first primitia—that he became restless. Thinks he is Christ's
plenipotentiary for healing the sick—extremely energetic—keeps his
own calendar, which stays five days behind. Speaks poorly of the
convent, claims that the crazy people locked themselves in there and
sent him, the sane one, to an institution." The capuchin, whenever
he feels better, walks from room to room. He reads out the patients'
names and tries to cure them by taking them for a stroll. Among
those people, there probably is Mr. Drużak, suffering from a "profound religious reflection," always smiling and rather happy; only
sometimes, in fits of rage, he would threaten to burn down the whole
city—which, coming from a chimney sweep sounds like a legitimate
threat. And then there's Mr. Nowak: one of the many suffering from
delirium tremens, who the morning after he was admitted screamed
that he was being "suffocated by a phantom." This outburst won
him an extra dose of opium, but it amounted to nothing since they
kept administering opium and a straightjacket the entire time. His
whole stay was just a string of bad luck. One day he even "beat up
Katz," but who Katz is, we don't know. Finally, after four months of
torment, his brother comes to take him away. But it doesn't seem like
he's taking him to a better life. Among the others cured by walking
with the nutcase priest is also Mr. Sendler, "a Russian government
official" from Michałowice, also suffering from delirium tremens—
cured, then readmitted, then cured once more; and Mr. Zaremba,
"employee of Archduke Charles Louis in Galicia" suffering from
"profound reflection with a notion of persecution"—depression with
hints of paranoia—and Mr. Maurycy Spira, the only Israeli in the
crowd, suffering from profound reflection, and a medical student

from Pińczów living in Krakow. So I attempt to find Spira; there was a doctor named Maurycy Spira who served in the Polish Legions, but mine would probably be too old to be a match. There was also another one (or the same one) in Rzeszów, president of the Bar Kochba, a Jewish sports club established in 1910, and, as I learn, one of the first Jewish clubs in Poland. I'm curious if the student managed to escape the "profound reflection" of his adolescence in one piece. And so, many years later, I wish for him to get it together and become a decent man. I can't do much more.

I read about this fellowship of the totally and partially crazy for the nth time; they're all dead, gone to the other side. I recreate, I try to figure what led them to Kulparkowo. Anyway, the very fact that Krakow's crazies were sent there, outside of Lviv, proves what Krakow really was back then: a satellite, a province, a muddy town with suburbs full of suspicious inns; a town with brothels right by the town wall on narrow streets that smelled like an outhouse. And the new, huge hospital was built in Lviv, in the then still-empty borough where the loonies wouldn't bother anyone. It just so happens that those who were sent from Holy Ghost to Kulparkowo were some of the first because the hospital was built in 1875, the same year in which the first hospital patient cards were dated. In those days, a midgety gnome by the name of Jan Matejko reigned over the souls of all those tribesmen in Krakow. (I need to write it down in order to believe it: these are the great people this city used to have, the giants it used to praise).

It's a sultry spring, it's raining, candelabra-like little blossoms start to appear on the chestnut trees; it seems as if they, and not the lanterns, are shining. You can walk and breathe in all that has accumulated: the smell of the soil, of blooming, of urine. It's spring, a season for walks around the town in which all those patient cards had been filled out; cards that I have to keep or pass on. It seems like the doctors sent their worst cases back home at the end of the year, as if they were handing out school reports. They took inventory and decided that the chimney sweep, suffering from "profound religious reflection," was cured, and that the vicar from Tyniec was incurable. How did they ship them back? What were the winters like back then? Did they need to put those crazies in straightjackets (probably yes, often)? Numb them with opiates measured by the tablespoon and tea-spoon (most likely)? What transportation did they use? Probably the train, since from 1861 there was a connection, courtesy of Archduke Charles Louis, between Krakow and Lviv. They probably had them travel in coach too, since better seating wasn't yet popular. Around 1875 this railway company became very popular, carrying almost one million passengers a year—I read this somewhere, amazed, and I even tried to research how long a trip lasted back then, and how long it lasts now. I don't have any data for 1875, but in 1914 a trip from Krakow to Lviv lasted five and a half hours; today it's six hours and fifty-eight minutes at least, but there's a border along the way and they need to change the train's wheelset to fit the different track size—whereas back in the day it used to be a smooth ride. This rail-way boom might've saved the patients from the Holy Ghost Hospital from a ride in a horse-and-buggy ambulance. But I can only imagine this part because I feel sorry for them after all those years; for all those suffering from "profound reflection" and lying stretched out as if nailed to a cross, too calm and deprived of any thoughts, staring blankly at the floor, those who don't talk for years until their fam-ily realizes something needs to be done. And I feel sorry for violent madmen, dreaming of shackles and wolves, screaming at night and soiling themselves, for all who must've grown boring to the staff of the Krakow hospital after months and years spent in a straightjacket; years of shock therapy, leeches, cold compresses, and opiates.

It's not that far of a stretch from the story of the train-car full of crazies being shipped from my town to Lviv, or Kulparkowo—formerly Goldberghof—to the stories and journeys taken a little farther; journeys I discovered in the notes recorded for the sake of others' learning. Half a century before the specters of Holy Ghost Hospital, mad from drinking, from sadness, or from love, a man named Krystyn Lach-Szyrma embarked on a journey to England and Scotland, where he was supposed to study economics. He was a keen observer, and paid attention to detail while still seeing the bigger picture, and knew how to sketch realistic images. His *England and Scotland: Recollections From the Journey of 1820–1824* is still interesting even today, at least in part. He observes Great Britain without spite; he's not some Frenchman who can't stand the food and doesn't like anything. Lach-Szyrma tells it how it is, providing information about how the country is organized, about its laws, prices, roads, and about its sick, including its madmen.

He was not the only one to do so. Mental hospitals were famous as examples of charitable initiatives worth bragging about, but also as human zoos, museums where, for the sake of knowledge, or pleasure, the better part of society observes the lesser one. Among these institutions, Bedlam undoubtedly held the highest ranking, the worst of the worst, a cesspit of madness, a dumpsite for those who hit rock bottom. I saw Bedlam before I even knew about its existence in the reprints of paintings by William Hogarth, a slightly cartoonish eighteenth-century artist who was very popular in his day. His contemporaries were particularly impressed by *A Rake's Progress*—the story of Tom Rakewell, a young man who inherits a fortune only to blow it all immediately—a series presented in eight paintings. The fall in this story is inevitable. Upon his father's death, Tom already begins to enjoy some of his inherited luxuries. He goes to London, drinks, gambles, and attends orgies in a brothel. He loses everything. Then he finds a rich old hag, whom he marries—and then he's rich again, and loses everything once more. The last two paintings depict a debtors' prison, in which Tom starts to go mad, and Bedlam, where he lies naked on the floor, among other madmen. He lies on the ground covered by a mere cloth patch that, due to the observed decorum, is snow-white—but this whiteness is discordant from a common sense perspective. He lies senseless, not recognizing the only person who loved him despite everything, named, ironically, Anna Trulove, who even in those dire circumstances came to help him. But he can't be helped. Tom the profligate doesn't recognize anyone. And, in the background, behind the darkness of this human vortex, curious ladies with handheld fans enjoy a leisurely stroll as they are sightseeing the reeking chamber of half-humans; ladies free and bright among the confused and dark minds. It is Bedlam, although a milder version, because otherwise it would count as pornography. I haven't seen Bedlam itself, but I've seen Hogarth's paintings *in situ*, in a kind of madhouse, but one designed to host objects of arts and crafts: Sir John Soane's Museum in London, the most crowded museum I know. Also the most peculiar one, and as if the three connected tenement houses piled to the roof with hundreds of thousands of objects of all kinds weren't enough, right outside its walls was a city sprawling out in its weird shape, within its islandish self. It's enough to step

Wojciech Nowicki

outside in the square to meet judges in their robes, with their case files, on their way to the park for a cup of soup from a Korean bar just around the corner.

"On the 29th of November, 1823—a month which, with its overcast skies, brings the English most of their splenetic moods and makes one most suicidal . . ." That's how Krystyn Lach-Szyrma begins. "I have visited Bedlam. Bedlam, as is known, is a madhouse in London."

What follows are the descriptions of the building and sculptures in the vestibule—because they do have symbolic meaning, after all, and so we need to pay attention—and later the author writes briefly about what is inside the madhouse. "For the most part, the madhouse is not entirely unlike the lucid world. The majority of its populace are those without thoughts and unable to act, only staring in a torpor at what passes in front of their eyes. The madhouse also contains the forgotten populace. It wakens pity, but is not interesting."—and, as Lach-Szyrma believes, that is because, just like in the outside world, all attention is naturally turned to the "upper classes where the empire's dignitaries, reformers, politicians, heroes, prophets, kings, and gods reside." The author then ignores the maddened mob, and walks quickly through the halls, as if they were empty. He doesn't notice those mad from drinking, the simple folks, victims of delirium tremens, those who wake in the morning screaming, the catatonics, or those suffering from profound reflection, or those religiously agitated and lying stretched out on the ground as if crucified, or the crazed priests climbing furnaces and throwing ripped-out bricks at everyone until the allied forces of a straightjacket, drugs, and bloodletting will exhaust them and make them—as one doctor from Krakow put it—refrain from "monkeying around." But even in the case of those he described as fate's chosen ones—all he ever does is helplessly shrug his shoulders: "It would be difficult to distinguish all the kinds of madmen enclosed there; I will make accounts of them as they appeared in front of me."

So he provides the description of the crème de la crème of Bedlam, of patients crazy in a colorful way, crazies worth admiring, as well as people locked in the hospital, possibly for the rest of their lives, but who (he expresses such suspicion) are not crazy, rather political prisoners of a small caliber. Lach-Szyrma sees patients who belong somewhere else: if not the madhouse, then prison or an even worse punishment would doubtlessly await them. The author is not interested in the disease—it's vulgar. He deals with what is more intriguing, albeit baffling, though he doesn't know how to organize the information.

"It gave me chills," the Polish traveler writes later on, "seeing myself suddenly surrounded by so many madmen," and it's hard not to be surprised—after all, he went to Bedlam of his own will and had to suspect what he would find. "Nothing makes one so distrustful and disgusted toward another man like the loss of the most needed gift of reasonable behavior, the gift of reason itself," he continues. It is not the superiority of normalcy over madness that keeps him from walking among the inhabitants of Bedlam, but the fear of them. Unable to make reasonable judgments, they would do things to him unworthy of a human being. The custodian, however, sets his mind at ease. Nothing bad should happen. They meet madmen of all kinds, free to roam, because "these beings were harmless, thus they allowed them to wander wherever they wanted, and even satisfy their favorite fantasies. The dangerous ones are kept behind bars, their arms and legs chained. I have seen a few with their hands tied so they won't scratch themselves or others." They meet a young man who knew many foreign languages and read books—it was a student from Heidelberg who "intended to save Napoleon from deportation to St. Helena." Lach-Szyrma ends the paragraph about the student by saying "*relata refero*" because he doesn't want to take responsibility for facts he didn't witness himself.

The reasonable and meticulous author of the memoir, an experienced chronicler, takes very little away from Bedlam: "Bedlam is a huge edifice, five hundred and eight feet in length, with a dome in the middle, an expansive garden in the back for the sick to walk in. Its façade rests on Corinthian columns and bears the coats of arms of the three united kingdoms: the lion, the thistle, the harp—as if all the Britain had equal right to the building." Later, he mentions sculptures: Madness and Melancholia. At the end of his visit, he relates that over five hundred madmen reside there; the women loose their minds mostly because of love and commit crimes less frequently than men. That's it for the facts. The rest consists of the astonishment of a free man, convinced of the unshakability of his own mental faculties, terrified by the conversations he's having, by the madness and the grandeur of tragedy he witnesses. But he seems to fail to notice those behind bars, because such treatment of madmen doesn't agitate anyone too much at that time.

The two Bedlams, Hogarth's and Lach-Szyrma's, overlap, but not closely. One shows the entire moral chain that leads a man (even the wealthiest one) to the bottom of darkness where he lies unconscious, naked, madmen crowding behind him like in Bosch's painting, only less skillfully executed, thus less colorful. The Polish traveler sees in Bedlam not the pit of degradation, but a laudable institution for the masses. But when you take away the lion, the thistle, and the harp, the Corinthian columns and impressive length of the building, when you forget about the garden in the back and, more importantly, about the stocks to which the most troublesome patients were cuffed, what's left is the same thing: a chamber without escape, a black hole with a tiny window at the top with solid iron bars, and Bosch's characters, only less exciting in their representations. What remains are the misunderstood stories and helplessness exhibited for the public to see. After all, Lach-Szyrma says that he doesn't want to "distinguish them by their madness" because he's unable to, just like the doctors must've also been unable to. Bedlam must be thought of as prison, an inferno laid out with rotten hay, and yet these words never appear in the memories of travels across England and Scotland. Krystyn Lach-Szyrma is focused on admiration.

I was thinking about all those crowded madmen while lying in my too narrow and too short bed—on a Swedish island—perfect for staying in for just a while, but when you sleep in it for a month, questions start to come to mind: why did they make it so small, what kind of punishment is this? They know how to make bigger ones, my own Swedish bed barely fits my bedroom; and this bastard son of carpentry seems to be in that hotel room only to remind that sleep is a luxury not everyone can afford; that it needs to be conserved like water. I was in bed during my last night on the island, unable to sleep out of fear I might not get up. I was in bed, unable to sleep out of stress, shaken by a *reisefieber*, thinking about madness and immersing myself in madness, thinking about the disease, trying to remember who was in a hospital and why, what was the order. I was counting all the stays, the visits, and promised myself I'd write it down, although I don't know what for. I suddenly thought it was important. And in the morning, as usual, I didn't remember a thing.

Bedlam won't leave me alone.

Lach-Szyrma only briefly, and without any indignation, says the shackles in the madhouse are a natural attribute of madness itself. I stare at a print I dug out from somewhere. It shows a good-looking man named Willam Norris—an American sailor. The print shows him on a simple wood-framed bed with a hay mattress; he's sitting up with a painful frown, dressed in a shirt and with a headscarf or a nightcap on his head. He's restrained with something that resembles metal suspenders, his arms tightly pressed against his torso and the suspenders chained to a wide pipe behind him. He can sit, nothing more; he can move his legs, but this legs won't go much farther; he can move his hands, but not his arms. This is how Norris spent thirteen years of his life.

A hundred years before Lach-Szyrma, in 1725, César de Saussure, a young Swiss traveler who arrived in London, reporting in his letters on what was worthy of attention during his voyages across Germany, the Netherlands, and England. He visited Bedlam as well. He described a corridor and cells on the main floor, with little windows in the doors enabling one to look inside. "On the first floor," he wrote, "there is a section designated for dangerous madmen, mostly restrained, and terrifying to even look at. On their free days, people of both genders, mostly the lower classes, come in great numbers to visit the hospital and entertain themselves with sights of those poor wretches who evoke nothing but laughter in them."

Even though Bedlam changed buildings and moved between different boroughs of London, the main principle remained intact, recalls Peter Ackroyd, the city's biographer: "The conditions of the interior were as sparse as before, as if once again the whole purpose of the building was a theatrical display designed to depict the triumph over lunacy in London. The two sculpted giants of madness, known popularly as the 'brainless brothers' were kept in the vestibule. Methods of treatment remained severe, and were largely dependent on mechanical restraint . . ." (The restraints, by the way, are called by their real names: whips and chains.) "Outside it seemed to be a palace; inside, it closely resembled a prison. The price of admission was a penny . . ."

The era of pharmacological treatment, combined with occupational therapy, began in the middle of the nineteenth century. Engravings from 1860 show idyllic scenes: therapy rooms look like gentleman clubs, patients are placed in spacious rooms with huge windows or little trees in pots. Every month a ball took place; supposedly it was a moving spectacle. But even though that era started in the 1850s, Edmondo de Amicis, author of *Heart*, who published his travel memoirs from London in 1874, doesn't even mention Bedlam anymore.

And since I went all that way back in time, I'll go a little further. Jakub Sobieski—father of Jan Sobieski III, future king of
Poland—who penned memoirs of his travels around Europe,
found himself in Paris on the day of the assassination of Henry IV
of France by François Ravaillac in 1610. It took place on Rue de la
Ferronnerie, the street of the lilies. Ravaillac—what became obvious
immediately—was sick in the head, and experienced visions that these
days we can treat normally, but which back then were treated with an
ax. Sobieski writes: "At noon, after the killing of the King Henry IV,
Paris was engulfed in panic. It seemed as if Judgment Day had come.
All of the city took to the streets upon hearing of the King's death;
women flocked outside their houses, screaming, crying, running with
their children, but not knowing themselves where to. Others roamed
the streets aimlessly in their buggies, without destination; some men
locked themselves in their houses, others, half dressed (as was their
custom at that time of day; the French would rest at home), ran barefoot in the streets, or mounted their horses, sometimes bareback, but
all with their sabers drawn, threatening, cursing, screaming. To refer
to them at the time as a *crazed nation* was accurate."

I thought this image may be exaggerated, too colorful, because
Sobieski describes a city gripped in madness, and no medic from

the Holy Ghost Hospital, nor an old fashioned doctor from Bedlam, would take it easy on a city like this: it needs treatment, a phlebotomy, a straight jacket, chains. And yet, I find in the writings of Samuel Pepys, half a century earlier, something of an echo of that Paris in the state of utmost agitation, of a fever that threatens life. In Pepys's work it is a feverish London in the times of restoration: "Waked in the morning about six o'clock, by people running up and down . . . talking that the Fanatiques were up in arms in the City. And so I rose and went forth; where in the street I found every body in arms at the doors. So I returned (though with no courage at all, but that I might not seem to be afeared), and got by sword and pistol, which, however, I had no powder to charge; and went to the door, where I found Sir R. Ford, and with him I walked up and down as far as the Exchange, and there I left him. In our way, the streets full of Train-band, and great stories, what mischief these rogues have done; and I think near a dozen have been killed this morning on both sides. Seeing the city in this condition, the shops shut, and all things in trouble, I went home and sat . . ." And then Pepys notes, poor soul honest to itself: ". . . in short it is this, of all these Fanatiques that have done all this, viz., routed all the Trainbands that they met with, put the King's life-guards to the run, killed about twenty men, broke through the City gates twice; and all this in the day-time, when all the City was in arms; are not in all about 31. Whereas we did believe them. . . . to be at least 500."

After the mass madness of a people—because Sobieski clearly states that he observed a nation of madmen suddenly awaken to their madness, just like Pepys did in his mild manner—there follow the necessary proceedings: a coronation, a court process and punishment, and only at the very end the funeral. That is the order of necessities: interregnum can't last too long, the king's assassin must be punished accordingly and swiftly, and the funeral is last because the guests coming for the ceremony will need time to arrive. Out of all of this, the description of the punishment is the most severe, due to Sobieski's completely transparent style, and without any signs of disgust, because what was he supposed to be disgusted about anyway?

Jakub Sobieski sits by the window facing Place de Grève and describes what he can see from there, how they torture Ravaillac in different ways. And I think that magnate Sobieski, whose portrait in Polish dress I still remember, must've looked a little bit like a savage in the Paris of those days. "First," Sobieski writes, "he was led to the street on which he murdered the king, and then he was given the very knife, covered in the royal blood, to hold in his hand; and this very hand was burnt, causing him unimaginable pain as first his fingers slowly fell off; then he dropped the knife and the rest of his hand soon followed; exhausted, they took him by oxcart to the front of the finest cathedral in all of Paris—the Holy Mary. He wore a shirt and some ragged, blue-linen pants. When finally there, a crier started to pronounce him a traitor, a criminal, and a cruel king slayer who had wiped the great King Henry IV of the face of this world. The crowd raised a great outcry, cursing and slandering him. From there, when they brought him to one corner, the executioner started tearing through his breast with pincers and then brought him to another corner and pronounced him traitor again; and they tore apart the other side of his breast. Then, they grabbed him with the pincers under his armpits and started tearing and the crier kept pronouncing his guilt; the crowd was so thick, with people on foot or mounted or in their buggies, that oxen could hardly have pushed their way through it. Finally, they brought him to a decent-sized square they call à la Grève, where the worst criminals in Paris are executed."

"The crowd," continues Jakub Sobieski, "was so thick, one could walk across their heads. But the roofs and windows were just as crowded, mostly with foreigners, and I was there too, with the Radziwił princes, and had rented one window, and was far overcharged for it, too. Soon, as they made room for the rowdy crowd, they prepared to execute him. He died being pulled apart by horses."

At this point I have to retract the future king's father's right to speak—he who, from a window like a theater box, watches the death of a murderer and a madman—because there are so many inexplicable things in this story, unacceptable in our aseptic times, which, while reading the quoted pages, I agree with after all. Here I am, taking the ripping of live flesh with pincers and being torn apart by horses for something obvious. In that, I think, lies the strength of literature.

It's similar with Pepys; the Englishman also describes such spectacles of his own day. He writes: ". . . I went out to Charing Cross, to see Major-general Harrison hanged, drawn, and quartered; which was done there, he looking as cheerful as any man could do in that condition." These are not the only words of admiration, or surprise, for those people who, at the time of their death, apparently mocked their fate. But I read somewhere else that that was the fashionable attitude; fashionable among the sentenced: not to be afraid, but to laugh. ". . . His head and heart," Pepys writes later on, "were shown to the people, at which there was great shouts of joy. It is said, that he said that he was sure to come shortly at the right hand of Christ to judge them that now had judged him; and that his wife do expect his coming again. Thus it was my chance to see the King beheaded at White Hall, and to see the first blood shed in revenge for the blood of the King at Charing Cross . . . I went by waterway home, where I was angry with my wife for her things lying about, and in my passion kicked the little fine basket, which I had bought her in Holland, and broke it, which troubled me after I had done it." That's all Pepys for you in his coded notes, mixing freshly torn-out heart, triumphing crowds, and small domestic worries, mostly caused by his wife: "This morning Mr. Carew was hanged and quartered at Charing Cross; but his quarters, by a great favor, are not to be hanged up. . . . After that done to sleep, which I did not very well do, because that my wife having a stopping in her nose and she snored much, which I never did hear her do before."

And Sobieski, the father, writes: "they, a few hundred men, barely got off their horses before they grabbed their sabers and in a great rage almost chopped him to pieces." But that was not the end of punishment regicide suffered that day, one that he might've deserved, an eye for an eye after all: "A great numbers of people carried parts of Ravaillac's body home with them in their handkerchiefs. There was one bookbinder," the author tells us, "a seemingly stable man with a large beard, who was so full of hate for Ravaillac that he brought a few pieces of flesh home and, in his great spite and loathing, fried them up and ate them with his scrambled eggs—that is what my own eyes and the eyes of His Majesty Branicki saw. He even dared to invite us to this banquet of his, to help him eat, in response to which we both spat at him and went away. I understand that the man went mad like a dog from his own venom running through his veins. Other remains of Ravaillac's body were thrown into a fire that was prepared beforehand, and his ashes were scattered by the wind."

And if that was not enough, numerous punishments were administered to the Ravaillac family and house, so that the infamy would befall everyone and everything that had anything to do with the king's death. But instead of a hole burned in the ground by Ravaillac's stake, there is an image burned out in memory, a description of the regicide and his execution; maybe deserved, but cruel and, because of the bookbinder's scrambled eggs, sentenced to an eternal existence.

Moorings

The train was leaving the station in Czerniowce. I stood on the platform; I hadn't managed to buy a ticket. That always happens at one point during travel—a mechanism grinds to a halt and there's no longer any movement. A hotel was out of the question. A man smelling of beer approached me, "What's up? You're not going?" he asked. "Then come with me, I live right here, right outside the city, there, not far." It was sixty kilometers. First we hitchhiked, and then we took a bus; it had started to grow dusky by the time we got there. He borrowed a few hryviens from me and sent a young boy to the store.

The house was well proportioned, and pretty; they planted cabbage and had some plum trees. In the corner of their property was a lone pig in its pen, and next to it an outhouse. "If you need to go, go there," he said. His wife came out, "You're drunk again," she stated sadly, "and who's that?" she asked pointing her chin at me. "Me," I started to explain, "I'm from Poland," and she immediately warmed up to me because she used to work in Poland, of course, and, as would soon become clear, also in Germany, Italy, Portugal, and soon she would go to Greece. But she'd have to come back because this one here would squander everything on drinking. She belonged to the legion of people always on the road, transients, seasonal workers for whom the season never ends; mainly Ukrainian women, and then

Moldovan and Albanian women who, just like the Greeks, Italians, Portuguese, Turks, and Poles decades earlier, roamed Europe and its outskirts, searching for decently paid but illegal work. She told the story of her life as Odysseus. Her husband sat next to her, sadly shaking his head, acknowledging her every word, all of her accusations. "I keep running myself into the ground," she said, "with no life of my own, and he keeps guzzling. All he can think about is drinking." And then he, without a hint of aggression, somewhat calmly, said simply: "Cut the crap, go, make something to eat." She went to the kitchen as if he had struck her. We ate whatever she brought, pumpernickel bread with cumin, pickles, speck made from the last pig they slaughtered, a little bit of pressed curd-cheese. We ate and drank, immersed in the yellow glow of a light bulb; no one uses light bulbs that weak anymore. We drank vodka, which the boy had just brought back from the store; we smoked on the bench outside the house and didn't talk too much because there was nothing really to talk about; everyone was tired. "And," he said finally, "she just keeps talking like that." "It's not my fault there's no money in it, I'm just a teacher, a school principal, here, in the village. School starts soon." "I'm a school principal," his aggravation increased. "School starts tomorrow, you hear me?" "I hear you," she answered, "go to sleep."

I slept under a line of holy paintings in their best room, exempted from everyday use. The bed was a wide bench layered with pelts and blankets, topped with a duvet that would be enough for the harshest winter; "and winters," they said, "are harsh here." They slept in the kitchen. Laid their mattresses on the floor and locked up the whole house "because," they explained, "there are thieves all around here." "Once they even stole our dog. To call them neighbors is too much, the living scum." The house was well heated; a fug filled the corners; he murmured something to her, her reply was quick and hostile. Then he left; I smelled the cigarette from where he was sitting outside in the darkness, smoking. Finally, he got up and went somewhere.

He woke me early in the morning. It was cold, and I quickly got my things together. His wife kissed me goodbye, wished me safe travels. He walked me to the main road. "It will come soon," he said. It is one of those village secrets; there was nothing there, and there has never been; just a right turn after the bridge, and you have to stand precisely there. And the schedule's in your head. "It comes from Przemyśl, and Przemyśl is a long way away," he said. "Should be here already, it's a little late." I kept shivering from the cold despite my sweater; he stood next to me in a short sleeve shirt, sweaty, reeking of a hangover, his pores releasing all that had accumulated over the years. He kept smoking off-brand cigarettes, smuggled from all over Europe; smoking one after another. Finally, he implored: "Not that I'm asking, but wouldn't you leave me something?" "I did, at the house, on the table," I said, and he left immediately. A bus emerged from behind the trees, filled to the brim with people, their wares, and the usual checkered bags, some things tied with rope and wire—nothing that would bring to mind a proper international trade. In the morning, I was back in Czerniowce, where I again had no ticket. I went to the bus station, and from there, I went somewhere farther.

It's that moment when the fear of not coming back disappears. I always have this sensation at the beginning. The first night, wherever I go, is always the most expensive one. As if I were looking for a comfortable casket for my precious body. The same with the first meal and the first train—they're always the best. And then I grow used to the circumstances until one day I find myself sitting in somebody's home; the home of the people I don't know. I find myself in a musty bed, unused for years, in a village the name of which I don't know. I drink with the men, whose names I never learn. I listen to their stories; usually these are modest. Their entire worldly possessions could be tied up in a handkerchief. Even if they travel, they stay in the cheapest dumps. Their women will stay ten to a room to save money, and their adventures—in the eyes of men—have nothing heroic in them; they simply clean other people's houses and bring the money back. When their children leave, it's as if they've dropped off the map on which all the places they know are marked. They disappear forever. They live somewhere and the name of this somewhere is an object of pride. They say: "She left for Sydney," or "for Toronto, she is an official now, sir," but they never add that she will never come visit, never come back; that she lost all will to do so.

Cities, villages, and hamlets; inconceivable metropolises. Roads between them. All of that was compressed into one big mass. I keep ripping out parts of it; the rest I fill in myself because it was forgotten. Places my clan decided to abstain from because they would rather nurture their gardens and melancholia, because they would rather sour the kraut for winter and look after the tightly sealed windows, brew tea and meticulously sweeten it. My clan sat motionless, breeding memory because nobody else wanted to, but somebody had to, after all. They kept holding a more and more intense vigil over it; one that kept building a taller and taller wall separating them from other clans until, one day, it turned out that they were just a miserable bunch in the middle of a sea; that, along with the crazies from Kulaparkowo, my whole clan would be locked away forever because nobody could listen to their miserable wailing. It turned out that the entire clan was on the same boat with St. Wojciech and St. Bruno, and any minute now they would all be decapitated because they believed in their past and still wanted to remember it. And all of this was done as if the whole clan was taking part in *dziady*, praising the pagan deity Kupała and the dead, a ritual only understood, in its own way, by so few. My clan was sitting and debating the past as if it were their children's future; as if they believed anything at all could depend on it. But all was buried already; others built their houses on this cemetery, on this dump; just like we built ours on somebody else's cemetery. I have forsaken my people and their silly obsequies, and now I'm ashamed. In return, I tell the story of what I've seen after my escape.

I was in Shkodër, I tell my clan, where in the middle of an empty road stood a boy, maybe five years of age, with a plastic bottle full of bread soaked with water. And it was this peculiar boy who was a foreword to all other cities and villages in Albania. One has to try and foresee, based on those first sights, what has been seen since the beginning; you have to figure out the rest. But he was a false prophecy, a decoy. Albanian roads are chaotic and loud, women stroll under enormous black umbrellas designed for a heavy rain—you can see those umbrellas everywhere, even in nineteenth-century paintings; or under rice-paper umbrellas, not because of some Japanese fashion, but because of the stores with Chinese merchandise that have settled down there like in all of our cities. The sun is scorching, scorching. Days spent half asleep, in the search of shadow. They burn wood by the side of the road, and fry corn in the fire; it's black and hard as a stick. Night in Durrës, Durazzo, displaying its Venetian chattels in full glory, its towers—but it's a port city like any other, maybe a little poorer. A scrapyard city, composed of car washes and inhabited by towel sellers—towels with an ominous coat of arms, an ancient warning: a red background—fire walk with me. On top, a black bird, a vicious two-headed eagle. Scare, burn, butcher the others; that's the Albanian coat of arms. They must've made it as a deterrent. Red flags for lying on the beach, for drying yourself after a swim in the lake; somehow I can't imagine drying a young body with such symbol—a talloned beast with tongues split like a snake's. And yet, they lie flat on those eagles, among bites of concrete blackened by the sea and slightly crumbled. Although, if you look you can tell there are hundreds of years of crumbling ahead of them; and even then they won't disappear by themselves. This concrete is what's left of the bunkers built by a mad ruler who, in the olden days, would have a colorful nickname, like Enver the Vengeful, or Enver the Evil, or Concrete Enver, after those bunkers, or Enver the Murderer, or the Idiot, because he wasn't the brightest. He did so much, it's hard to pick the right thing. In any case, the concrete is what's left of him. And it imitates the rock. This is the crop of the sea here, bunkers and concrete, and not the stones.

Durrës, Durazzo, is of a density and intensity of all that seems initially unfriendly and hostile: sticky hotness and the sea throwing out rotten matter, stores with an amalgam of merchandise, internet cafes like a convent locutory. All of Albania communicates with the world from those cafes: with Germany, with Italy, with some place where one can settle for a bit, earn a little money and then build a house, or at least live a little better. Families stand in front of those computers, staring at those on whom their fate depends. And those on the other end will be suspended between two lives for years, until they realize that it's enough, or, on the contrary, they'll understand that they alone live their new lives, and that there's almost nothing that connects them to that family on the computer screen. But for now, three generations gather to stare into a camera, they say "son, dad, dear," and the one on the other end gets emotional. Where in line is the Albanian nation, in embarking on a journey to conquer the world? Where, after the Italians, Portuguese, Greeks, Turks, after the Poles and Ukrainians? Our whole continent wanders, and it's not the only one that does so.

Durrës, Durazzo, and its sister Marseille-Massilia with its dense boroughs and dark alleyways close to the market, where the scents are from a different world, from across oceans, and where a police patrol ends with a brawl and a roundup, with the barking of a megaphone; it ends with somebody's tragedy—just like it started; only somewhere else, on a different continent. It started with a tragedy that brought that somebody to this port city that smells of fish. Durrës, sister of

Casablanca, black from its black population, from the inhabitants of a different Africa, who came from afar because from here—it's closer to the better side. They walk around with their lives packed into checkered bags, they sleep wherever, do simple jobs, and sell merchandise so shiny it has to be fake. Sister port cities, at the doorstep, with a human wave rushing somewhere.

"In the morning, in Skopje, from the room in the Motel Vien, you will see blocks of flats," I go on, telling the story to my family in my thoughts; family that could never be convinced to step on the evil path of travel, "and you can see minarets rising from between." This hotel was, like all other hotels in the Muslim neighborhood, inserted between blocks of flats; there was no room anywhere else, only here, on the former lawns, driveways, where normally you'd find garages. Between blocks of flats—a network of pathways, trails, concrete tracks; some sectioned in half by a chain so that no one can drive onto them and park; not all of this is private property. The smells from the nearby market strike like from any other market in the world, but you can't actually find much: yogurt, dried apricots, bread, figs, and herbal tea. "Muslims" says the seller and makes a gesture of hopelessness, as if the religious affiliation binds him not only when it comes to beer.

They drink tea at the bar by the market, they stare at the TV tuned to a Turkish channel—one that broadcasts local dance music. That's what they like here. The owner has a leukoma in one eye. He wrapped the remote in plastic and he rules the TV. He keeps track of every tea in a notebook. One client, so he puts a "|" in the line for tea. Another client, "|" in the cola line. There's nothing else. They sit and smoke, slowly slurping. They listen. The teahouse is on the street of the smiths, the doors to their shops opened; you can see how those who have a job forge. Older smiths don't get new jobs anymore, they sit outside their workshops. Next to them are the jewelers. It seems like not much changes here, a hundred years ago the description of this place would be similar, even the merchandise almost the same, only the crowd would be slightly thicker back then: a market in a Muslim neighborhood, mosques, muezzin, teahouses, and those half-unemployed elders; except jewelers were always in demand because the thirst for gold is never quenched. They drink tea and sit in silence. They drink tea and talk—depending—calmly; only a young clerk at a grocery kiosk is nervous. He hands change back too quickly, distractedly, because he has a computer on his desk and is watching a soccer game.

The hotelier is serious, his gestures are subdued. His mouth is surrounded by an already grayish beard; it reaches his chest. His assistant also has a beard, but it's still more like a goatee. The hotel's is called the Vien because the owner saved up the money for its construction while living in Vienna. I wonder what he did there. He named his hotel after a city that—yes—gave him a rough time, but also gave him money and a new life. The hotelier's name, and I don't even have to come up with a fake one, was Imer Osmani. During the day he sits in an alcove under the stairs because that's the only place with a little bit of room, since everything is slightly crooked in this building built without a second thought, as if the architect wasn't present at the construction site. On the shelf behind him is a Turkish flag. In the drawer—*The Book of Commentaries*. In the morning there is a young couple sitting in front of him. She's dressed properly, wearing a hijab. His dress is also modest, a shirt and pressed pants. The hotelier holds the Book in front of him and explains life to them. They fall quiet when I approach. The hotel is just a side operation, a necessity, whereas the true need is nestled in this alcove, at that pulpit for conflicted spouses, for the infertile, for the brothers who took to drinking.

There is an upheaval on the stone bridge. In a split second, all the merchants gather up their stands made of carton, grab their goods, and, suddenly, the bridge is deserted. No more chestnut sellers, no more CDs and movies on VHS, toys, socks, and knee braces; nothing's there anymore—in the blink of an eye. A man who looks like a civilian comes along, but the word "Police" is printed on the back of his jacket. He makes a ritual of his arrival, so that everyone has time to run. I saw a similar scene in Vienna, the city praised by Imer Osmani. Two youngsters were selling things off a cardboard stand. The police arrived and chased after them on their motorbikes, on the sidewalk—the boys didn't stand a chance. Here, it's different. Here, these are still different times.

The yellow-green hills surrounding the city are covered with snow. It's sunny in the city and a strong, chilling wind. People sit close to the buildings for warmth. Diplomats in suits drink coffee on the main avenue. The light is low and the poplars appear white. Everything seems to be shining with an internal glow, the bridge, the Vardar River running under it, the people walking over it. The bones protruding from a beggar's stump-leg are more pronounced. The ruins of Ottoman houses have sharper edges. And at night, the light in the bar window glows red and there's one beer left in the fridge, but people there wouldn't order it anyway, so it'll be there when I arrive. They smoke cigarettes and stare at the TV where dark-haired, dark-eyed beauties squirm; tense, to a point where you wish you could reach out and touch them. Thirty men stare at the women on-screen; each man has a mustache, smokes, and never smiles. They lust after those women but won't do anything about it. They drink their kefir and unconsciously maul cigarettes between their fingers, eventually lighting up one after another.

I wanted my clan to know how, in Belgrade, people run across multi-lane streets, between speeding cars, and everyone has something for sale—small children and adults, even the elderly—because they all belong to this dark-skinned nation and they all run, risking their lives. They are the local Indians, from the local reservation by the Danube or the Sava rivers. I can't remember where their city is; it's not a camp, but an actual city—with actual addresses for the mailman's sake, painted on the plywood of their abodes, which have backyards sometimes paved with wood planks, and sometimes even stone, with tires holding down the roofs made of aluminum and leftover paneling. Between the houses, their rags hang drying in the wind, and a plant grows out of a cracked bowl—something green for decoration; and a decoration means it's home. There is one real home in the middle of this city. And it's not the house of some outside master, but of a tribesman for whom they all do honest work. The King of scrap and rags, the emperor of waste paper; he'll buy the handlebars for a child's tricycle, and any amount of tram tracks collected God knows how from all over Belgrade. He doesn't ask any questions. You don't ask questions here. He'll buy a pile of yellowed newspapers wrapped with string and a reel of paper that his people will roll down from the printers. His house is like a town hall and Supreme Court all in one; the epicenter of power and justice, the last instance. And to the side, across the road, is a crapper. You get there by a linoleum path that leads through the mud; a red path, as if you were in Cannes walking the red carpet reserved for the stars. On the other side of the river, on the flat part of the shore, is a smaller kingdom; one wonders if it has its own ruler, or if the power reaches there from this side of the river. Maybe they're outcasts? Exiled from the city? I see the inhabitants of those bum kingdoms everywhere; they try to wash your car window with dirty water, they try to spit on your car, or make a deal of some sort. Most often, however, they carry some kinds of scraps, God knows from where; they're like ants, like bees that feed their queen and in whose hive the drone is growing; a fat baby ready to inherit the crown and continue to overwork its people, but pay them even less.

From the hills, all of Belgrade seems to be entirely white and waving; Belgrade, like a stone sea, luxury at its center, serving professionally brewed coffee straight from Italy, reading books in a coffee shop and eating cookies. Up close, Belgrade seems covered with filth, worn thin and cheap, even though it's indisputably magnificent. Belgrade—you can see it when you wander between its buildings—is proud of its grandeur, shines with its massive bulk, and yet is falling to pieces at the same time. There's a policeman standing by the pothole at the crossing, eating a *pleskjavica* bun filled with meat, and watching a high-voltage cable because the trolleybus pantograph has come off the wire. All the shoes at the shoemaker's are the same—black—as if any other style was forbidden. There are new buses on the streets, but the red trams screech as if they were about to fall apart, still remembering different times, a different country. People meet by the river, recalling their glory days over beer, talking about the country whose citizens they used to be; a country that is now gone, and what's left—nothing, pitiful remains. One says to me, full of bitterness and pride: "When I was a kid, you were the poor ones." That's what he says and he keeps drinking his beer. He keeps listing old privileges, benefits, "and now what?" And I don't know what to tell him.

I tried to tell my family how I wandered day and night around Delhi; I would begin at the edge of the merchants' district and would go farther and farther, catching glimpses of the insides of the shrines, houses; inside offices, trying to communicate with people one way or another. I would walk around and keep asking myself the only questions I was interested in back then, mainly: what am I doing here, why did I come here, where in my head is the beginning of this journey? I walked in circles between the new and the old town. I went to see what was in the bookstores. There were books about the British legal system, several used Harlequin romance novels, a few out-of-date guidebooks, most likely supplied by the hotel owners—trash left by tourists; nothing interesting, but at least they were within the realm of the known. The rest of the city didn't seem familiar in any way: walls splattered with red betel vines, as if it was blood; the days were too long, too sunny, I had vertigo and the fear of falling somewhere, unconscious, or that I would get lost for good. I hated this city, damn Delhi, an open sewer reeking of human waste, a rotting organism exposed to the sun. Back then, I didn't know any other place more poisoned than this ant hill, and I was haunted by the fear of a place where everybody was too close to one another, glued together.

In the old town the smells were more poignant, more stimulating, and nothing in-between: the sharp smell of ammonia, of rotting, of cooking oil, and on top of that various spices, chili, cumin, ginger, and the smell of poorly tanned leather, of shit, of ambergris, of incense. It was an endless parade of smells; after a while it all starts to flow together, it's easy to forget which smells are good and which are bad. The new town was less dazzling: just exhaust, asphalt, and dust. The old town was dilapidating before our very eyes, but also as if it were tied with twine, glued with spit and word of honor, and covered with cow shit to better hold it together. Out there, people prayed with zeal, ate gluttonously all day long, bartered and slept on the streets. In the old town, skinny, muscled types kept running rickshaws and smoking hashish, shooting heroin, drinking local brandy—that was their fuel. They had no access to the new town because it was supposed to be modern and blocked poverty right at its gates.

I was standing at the Connaught Place, in the heart of New Delhi, and reminiscing about my first airplane flight some twenty years before. I was flying on a ticket in my brother's name; those were still the days before having to take off your shoes and belt. You simply showed your passport at one checkpoint, then your ticket at the gate, and you were ready to go. But flying was still a novelty back then, not like today when it became more like a ride on a tram. In Paris, there were announcements hanging on the "wailing wall" of the Polish church: three workers for tomorrow, this or that kind, a job off the books for people from the East. There were also offers: one ticket for a male, will sell by the end of December; by next week, a ticket for m and f, urgent—at the airport, it was enough if the genders matched. The interior of the plane smelled a little bit; "We apologize," the stewardess said, "we had a rough flight this way," as if the flight itself was a disease.

That's what I was thinking about at Connaught Place, the so-called jewel of the capital, but overgrown with betel, filled with hackers and spitters as if it was a hospital tuberculosis ward. This square was just like the airplane I had my first flight on—seemingly wonderful, but ultimately a smelly and corroded machine; the ugliest plane at the entire airport. Failed sparks of genius: a square like a palace inherited after the British, and a flying machine from our part of the world—that is what I had before my eyes and on my mind.

Entire families lived on the sidewalks at the edge of the new town. I kept passing one such family every day. She—in complete disarray; her kids unconscious, scattered all around. Her man worked as a rickshaw driver, but mostly smoked heroin; sometimes he would lie naked like a slab of meat. He had his eyes open, but he couldn't see anything. That's why he was smoking, to cut off the mental electricity and sail away. Mother India is extremely skilled at shutting down your higher sensibilities. It teaches you to get rid of an intruder, pass by families like that one quickly and without a word—the families who were stopped at the entrance to the wide streets and lawns as if by an invisible gate.

"Mother India is a whore," I kept thinking to myself, "What am I doing here anyway, where did I get this need to come here?" To get lost somewhere, to hibernate—that's all I wanted at that point; to sleep, read for hours, not to think too much. I was standing at the Rajiv Chowk station and dreaming about disappearing for hours, shutting down; a restart. Poof, and I'm gone.

In Sighetu Marmației—though the city has many more names, in German, Yiddish, Hungarian, Slovak, Polish, and Ukrainian; after all, Ukraine is right over the border—so, in *Syhot*—let's stick with the Polish name—I stayed in many different places, and I don't remember all of them. Most often I stayed in a hotel in the middle of the city—Hotel Coroana, formerly Tisa, and even earlier Korona— with faux leather armchairs on the landing, and ashtrays with fig plants right next to them. From the street level, or rather from the square—the main square of Syhot—city's colorful; huge windows of the hotel's restaurant, some repurposed barracks in the back, the cook's assistants walking across a plank laid over a puddle of mud to go peel the potatoes. That's how it is in Syhot, that's how I remember it. From the street it still looks so-so, Mr. Fix-it is standing on a ladder, slapping paint all over the plaster wall; go through the gate, walk past the bumpy courtyard, and then the concrete begins; slanted balconies, overgrown gardens—as if it all belonged to everyone and to no one at the same time. Exposed to inclement weather, weeds grown into the stone, and moss and humidity are impossible to keep away. The city shrinks with every step. Right around the corner from the main square are communal blocks of flats with broken windows, children playing on an abandoned sofa. It was just like the city I used to live in; just like behind the basalt snake of Wiejska Street. Just like in its pre-war neighborhoods of houses, decent tenement houses with sturdy, but slightly dented floors; like in those apartments filled with fate's rejects, drunkards unloading anger on their children, wives, and dogs; just like in those houses where there's never enough money and the dominant smell is that of moldy and stale cooking oil. I knew all of that, but here—it was different, happier, and somewhat racy. There was firewood neatly piled for winter outside the blocks of flats. Tenants had knocked holes into the external wall to run the stove pipes outside; the whole wall was black from smoke. This is how you heat your apartment in the winter here because the walls are thin and windows are drafty. There's a doghouse at the entrance to the stairwell. The dog barks at outsiders, its chain digging into its neck. In place of a lawn are shanties, little garages made of wood and metal sheets. Between them are dumpsters, the garbage compressed under its own weight; stench crawls all over the city.

I slept at the Ukrainian guy's place, right by the station. He murmured slightly more comprehensibly; as a Ukrainian he was well-known there and he tossed rumbling words at everyone who approached the door: "And you? Want to sleep at my place? Who sent you? Got any money? Here, you pay up front." He would piss into the bathtub, he must've forgotten what it was for; a boor thick with dirt and with a cigarette hanging from his mouth. I never saw him without a cigarette. "One bath," he said and he showed me one finger. "Light goes out at ten," and he spread the fingers on both hands. He ran this little business, a one story house by the train station, somehow always empty. He swore his was the cheapest place in town, that he basically robbed himself, but a price for one bed was like in a hotel with breakfast included, an actual shower, and a free folder with information about the city. But when there was a wedding party at the Hotel Coroana, and the other hotels were even more expensive, I would always end up at the Ukrainian's place. I could smell his sweat a mile away, but I would stay anyway, wondering if the bed bugs would bite me again, if I'd catch some skin disease, if he'd try to screw me over for some extra cash. Because you have to be crazy to pay so much for one night—that was his reasoning—crazy to go around like this, without a clear purpose; so why not ask even more? He'd mostly sit inside the house, staring at the street through a yellowish curtain and mumbling; he had no better listener than himself. He sat and kept watch; and talked.

North of the city's border runs the Tisa River, a bundle of waterways with islands of gray stone that serves several European countries—a benefactor river, supplying the Danube with water. People occupy its banks on Saturdays and Sundays. Long ago they would come on foot, now they drive cars and park almost in the river itself, gently maneuvering among the rocks. They drive their cars there, but do the same thing they did before. They stay for the night; they drink and roast a ram. The shore is sprinkled with jawbones, ribs; sometimes you can find a whole skull. It looks as if an earthquake displaced some underground layers, as if, from underneath the rocks, it exposed a cemetery of wise—and beautiful in their wisdom—animals that used to come to this one place to die. But that's not the way it is. This is a stage for uncontrollable gluttony, giggles, promiscuity under the open sky; this is the ripping off of clothes in a hurry because you can't wait any longer. They eat their fatty ram, down it with beer and *pálinka* and hiccup; and then they wrestle on their blankets. In the morning they get emotional, they look at the water, in each other's embrace. They smoke shivering in the faint light, right before dawn. That's where I walked to from the city, stopped by farmers wearing only pants, a remnant of their fancy Sunday suits, stopped by bare concave-chested peasants in hats who were convinced that I was lost, or planning something sinister; as if the thought never left their minds that someone will take away the corn they've saved for their cattle. Or I would be stopped by rugged border patrol soldiers. We would stand in a cornfield, them checking my documents to kill time, giving warnings in an alien tongue, repeating "border," as if I was committing a crime just by getting close to it. I would go for walks by the Tisa and stare at its waters. I would watch people wearing high galoshes and rubber gloves, dragging spools of cable from their houses and dropping the end into the river; and the fish would surface, belly-up. They would collect them, laughing as if they were just out to cut some grass for the cattle. They just came to get some fish for dinner, maybe a little bit to sell. But people here didn't like fish that much. They only ate them sometimes because they were free.

And then came that one year, an even number—the year two thousand—when I went by the same river, but in a different city, and the water smelled like a city dump. The shore looked as if it had torn up by heavy machinery. I hadn't wanted to go to Baia Mare, Romania—I was running away from that city; we had some unfinished business. But instead it came to me. A tailing dam at the Baia Mare gold-processing plant had broken, spilling cyanide into the water and killing the fish. I was still in Bucharest when I saw the news report on this wild river and its dead fish. It was an unsettling year. A month later, a different mine poisoned the Tisa, this time with heavy metals. A cocktail. "Insufficient safeguards," the commentators sighed and kept preaching about a deluge, a great catastrophe that cannot be undone, just like Chernobyl. And now I was standing on a shore that only a year ago was covered with the bones of sheep, signs of human activity, of a brotherhood between man and the river. What seemed irreversible back in Bucharest, like the death of the river, here—on this shore—looked like the mere workings of an accident. Kids played with the dead fish. Farmers scratched their heads, wondering if the corn would be all right—it was slightly inundated, a little rotten, but all this talk of heavy metals didn't affect them. They debated in the streets over beers, but didn't see any reason to despair.

They knew that all would be reborn. In order to understand that, all you have to do is look at Syhot. This city is alive, even though it almost perished once. I walked around it, as if I was drunk, through the park in the city center where it was enough to sit down on the bench for someone to immediately join you with urgent business; with an urgent question, for example, if I was British, if I was an Arab, do I have any dollars for sale? "No," I kept replying patiently, and those answers allowed them to drag on the conversation. My speakers ranged in age from twelve to eighty. Just in case, they kept praising my country, or remained elegantly quiet, would simply sit with me for a moment and then leave. I felt good among them. There were nuns standing by some wall, one with a paper sign on her chest: Be kind and make a donation for the Orthodox Church. White face, dressed like a crow. Farther down the street—peasant women with turkeys for sale. They hold those giant birds in their arms all day, to display them better, to have something to do. If they didn't use their hands, they would feel useless. There was life in Syhot, even though not so long ago it was a sad city, a prison city; a city with a void after the Jews, a city on the border, and fearful of it.

There was only one man who didn't know that the city had come back to life. A skinny, stringy patient from the local hospital stood at its gates and looked around frantically. He kept running away, running straight ahead. He'd beg for a cigarette, ten leu, matches, anything. He would snatch whatever I was ready to hand him and run, looking behind him, even though no one was chasing him, no one was looking for him. He was free to go. He kept tripping in his felt slippers. He was free, just like the people of my clan were free, but they didn't do much with their freedom. He was free, but became insane; only he didn't know it.

I wandered, I talked, and I ate with the pilgrims. I can't quite remember now what for. I do remember how one night there were prayers taking place in the monastery where I was staying; I was in the attic room, wide awake. The attic was as big as a town, with a few light bulbs on an exposed wire that were the only source of light. I couldn't sleep because it was freezing. The friar had given me a blanket and a straw mattress like everybody else, and I was lying dressed in everything I had—my winter coat, my hat, and gloves—and waiting for the attic to warm up from the collective breath, from the snoring of people who had stripped down to their long johns, neatly folded their clothes, and put them under their heads so that no one would steal them. They would pray the Rosary; you could hear lung-wrenching coughs, children's cries, and sleeptalking—conversations conducted as if nobody was around. I couldn't sleep. I was annoyed by everything: noises, cold, the musty smell of the mattress. I would go down the stairs at night, where the smell of wood and dust vibrated in the air, and watch those sleeping in the church. They looked as if they had been sculpted by Veit Stoss: twisted, sick, supporting one another. Their faces were concrete, the skin leathery, their fat fingers unable to grasp small objects. The pages of their prayer books resisted them. They sat, snoring, behind the altar, in stalls, and in confessionals. They lay piled in galleries, the more vigilant ones opening their eyes whenever someone passed by. It was torment, not sleep. God's people in beds made of sculpted wood; worn out jackets, the women's heads covered with brown-and-gray checkered scarfs. The church, even though baroque, filled up with people reminiscent of the middle ages, people coming on a pilgrimage and sleeping under the roof of a temple. The divine roses, reds and blues of the paintings couldn't help; the basilica smelled of sweat, manure, bad breath. I would go outside and read the names of countrymen who had passed away on a plaque: Fidelis, Angel, Kapistran, Servacy. But these men were just like those in the church, peasants from the near-by villages, whose mothers christened them John, Klemens, Edward. And they went to the monastery and picked beautiful names that nobody here ever heard of before. It was the middle of the night, and groups of pilgrims holding candles kept passing by me. Just like me, they were lost in the dark, bundled up in fur coats, Sunday's best hanging in the wardrobe for forty years. And they kept praying, illuminated by those candles. One read from a notebook, the rest would repeat. At night, they were phantom-like and quiet; in the morning they would come back to life. Smacking their lips, they ate thick slices of bread and opened their canned preserves with knives. Those better off would go down to the church cafeteria for tea, and every zloty spent was like showing off in a casino. Those less well-off went to the fountain outside to down their bread with water, and were ready to go. There was still snow on the road and under it was deep mud. We walked single-file, and when someone fell down the rest would follow.

I've been traveling like this for years, I can't even remember the names of towns anymore. I traveled, I took pictures. The camera was always a great excuse to hide from people or to start a conversation. In Barda you walk up the mountain carrying stones in your hands to make it tougher, to commemorate the suffering. I talked there to an older man walking next to me one year. He was hacking as if his throat were being cut open, and he kept spitting. When we finally stopped, he stepped aside and lit a cigarette. "Jesus," he said, "I can't do it anymore, I have only one lung, I walk for health."

I went to Rome. When the pope died, my friend and I slept on the lawn; both of us bundled up because the mornings can be harsh there. Firefighters gave us some boxes, but they were damp from the dew. And in the morning we drank coffee at a local bar. We were soaked and you could hear our teeth chattering and we beamed with pride. I went to Oława, where a man who had visions had founded a temple, because I wanted to see what a church for the excluded look like. They had clergy house, a chapel—everything. I remember I was walking there from the city, and in the road ahead of me were people—walking on their knees with their arms above their heads so it would be even harder. They were led by a man with a bicycle. He was holding the bike in one hand, and carrying a figure of Christ in the other. He wanted to switch hands, so I held his bike for him. He quickly embraced the figure of Jesus with his now-free arm and dryly said "thanks, brother." I went to see their chapels, decorated with crutches and eyeglasses no longer needed, rejected; the caption under the painting said: Jesus said unto Mary of Szczecin: "Come to Oława. I heal, and so does my Mother." During the service, women lay prostrated outside the church. When mass was over, the founder had some visions, which were meticulously tallied. They were already in the upper two hundreds back then. I saw his followers for the first time from the train to Wrocław. I saw a crowd gathered in the community gardens. They waited for him to come and preach by his gazebo. They would wait for health, better times—anything for a change. A dozen years later he had everything built and stable, and the visions occurred every Sunday. That's what people came for; they couldn't do without a miracle. Without his prophecies, these would merely be buildings by the road. He had to keep seeing and keep talking about what he saw. He spoke in the first person, as Mary, "My son, John Paul the Second, is old," he would say, "and he will soon die. Keep praying for my son," he would wail, his voice breaking, a bland man in a wrinkly suit, a former employee of the Rolling-Stock Repair Company who built his own temple. He would wail and people would sob. Women would shout at me, "Kneel when brother Domański speaks! On your knees!" Before he died, he went for confession and repented for his sins; and his church of outcasts came back to the Church.

"I expect to see you tomorrow at the Orthodox temple," said the priest. We were sitting in his office and he was sucking on a pipe that had gone out some time earlier; he blew through it, tapped on it; I kept cracking my knuckles. He sat there with his yellowish beard, silent almost the entire time. He wasn't a great speaker. He was afraid of making mistakes when he spoke French, he'd rather keep quiet. He would show me French romances, crime stories lying around, mixed with church prayer books on the shelves behind his desk. Sometimes visiting women would interrupt. They would all come in, bowing, and quickly and quietly attack, "shu, shu, shu Father" and he would brush each one off with a commanding gesture, saying "Not now mother, come later. I have a guest." We were sitting in silence, bored. I was staring at the worn carpet and the scuffed furniture. I was thinking what he must've been through before he came to sit here, comfortably, far away from his noisy wife, who kept ordering people, peasants, and deliverers around the house. The priest was nervous and kept chewing on his beard from all this stress. He kept composing mutilated sentences in French, sometimes covertly looking up something in a phrase book. It was because of me he kept carrying it around in his pocket. His wife was a violent perfectionist; her accent was cautious, and her French carried marks of former greatness, despite the fact that she was wearing a flower-patterned gabardine and had black dirt under her fingernails. She would buy fruits from the villagers to make preserves and for distilling. She sold homemade alcohol to the local restaurants. Often when I stayed with them, and was about to go to sleep, somebody would knock at the back door. You knew immediately that it was one of the neighbors coming to beg for a bottle. In the morning, she would put a loaf of white bread in front of me, a dozen hard boiled eggs, jams, sausages, speck; she would bring coffee or tea. She tried to shove as much food into me as possible. I would come back late at night, and she would often be already asleep, so she wanted to make sure I ate well in the morning no matter what. It made her feel better, she claimed, and I knew she'd tick off another box: yet another thing under control. From her dark kitchen—because the kitchen was in the basement and she was saving on electricity—she commanded her husband, their daughters, the Orthodox temple. She gave orders to wash the floor or put out flowers. She commanded her guests—she ran the village. "I have to look after everything," she would say, "I'm the richest in the village," as if she lived and ruled there all by herself. And when I'd ask how it happened that they made it through the dark years without losing anything, or maybe losing everything and rebuilding it all in an instant, she kept quiet. But I wasn't trying to offend her. She would leave then, ringing her keys, her willingness to talk lost.

On Sunday morning the priest met me in the vestibule and simply said "Come in, please." There was no escape, but I stood at the back, to make my exit as quickly as possible if need be. The service was just a cover up, there were trucks parked outside the temple. They loaded people in the back. Not everyone could fit. The Priest had one woman get out, and told me to get in instead. I didn't want to. And he just said "Don't be silly, sir, you don't even know where we're going." We were driving on a road I already knew. Next to me, a young Orthodox priest eyed me suspiciously. All the women were wearing their Sunday dresses, surprisingly short, always black, and the older women wore white shirts and sheep-skin vests. There was a boy who didn't see anything the entire trip because his head barely cleared my waist. He held his mom's hand nervously. We were going through a village, later the houses ended, and so did the farms—only hills spotted with junk that always carries the same smell of rust and grease. You can smell it long before you see it. And then: nothing for a long time, only little springs coming from nobody knows where, their water caught by a piece of rusty pipe, collected in an old tire or a hollowed log. Above those springs you could sometimes spot signs, like the ones you'd expect to see in health resorts; for indigestion, hyperacidity, kidney stones—you could roam from one spring in the village to the next and be cured of almost everything. Only I couldn't be healed, because there's no water for my afflictions. No water coming from a pipe sticking out of the wall of an old farmhouse can help me, even if I came every day and drank from my cupped hands. (You couldn't drink it otherwise. There once used to be a leaky cup hanging on a string—I know because I saw ones like them by other springs—a cup with a smallish hole, and though you could still drink, the little hole turns the cup into a worthless object. How desperate do you have to be to unwind the rusty wire and steal a leaky cup? How little do you have to feel the desire to steal an object like that?) Around those springs, water would collect in puddles, boots would smack, trouser hems would grow heavy; I had been by this spring the day before, drinking with hope, but nothing happened. Now we were speeding over the bumps and passing the springs; we turned many times and finally the truck stopped and we had to get out and walk.

There was a chapel there that was being consecrated. There was a Patriarch and some nuns—all in black—their faces tightly wrapped in white cloth. There was a whole regiment of them. My priest wanted just that, he wanted me to observe that particular day. "I expect you tomorrow at the temple," that's what he had said, for the first time since I had started truly living with them, since I started eating their food, since we started saying good night to one another on the stairs. He spoke in a tone that did not take no for an answer. I was supposed to come and see that it was not his wife—educated in Bucharest, the daughter of a merchant—who ruled the house, the village; that it were his priestly matters that had brought the Patriarch from the far-away city, that brought the nuns who set up tables, made coffee, sliced bread, and, even before that, baked it at their monastery, who served water to the thirsty and provided shade for the clergymen—all before we had even arrived. The service took place under the open sky. My priest glowed with happiness; it was not his yellowish beard, but his sparkling eyes that caught the attention of others. People were kneeling and I could see their cracked feet. Drenched in sweat, we drank water from a single cup, we shared bread; my priest beamed like God the Father himself and afterward left together with the patriarch in a car. The nuns loaded everything back on the carts, people climbed back into the trucks, and I walked away through the hills.

From my homes, and with homes in my head, I would leave and feel homeless. Because anything can happen when you're traveling long and far; that's what I've been taught. The road ends suddenly, even though it's on the map. The overpass hangs suspended in the air and instead of the rest of it there's a rusty road sign; instead of a road there's only sand; or a group of gypsies in the middle of the road. The gypsies take of their sandals and dance as if they had an epiphany, with their arms thrust up high. It's not an epiphany, but happiness about nothing in particular, inaccessible to me and the likes of me. A few plastic bottles of beer and everyone's dancing with everybody else, and one elder lady dances alone because she likes it that way. And soon my companions and I dance too, and some young girl starts to yell, "Hey, you, give me your *sapagi!*" and she indicates that she's barefoot, while I'm wearing shoes. But her sister hits her on the head to shut up and keep dancing. That's what happens on the road; and I either dive right in, or tremble with fear.

And so, when the day ends I fall in love with a hotel. I need a hotel, a motel, a temporary home, anything; a place to collect my thoughts and catch my breath. I need a shower, or at least a sink, and a bed. I need a TV that speaks another language—everything's always more interesting in a foreign language, even though I know the movies and all the shows, even though women in the same makeup make serious faces and announce catastrophes on the news, even if it's not the season for tragedy and they need to make an entire circus around fifteen people protesting against stray dogs, or about a temporary power shortage, or a council of old men in worn-out suits. You need that when you travel, you need to immerse yourself in that; you need to fall asleep while watching. And you need a hotel restaurant, even if just to reject it in the end, because there's nothing more disgusting than a hotel restaurant.

Only road signs pointing to Hotel Naţional will lead confidently to Kishinev's downtown. There are plenty of those little guideposts, everywhere, as if they were leading to the center of the Sun City, the only place worth visiting. And when the pot-holed asphalt rumbles beneath your wheels—it's night and almost thirty degrees Celsius— you want something to be there, at the end of those guideposts; you want a bed and warm water, not another hour in the car. So we follow the tracks leading to the Naţional, we become powerless and blindly follow the lead. At the end of the line is a black monolith backgrounded by a dark sky. There's no light in any of the windows. The multistory, gray concrete building is empty. Glued to its side is a smaller building—a restaurant according to its boastful neon. But there is no restaurant. There is a hotel casino, though. It's the only thing that is what it claims to be: pasted all over with pictures of slot machines and lucky numbers, the casino glimmers with lights. The guideposts lead to the city's only hotel, which was closed long ago.

These are the moments when I feel discouraged, I feel like going back, or sleeping in a car. Let it happen in Kishinev or anywhere else where there is a receptionist who lets you know it's time to grease the hand, or that she's done with everything—like in Bańska Bystrzyca, a hotel the size of a cruise ship, another concrete block with dark windows where a blonde bimbo behind a glass screen (I don't even remember her face) told me there were no available rooms. And there were maybe five cars in the parking lot. It's night and she would have to lock up the reception, go up few flights, maybe change the sheets, or at least call up the maid. And she's sleepy and has no strength left, so she says: "there are no vacancies" and shuts her screen. You have to move on.

I know hotels that are spotless, with huge swimming pools and urinals like sculptures; with quiet—when needed, multi-lingual—service personnel. And I often sleep in places where a beefed-up guy with an open shirt offers you prostitutes without embarrassment; "If you want girls," he says, "girls are nice, skinny, young." That's in Tiraspol, at Hotel Ajst by the Dniester River, where at night the city is covered with a sheepskin of moonlight, and there's a deadly battle resonating in the room next door; shrieks and hacking. They rented the room together. I saw them at Café Eilenburg on Sverdlov Street, a small fellow in a red shirt open all the way to his belly button and his bear-like friend—his muscle. The little guy had dark hair, slick with hair gel, and a trimmed mustache—a comical character, you could say, but he'd blow his money and never go anywhere without his bodyguard. They were sitting on a terrace, at a plastic garden table, being served by a busty waitress; you could tell the owner had a good eye for detail. The little man had a cheap camera; it didn't really fit someone who'd spent two paychecks on a dinner. He grabbed the waitress, turned around and asked me to take a picture. He shouted, "Oh sweetheart, what an ass you have, and those titties, fuck me, heavenly!" She laughed and put her arm around him, his head reaching her armpit. He put his face between her breasts and loudly inhaled their smell. Click, picture taken. He emerged from between them and said: "Hi, I'm from Hungary—and you?" The conversation didn't last, just a few sentences, and I finally asked what exactly it was that he was doing there. "Well," he waived his hand, "business, in general."

He seemed reckless with money, but he wouldn't go overboard. He and his bodyguard stayed in one room; they slept in a king bed together and washed their own socks. The nocturnal shrieks also had a simple explanation; it's cheaper to have the same prostitute. One smokes on the balcony while the other wrestles in bed with a woman who's vocally gifted and makes sure they're happy. The river is wide at this point, and the silence has a dimension punctuated by sounds that carry like a heart beating in an echo chamber. You can hear the clinking of bottles from miles away, from all over the city. The river's current carries distant barks. The woman gives a high-pitched moan and then silence. Finally, a break. Then the cigarette smoke starts wafting into my room. They smoke, and a languid conversation begins. The little guy, finally less excited, and the girl; she speaks in a hoarse voice, as if she aged thirty years all of a sudden. "Sleep, Christ, fall asleep" I say to myself, because they will soon start again. The bodyguard is next in line and I can't close the window, the room is like a tin can—it has no ventilation. The chill won't come before morning.

I have known these places only in passing. "The Dniester River gorge," I read the caption on the back of a photograph; "The După River gorge," the caption on another. An old box, and in it—pictures from the past: torn-down bridges, grape picking, grapevine celebrations. All from here. Dniester, a typical river of the plains, cutting deep into the earth. Bridges thrown over it like spider webs, God knows how. But the Dniester is wide, broad. Tiraspol, out of thriftiness, was built only on its northern shore: one bridge is enough, one ferry will do. That's how it is today still.

In our hotel by the Dniester River, the day starts at 6 A.M. with the penetrating roar of a drill and a housekeeper's laughter. Time to wake up. It's enough to show your face around the reception desk for the watchmen to start chatting. He has his own little room, he oversees the parking lot, collects tips from the drivers; he has his own little herd of women that put out with his blessing and for a cut of their profits. So he approaches us, hands in his pockets, "Hi guys, if you need anything, you know . . ."

The next day, in the capital city of Kishinev, I find his brother and soul mate: a janitor at a sister hotel—Hotel Turist. Go anywhere you want, be it Odessa or Minsk, and you'll be always stay in the same room. There will be the same red pone in the hallway, you'll meet the same mean housekeeper. Identical hotels are all over the old republics. So the watchman, with his hands in pockets, starts a conversation under the cloak of night: "If you need anything, come see me." And an hour later, the door to the neighboring room will creak open; first, a crooked, tired high heel shoe will emerge—it walked a long way— and then a fat leg, and finally, in the light of the incandescent bulb, the drunk face of a hotel prostitute will appear, layered with eternal make-up. Behind her is a shadow; a clone of the watchman from the hotel by the Dniester River. Not so friendly anymore, not so open. At the sight of a stranger he will hit the light switch. The darkness will fall and he will dissolve into it like a rat.

And there are two fold out beds in the room I'm in, one broken. There is some dirty winter bedding—even though it's the middle of summer—some worn out towels, two landscape paintings, a chandelier, carpeting, and hot water only in the mornings and in the evenings. Everything is itemized, except the water, on a list nailed to the door with a round stamp at the bottom. There is a desk, although nobody knows what for. A stifling heat has accumulated in that room, in all of the rooms, so it's time to run. We have to go to the bar next door to let it all out, to drink it over, and the receptionist informs us in a serious tone that we have to check out in the morning because there's no more room for us at the Turist.

In those moments, when you're being thrown out of a hotel, not even rage can help. Images come to mind of other hotels, on different latitudes, pampered to a point of ridiculousness and overprotectiveness; images of chocolates found on the pillow every evening, of newspapers from all over the world, and monogramed slippers. You can hear the echo of the masseuse's voice and the hissing of the espresso machine in the air-conditioned lobby. And here: a group of Americans wanders around the lobby in the morning—a whole group lost in a typically American way—and the whole group is, in a typically American way, cautious. I observe their way of dealing with Kishinev's hotels. They bought checkered Chinese bags, twelve packs of Coke and water, and now split the rations among themselves, right under the plastic clocks showing time in the capitals of the world without clear purpose. And the old lady polishing live plants with the window cleaner watches them closely. One room, two people, two Cokes, two bottles of water—and faith that it will help them survive in a city they consider savage. The hotel expelled us in favor of them, rightfully assuming that we'd make it work somehow.

In the end, we find a place, an apartment in the block of flats on bulevardul Cantemir. Blocks of flats have been sprouting up there straight from the ground, without stairs or landings leading to the stairwell inside. Those were only welded together later, and the concrete finally poured. But people had to get to their apartments even during construction, after all, so there are boot and paw prints left in the concrete. Water collects in the imprints after the rain. You have to be careful not to fall because it's slippery. When you look up from the foot of the buildings, you can see strings running from somebody's kitchen to the living room and lingerie hung out to dry. It's not the colors, but the sheer image of somebody leaning out the window to hang it that makes an impression; the thought of a woman leaning out of this window, below her a dozen stories and a slippery landing marked with footprints. When I think about the space separating her from the concrete I feel dizzy.

From that window, you can see merchants packing up in the afternoon after a day at the local market. They form small groups, they joke around and wait for a car that will take them home. You can see pedestrians zigzagging across the busy freeway, and the cars won't even slow down. You can see a man in another block of flats across the way, how he smokes on his balcony, among the bed linens hung to dry, and keeps nervously glancing over his shoulder; maybe he's not allowed to smoke and he's afraid of his wife. You can spot a 24/7 store, a small kiosk on the corner; and inside—an old babushka selling sunflowers with seeds ready to husk straight from her blanket spread across the floor.

Chaos surrounds the buildings, and nobody seems to notice because it has made itself part of the landscape: cars parked in the bushes, muddy hills, those bed sheets waving high against the gray wall; balconies patched with whatever's available, wood, plastic, metal. And inside those buildings—dark stairwells, painted in bold colors, azure, navy blue, and green; they help you notice that everything else is not so happy. Doors are open throughout the corridor, there are buckets full of potatoes standing outside, someone's pancakes, somebody else is peeling onions, and two women are sitting and smoking. It's summer and it's unbearably hot in those apartments, so you open the doors to air them out, and you find a neighbor to talk for a little while around the corner, where the sun can't reach you. But when you go inside the apartments, as usual, they're clean, neat, and homely—as if the Russian mess stayed behind the door.

And also this: you exit the elevator on any given floor and there is only a tiny bit of free space. The rest has been claimed by the residents. They've walled it off with steel doors, created extra hallways, and extended their balconies from the inside so that now they are like verandas. They jostle around their compact space, claiming as much of it for themselves as they can.

There's more still deposited in my memory. Hotel Krajina in the Serbian city of Negotin: two buildings, one next to the other (the image slowly takes shape in my mind), the hallway carpeted in gray, and a group of tired men standing on that carpeting; it's evening and they've just come back after being out the whole day. They smoke cigarettes and hide them in the palms of their hands. They stand around in flip-flops, in their rugged boots. They don't look like they're waiting for anyone, or like they're guests in the hotel. They simply are, they're standing and smoking under a sign that says smoking is forbidden; right by the flowerpots with dry soil. The sleepy doorwoman pays them no attention and they keep on smoking and staring at the TV that shows only muted static. The doorwoman writes down the prices on a piece of paper and shows them to us through the glass screen. The room is on the second floor, but the smell of laundry is already overwhelming enough in the lobby. On the first floor, in front of every door, is a drying rack with bedding hanging on it, checkered shirts, leggings from a previous era, anything you can find in any second-hand store for a dime a pound. There's no laundry on the second floor, though it starts again on the third floor, and so it goes all the way to the tenth. Nobody comes to Negotin, a forgotten hellhole near the Bulgarian border, close to the mining town of Bor. The hotel is inhabited by immigrants, unemployed, a gray mass that you don't usually see together in one place. There's nobody on the second floor—the only regular hotel floor. No one is using the bathrooms, tiled in a dirty brown; nobody lathers up the soap with its long-evaporated smell of generic cleaning agent. Nobody looks out the windows, from which you can see the grand prize at the local casino—a Yugo.

Then there's Hotel Kiev in Czerniowce. Before the war it was a classy hotel, modern, representative of the decent-sized metropolis that Chernivtsi used to be—and still is now, but in a different way. Although I'm not sure if I should believe the stories of its former glory: in 1919 Katarzyna Sayn-Wittgenstein complained about the local hotels, particularly about Hôtel Central. In her diary she wrote: "It is only our second day in Czerniowce, and already it managed to bring us down. Our hotel accommodations are unpleasant, uncomfortable, and expensive." And almost a century later the hotel has changed, room by room, meter by meter. With every visit a new part of the hallway becomes available to the guests. There used to be little rooms with space for two beds, thin walls, and creaking floors. Now, there are hallways big as Ali Baba's cave, covered with colorful, Styrofoam stuccos. Clean plasterboard covers the dingy plaster. The floor manager is no longer nestled at the end of a corridor, on a sofa; she doesn't have to get up in the middle of the night to every creak, be on the move in her high heels, fully clothed, and out from under her thick comforter. I always admired the resilience of her perm, untouched, as if carved in stone. Now, opposite the stairs, there's a huge hole in the wall behind which is a spacious room and two fold-out beds with rumpled bedding, and two female custodians talking about a wedding. "It was beautiful," they say, "so many guests." "Let me see your receipt—your room number is twenty-three, end of the hall."

I remember our rides from place to place, cities, streets, people, even the weather. I greedily take notes on restaurants with people who dance until they can't dance anymore, because I will be back for sure, or so I tell myself. I cast from my memory the hotels, empty spaces, gaps in my biography. Later, when it's already too late, I try to recall those hallways with plaster crumbling off the walls, the elevators that stop only at certain floors. I try to remember the face of a crying housekeeper whose son had just been stabbed, and she couldn't go to the hospital from fear of being fired. But her face disappeared somewhere and all I remember is a blue apron and words of consolation from the fat janitor-pimp. I recreate hotel bars, empty and dusty, with drunk staff; I recreate hotel restaurants—that one with a pimpled waiter who refused to serve anything, or this other one where shady businesses are discussed in the morning, and elegant older ladies have half a liter of vodka with their breakfast.

I was riding on a tram, a guy in a checkered shirt behind me, sweaty and possibly a little drunk. He's gripping a handle, and has a suitcase in his other hand and a coat over his shoulder. An expressionless man, glassy-eyed, he keeps pushing me, but the person in front of me holds his position. I'm stuck in this vice, and the hand of a third man (also with a coat over his shoulder) pulls the money out of my pocket. I can see all of it; I read the gestures as if I was watching a game in a slow motion. The only thing that is left for me is to fight them, so *whoosh*, I grab the hand that I can feel, that I can see in my pocket; and I start to yell and these three yell back at me. The entire tram turns their backs on me, nobody sees anything, nothing ever happened. The hand escapes as if it was slippery with soap; the seemingly drunk guy has already passed my money to the third man. The first two are still shouting; the third disappears. And when the tram starts up again I can see him at the tram stop, standing there calmly. It was the ticket controller who pointed me out to them, the bitch, I want to yank her by her dirty hair and kick her ass. The other two have already moved; now they watch her and she indicates someone with a jut of her chin. They start to work on a woman carrying groceries. I'm standing where I stood before, I don't do a thing, I don't exit; just keep your mouth shut and keep going, I tell myself.

Lviv's trams—a noisy whore that sells people out instead of taking care of them. The ticket controller's a thief. The city is despicable. You already know how it is, when somebody steals your money and the rest of the world pretends that nothing's happened. You've already experienced the Lviv school of pickpocketing first-hand. Everyone refers to it almost with pride, as if they were talking about the school of mathematics. They are proud because—one—it's so incredible and—two—it's so *them*; it is so *them* because it comes from the borderlands, and because it's a lost art. The Lviv school of pickpockets, one of a million reasons to miss our poor motherland that is no longer ours. And so the Lviv school of pickpocketing shoved a stick up your ass, took whatever was yours, and kept on doing the same to others—and you were scared, you stood like a pillar of salt, in silence, fearing the cold of a knife. And when they left—those representatives of this famous school—you went one more stop and also exited, all sweaty, looking for objects missing from your pockets while knees kept wobbling. J. kept trying to calm you, as if you were a child, "Nothing happened," she kept saying, "stop, it's just few zloty." Now you know how it feels.

Truth be told, you knew the feeling from before. You knew it perfectly well. But you didn't want to tell anyone. You were on a train from Bystrzyca to Bucharest, because it was in Bystrzyca were we stopped on our way to Syhot. The trip to Bucharest takes I don't know how long, so we stop there to see the city and spend the night in a motel. And these five men who were on the train with us kept drinking all the way. They were smoking in our compartment, even though it was forbidden. The ticket controller caught them, they paid the fine, and started shouting, mad about the money I guess, that it was our fault. So they kept smoking, blowing smoke in our faces and yelling. The controller walked by but didn't say anything more. He checked our tickets, not theirs, because they had stopped being nice and were already telling him to go fuck himself and that he was alone. So he checked our passports not to lose face completely, and went on. I said: "Let's go, I can stand the rest of the way, come on." But B. remained seated and said "No, we're staying, because if we go, then I'll snap." So we stayed.

The landscape outside the window was rather flat. The leg of the trip north of Salva and all the way to Syhot, is a ride on precarious mountain-side road: bridges, tunnels. You could lose your mind. But so far, in the lower region, it was rather calm, except for those guys. We were pretending to be asleep and they kept singing some army songs right into our ears. So finally, I don't remember how it went down exactly, but I found myself choking the one in front of me, the big one. I was choking him and the others were kicking me and B. was trying to do something about it. But there wasn't much to be done.

"Fags!" they kept shouting, "Just you wait!" And then: "Passports, you fuckers, give me your passports. Wallets. Money. Luggage." (The controller passed outside the door, took a quick look in, and disappeared). They couldn't decide, as if this was some kind of game, and kept laying our stuff out, picking their prize: credit cards were out of the question, and we had almost no cash. In the end, the big one said: "This." It was a Roamer from my great-grandfather, a cheap watch, but the only thing I had to remember him by. I had never met my great-grandfather, the one who hid out in London; the watch was all that I had of him. The rest of him, the memory, is in me and will die with me. He sent these watches one time for me and my brother. "This," said the big one, and that's how great-grandpa and the only tangible souvenir that remained between us went to hell. The other two men held me, the fat one took off my watch and I did nothing. I just kept screaming, "You leave that alone you fuckhead, *ty chuju*!" I kept screaming in my own language. And he, as if nothing had happened, simply strapped on the watch and pressed it to his ear. It worked nicely, although it ran a little late; such was my great-grandfather's revenge.

I kept screaming; my ears had turned red and I screamed like that so that everything that needed to be said was said. That was the first time, and I've never talked about it before, I experienced the adrenaline that comes with theft, the bad kind, and it was a huge dose. It was bad because it felt like being publicly raped; and there's also the question of honor. You feel as if someone injected you with pure alcohol and, to make matters worse, later you have to collect your shit and leave quietly. Those who just robbed you will kick you in the ass in farewell, so you leave amid peals of laughter. "Motherfuckers," I thought, "I'll kill you all"; and simultaneously: "Thank God it's only a watch"; and also: "I hope they won't look for us later, on the train"; and finally, without making any sense: "What will I do without the watch, without my great-grandfather on my wrist?"

All of Romania was like that, just my wanderings. One time I slept in the corridor and nothing bad happened. I slept in the first-class waiting room in the town of Dej because the waiting room was empty. People with tickets for second class were afraid to come inside, even though the train was already a few hours late and they could barely stand. But they had tickets for second class, so they sat on the concrete floor of the train station. I had fallen asleep in the waiting room even though, just like them, I had a ticket for coach. But I didn't give a shit, because I could always say that I didn't understand anything. And when I woke up, I was lying in a sea of Gypsies. My head was resting on the lap of a fat guy with a mustache. When he realized I was awake, he just tipped his hat and pointed to my backpack to let me know he was watching it. A child was asleep on my stomach. Everyone was smoking, we shared, we drank some vodka. There was always somebody behind the train station with a barrel of it; you could buy yourself half a liter in a plastic bottle. Someone would always host me in Romania, someone always took pity. When there was nowhere to go, for example, these two boys from a tiny hotel appeared—although "hotel" barely fits this regular house with a garden and a regular family, all crammed into one room so that they could rent the rest of the house to visitors, down to the last bed. These two boys would sleep in one bed together, so that I could also fit. And right after I woke up I took a ride to the train station in a rusty bus—but maybe that was in a different city, a different summer, and only I think that it was then. I had my backpack between my legs; a man got on the bus. He leaned over to the driver, his jacket over his shoulder because it was getting hot. And I could see under this jacket he had already opened up my backpack and was trying to pull something out. I grabbed him and he started to run, and just before he took off—he took a swing at me, but missed. And then it turned out that everybody had seen it; there was a French teacher sitting next to me and she told me, "Oh, mister, I know this one in and out. He steals here all the time." "So why didn't you say something when he was working me?" I responded. How is it that when you're somewhere far away and there's poverty all around, and even though you look just like everyone else, for some reason you seem to be the better target?

I intoxicated myself with Romania, year after year, forgetting— or no, bartering rather—bad deeds over good ones: like this guy at a hotel next to Gara de Nord who tried to screw me over, he was replaced by the memory later that evening when the house of a drunk in Moisei burned down, and the whole village stood watching, smoking and drinking, giving advice to the youngsters who were climbing on the roof, trying to salvage whatever they could. The entire village stood there and debated the crime and the just punishment. Memories of attempts to extort a bribe from me have been traded for a day when the priest's wife presented me with her cunning goodness; I say cunning because the goal was not to feed the traveler, but to secure the future of her daughter, a medical student in Bucharest (who, unbeknownst to her mother, had a boyfriend there); or for dozens of less significant moments: all this inexact change I got back from a cashier, attempts to fool me at a currency exchange kiosk, some conmanship here and there. But I still keep coming back and trade for more memories: petty theft for a grand experience, and I get what I want. I don't know myself where this mercy comes from, maybe from the fact that there's no price I wouldn't pay for what happens to me out there; to eat cheese with highlanders in a cable car sliding, it feels like it, into the abyss. A woman holds the bread to her bosom, a man tears off a huge chunk of cheese with his hands, cuts it with his little knife into pieces, shares it, even though he was supposed to sell it at the market. We drink vodka, we drink water from a brook—the train stops and you can get off sometimes, stretch your legs. Together, we save a drunk who sits on the steps of the train car the whole way and who keeps vomiting, or hanging low and trailing his hand over the ground, which moves too fast for him and makes him laugh.

"You've lost your mind!" says J. "You're starting to see thieves everywhere." But what am I suppose to do, it's a litany, a chain of evil hearts. We barely got of the plane in Madrid and already on the subway some man knocked into me from behind, hurrying to grab a seat. But before he sat, he slowed down and stopped. And I see it again: shabby clothes, his eyes meeting those of a guy behind me, and of course the jacket—always the jacket hanging over the shoulder. Only the slight tremors of his muscles reveal what's actually happening: it looks like he's nodding off while standing, but in reality he's looking through a crocodile-skin bag. Its owner doesn't understand English, so I gesture to her what's happening. And it's as if she was kicked by a horse, her face all flushed. She's screaming, and her husband is grabbing the thief, who is barely responsive; he's pushed out onto the station platform, someone grabs him and his being taken somewhere immediately. That's how I am now, even in

Palermo—instead of enjoying the city, which is covered by turns in dirt and the baroque, with bushes in places where bombs fell almost seventy years ago, instead, I keep staring at a guy on our bus ride, and I know. A beginner, although not young, or maybe he's just poor at his job. He's working on some fellow. He's trying to open his backpack and it takes him almost ten minutes. I can see how he's sweating because the zipper keeps grinding to a halt, until the one who's being robbed realizes what's going on and the usual happens: shouts, the thief and his partner exit the bus. They'll wait for the next one.

That's what has become of my travels. I've caught the bug and I can't help it. Am I supposed to pretend I don't see those two Tunisians who have been sharing the contents of wallets outside the same restaurant for years now? Or that I don't see this nice Egyptian. I met him at M.'s party and then he disappeared. I stumbled upon him some time later in Warsaw, on Kościelna Street, working tourists outside the hotel; or those two men who come into restaurants late in the evening, wearing suits, speaking French, and always sitting close to the drunk guests? They go through the menu thoroughly, exchange opinions, and the waiters pretend they don't see them.

A brief catalog of my travels, very much incomplete. In it there are the lost watch and humiliations, there is extreme vigilance and the resolve for this time to be the last one. There is a readiness, against all odds, to slaughter the next thief.

In the *Geographical Dictionary of the Kingdom of Poland and other Slavic Countries*, published in 1880, you can read the following about Tiraspol: "The county town of the Kherson Governorate" that "lays on the left shore of the Dniester River, opposite Bendery." All this is true—once you're past Sheriff Stadium you're already in Bendery. "In 1870 it was composed of 3,546 houses (146 brick), 16,692 citizens (1,500 Old Believers, 3,614 Jews), 3 Orthodox churches, 1 Edinoverie church, 2 synagogues, 1 Jewish house of prayer, 12 depots, 123 stores, a county school, an alms-house, a hospital, a post office, train tracks, an a marina," the *Geographical Dictionary* continues. I skip the incomes, they don't tell me anything, I can't figure out what it would be in today's currency. But the citizens "deal in merchandise, orcharding and gardening (347 gardens occupying 950 dessiatin), and factory work (tallow-works, tallow candles, tobacco, and a giant steam mill)." The dissidents are the most interesting. I copy the text on the Don Cossacks in the work entitled *Polish Extracts, Both in Prose and Verse, Collected From the Works of Past and Present Polish Authors, for the Amusement of Fine Individuals and Youth of Both Sexes by Tomasz Szumski, the Teacher at the Royal Gymnasium in Poznań* (1821): "Old Believers, or the faithful, would cleanse their chambers and use incense on every piece of earthenware that had been touched by a Russian who was not faithful. If a non-believer were to smoke a pipe, the whole procedure

132

had to be repeated several times, and a truly religious Old Believer would be ready to remodel his entire abode. Every household had a glass case that contained the silverware and goblets from all over the world, and other such artifacts, that, to this day, hold the family's coat of arms." None of this explains much, just that those Old Believers were seen as eccentric and that the country was full of surprises.

Tiraspol has wide streets, as if for a parade; but it's hard to say what for because there are very few cars. There's a cinema that stands there like a spaceship in the middle of a training range; it only shows old movies. The church, gilded and painted in the colors of heaven, is permanently shut. The park behind the cinema and the church resembles a meadow, and people walk around it in circles with their dogs, practicing commands—"Sit!" and "Fetch!" and "Sit!" again; and "Heel!" There is a statue of Alexander Suvorov on horseback, and Russian tourists take pictures with their children beneath it. People come here as if it was a reservation. Tiraspol reminds me of the old days—cranky, tired women working in hotels and offices. You cross the border and have to go and get your passport stamped, all those visa forms in Cyrillic with the boxes you can't possibly know how to fill in; the name of the hotel you'll be staying at, the purpose of your visit, how long. Ministries of God knows what, since this country doesn't even exist, with its headquarters on the main floor of a residential block of flats. For entertainment: you sit on a bench and wait. And have a drink, but in moderation, unless it's night, because the police are rough, but they patrol less after dark. There are barely any cafes; and all they serve there are potatoes and pork cutlets anyway.

"The main river of the county is the Dniester River, constituting its western border and having many tributaries found in the plains. It is flush with water in the spring and dried out during the summer," the *Dictionary* continues its list of facts. The Dniester River is a safe haven for all the living things. Framed by concrete, with poplars planted in its sides—their trunks smeared with lime. During the day, the beach on the other side, toward Bendery, becomes populated. After sundown, in the bushes, the young couples couple; young males with chains around their necks fight bloody battles for the females; and the females, for their own peace of mind and to kill boredom, raise their skirts for the victors and the defeated alike. The police walk around, checking IDs. Prostitutes spend entire nights waiting around the Gnome bar. Nobody ever comes. Their fridge is out of order. The stench is so bad, you can almost feel it on your skin. They sit there together, as a family; the bartender the mother, the prostitute her daughter. Mother says "Have pity, comrade, she's young, pretty, take her to a room." She's the one from the neighboring room, the companion of the small Hungarian guy and his bodyguard from before; drugged, drunk Lolita—too young to be awake at this late hour. The janitor's drinking beer with me, the national anthem is playing on the TV; it's 1 A.M. and the nation is going to sleep. Crops wave in the wind, people are marching, and youth are dancing. And then the payback, we drink knock-off cognac in the janitor's little room and the receptionist tries to eavesdrop through the slightly open door.

We were eating dinner in one of the blocks of flats behind the market. All the blocks are identical. Broken light bulbs, stains on the walls, crooked stairs. Garbage underneath the windows and withered bushes. And in the apartments—chocolates; always in a crystal bowl, because there might be an unexpected guest coming any time; there's always a shiny bedspread on the bed. As if the world was contained within those forty square-meters of fenced property; and the rest is some worthless *ubi leones* that you have to make your way through. And no one wants to care about and nobody really notices what's on the outside, behind the bars. We were having dinner in one of those apartments and our host said "You see, comrades, we have higher education—the elite of our nation, one could say. My wife graduated from the music academy and I'm an engineer. We live well in our republic. We run a store at the market, or a stand, rather, and our daughter has a stand next to ours, too." We were eating fried fish, potatoes, vegetables, and drinking sweet wine from the Kvint production plant. "It's the best champagne in the world," our host would say. It would be rude to disagree, he was paying after all. "To your health, comrades, and to ours as well. I raise a toast to our meeting."

The square consisted of flattened dirt shaded by poplars. There was a little kiosk right next to it, and the kiosk had all the usual things—plastic bottles of vodka with fruits on the labels, cigarettes, instant coffee, and a can of sugar set out on the counter. The counter lost its shine a long time ago. That was in Romania, in the city of Bystrzyca, or Bistriṭa—which used to be called Beszterce in Hungarian, but the Hungarian town is long gone, disappeared without a trace; everything here was Romanian now. I was standing under the poplar with my coffee and a cigarette, half-awake, and around me people were on their way to work, carrying lunch or any number of things in their carefully-saved plastic bags from the supermarket. The mess at home always feels more bearable than abroad because it's already tamed. When I'm at home, everything seems to be slightly more meaningless to me. But there—I was the king of the world; standing by the kiosk, buying my cigarettes cheap, drinking my coffee with half a cup of sugar, because otherwise it would be undrinkable, and telling myself: how beautiful and how disgusting. Or something along those lines.

I have no clue why I stopped in that city. There must've been a reason, but I can't remember now. I was tired. There was no train. First I had been to Budapest, and slept on a train station bench; in

the morning I took a train to Oradea, Romania. There were gera-
niums hanging under a little canopy at the train station, a woman's
touch, a southern sensitivity. So, I guess, you could've expected some
kind of sensitivity in the poverty that at that point in time reigned in
the entire country. I went to the park. An old janitor lady was sitting
on a bench and smoking cigarettes. Her broom was standing next
to her, casually propped against the same bench. The woman was
smoking and laughing. In the shade of the dying trees, her golden
teeth sparkled like sun shining through the holes in a circus tent.
From that park I went to Cluj-Napoca. On the street I saw a group
of people, all wearing hats; one man was missing his leg from the
knee down, and the other leg was sticking out to the side; he was
dragging it. The only vacancy we could find was in a small hotel by
the bus station. There was nothing to eat. B. came back from the
bathroom all pale and said curtly, "Don't go in there, don't ask." But
at least we had a place to sleep. The bed bugs came out at night and
we slept with the lights on.

By the next day I was in Bistriţa, or Bystrzyca in Polish, by the river
of that same name, again king of the world, with a TV and a shower
in my room. And yet, there was something broken about this part
of the world that was drawing me in, something far more tempting
than your obligatory tour with a tour guide. Besides, there's nothing
more boring than a guidebook for this part of the world. It lies all the
time—that's its role—it always shows how interesting the country is.
In the section on Romania it kept pointing to the mountains, naming
a camping site with shitty cabins for the lovers of humiliating experi-
ences. It encouraged travelers to indulge in winter sports, but it was
summer. It kept telling stories about the merits of hunting, about the
bears, about the Saxons, as if they were yet another element of the
local fauna; and those necessary bits about Dracula, shameful pages
I keep leafing through nervously. And when it finally happened, I
found myself standing one morning, well rested, in the middle of

Bistriţa, and saw for the first time all that I would be seeing for years to come, all that I have been on a pilgrimage to, and all that I have later despised in this bed in Gotland, because it occurred to me that it was time to stop for a moment. It was a city of a questionable charm, like Baia Mare for example, were Roma women shoveled hot asphalt from the bed of the truck in the afternoon heat on Strada Victorei, while others patted it into a road. The overseer kept shouting from the bushes: "Faster, faster I say," and they kept pretending he's wasn't there; pretending that the entire street was empty. They were doing the most physically demanding work with the most primitive tools, and their dignity depended on showing him that they didn't see both him and the beer he was holding. A small steamroller kept going back and forth along the entire length of Strada Victorei, pressing the asphalt laid down by the women into a decent street. Half an hour later the first cars were driving on it, creating new ruts. In the newer part of town, in a fancy hotel, there was a pile of rubble, tall as a man. There was a decent-sized, but badly beaten up palm tree standing in the corner, a piano covered in dust, and the currency exchange office. Next to it was a bank, already closed, with a stuffed bear in the atrium. In the evening we drank warm alcohol, sitting on our beds in the hotel because, even though the guidebook encouraged us to explore the city, it was dead, crusted over. And the only thing left to do was to wait until morning. It was getting dark, and I remember the violet of the sky. Baia Mare, Nagybánya—a one-night-stand city. New residential areas stretched beyond the railroad tracks. Children, sheep, and stray dogs wandered aimlessly, people walked home along the tracks after work—everything in a great, symbiotic coexistence with the train. But this intertwined life wasn't perfect. Along the tracks was a line of crosses rising from the ground with fake flower wreaths resting at their feet for all who died tragically in accidents. Anyway, all roadsides in Romania are spotted with crosses. Baia Mare. You think it means something beautiful, but all it means is a Giant Mine. Fuck Baia Mare. Imagine a city for which there is no better name. Giant Hole in the Ground, Giant Black Hole Full of Stink. We took off in the morning. And now—I was lying, as if there were no walls or windows, inside the tempest that was inundating Gotland. I was scheduled to leave in the morning, and here I was remembering Baia Mare, with its smell of asphalt and dust.

But I would come back to Romania because it was not about gloating over its poverty that, back then, was still very apparent; the level of neglect had nothing to do with it. I would catch a cab that wasn't really a cab and kept repeating to myself: "Fuck, fuck, in the name of the Lord," and the young driver, speeding like a maniac even though he was in no rush in this rusty Dacia of his—and repeating that there're no jobs out here, none; and he would dance around the word "unemployed," as if he didn't know it in the first place. For a guy like him, raised in the suburbs, it was shameful to admit to unemployment, to the peanuts of severance pay he got a few months earlier from the bankrupt factory, and his current, almost non-existent income. A temporary change of plans is what he called it; a temporary lookout camped outside the train station in Syhot for people like me, to take us wherever we want; "as long as it's not too far because my parents get worried," he said, but it was more him who was worried about his Dacia, so that it wouldn't die on him somewhere on the road. It ran on diesel fuel; diesel was cheap. Everyone bought it from the bus drivers. I've seen it many times, buses won't go back to their base at night, but instead park in villages, outside the drivers' houses. They wouldn't even wait for night to fall, they would just sit outside in the garden, in their white undershirts, sipping beer, and the neighbors just kept coming as if they were going to buy bread. The driver would suck on a plastic hose and the clients would put their pots and buckets to catch the fuel. That's how it was. That's how my driver bought his fuel. He also had to keep his rates low, he knew best; if he weren't cheap, he wouldn't exist at all.

Those were the days when a hustler was a king. They wanted to fit everyone on their wagons and motorcycles; a few thousand leu for a short ride to the market in a neighboring village, but they wouldn't charge extra for whatever people might be riding with; sometimes you'd ride along with a pig, or chives would tickle your calf. They would charge ten thousand leu for longer rides, but wouldn't drop you off at the house. You had to exit somewhere along the route, at a crossing, and walk the rest of the way, those few kilometers to my old host. My old host would never recognize me, always welcoming me with a surprised expression; as if she was seeing me for the first time and as if no one had ever rented a room from her. I always stayed at her place and it's always been a pain; we always reenacted the same scene: she wouldn't want any money and I would insist on paying. She had two houses, a small wooden one with a summer kitchen—that's where she lived—and a much larger house on the other side of the backyard—for showing off—currently covered with plastic siding. She would rent me a bedroom in the larger house. Nobody had lived in it for a long time now. She was the only one left, the oldest in the family, and she walked back across the yard to the little cottage where she had raised her kids because she preferred this old way of life. Her daughter was far away, her son died in a car crash, and her husband—like every man—drank too much and one day didn't come home because he'd hanged himself, she would explain patiently one evening in the backyard. She was wearing a quilted vest with the filling sticking out. We were constantly lacking words, so we replaced them with gestures, putting on a pantomime. When she was talking about her husband, she made a dead face and wrapped an imaginary rope around her neck. She had a gift for that kind of thing, you could talk with her for hours. In the corner of her backyard, there was an outhouse stocked with a book printed on glossy paper, entitled *Partidul Comunist Român* and with a portrait of Ceauşescu on the first page. When in need, you'd tear out one page. The old lady would step out of the outhouse and wave at me happily with the party book, you could see it well from a distance because the cover was red; she waved to indicate what she thought about it, what she thought about the *Conducător*. She probably never had the opportunity for jokes like that before. Behind the outhouse was a pigsty. When she woke me up in the morning she would serve me eggs and speck, sometimes cucumbers and instant coffee. Everything came from her own backyard, except for the coffee, which came from the store. The pigs were given scraps, their diluted manure was used in the vegetable garden, and so on and so forth. When the pigs were fat, she would get a visit from the butcher—a next-door neighbor—who would take care of them, and get paid in meat. She would set a table in the middle of the backyard, she would serve, bring more coffee and eggs; and neighbors from all over the village would pass by behind the fence and she would stand by the table covered with an oilcloth repeatedly asking me if I need anything. She wouldn't sit because that would be a disgrace. I was her prize, her reason to be proud, her guest from abroad, a connection to the outside world. She would eat her own breakfast around 4 A.M., usually plain bread. She would wash it down with milk. From behind the fence you could hear horse hooves on the sand, a herdsman was leading his horses to pastures farther up the hill, so they could put on some weight. It felt like it was still summer, but you could feel the winter in your bones.

Then I would leave the old lady and she would stand in front of the house, on the road, with a wad of money in her hand, helpless; she always preferred dollars to leu. I wonder if she ever exchanged them for anything. She had everything. She lived alone in two houses, the bigger house was meant to show off wealth. The white walls were decorated with holy paintings, from which hung embroidered towels. There was even a refrigerator in this house, although unused, and an unplugged TV. All of that just in case, useless—and with security blinds in the windows, never fully down, with a tiny crack at the bottom so that you can find your way in darkness. Everyone built houses like that. Those houses were the source of happiness and the source of anxiety. People were afraid of the aliens, burglars, but not of cutthroats and drunks because they were your neighbors, you could meet them in every village. When it got noisy outside the store down the street, the old lady wouldn't hesitate to go and shout at the drunk herdsman and the lumberjacks. They were sitting on the porch, drinking beer and *pálinka*, they would drop by just for one drink and end up wasted, lose those funny hats that normally stuck to their heads God knows how. She would stand over them and threaten them with who knows what, because no police ever came to that village. There was one policeman, true, but he was also a neighbor and a drunk. She must've had some methods older than the apparatus of repression, because they would grow quiet and mumble their apologies.

I would leave her and her vegetable garden and her pigs; her out-house, the inconvenience of washing in a basin in front of the house when it got dark because there was no bathroom, or even a corner to hide in. There was always a cracked bar of soap, a basin, and a pitcher of cold water an the bench, gray from the rain and snow. The crickets would go nuts. The horses were coming back from pasture; you didn't have to urge them, they would turn to their stables on their own. I could hear their hooves on the sand from far away. I was washing in the dark and the herdsman would cordially greet me from behind the fence. She wouldn't go to bed because it was a disgrace to go to sleep before the guest. I would sit on the bench, already washed, staring into darkness and not wanting to go inside; it was damp indoors because she stopped heating the house—there was no one to heat it for. She put me in her old marital bed with her old comforter and a pillow; there were ten other pillows stacked on chairs. When I came in there for the first time, there was a pyramid of them to the ceiling. Two pyramids made of pillows: one for her dead husband, the other one for her—even though she had been living in the other house for a long time. Yet another sign of wealth, doesn't matter that it was invisible for the outside world. I would leave, I would come back, and she remained, standing in front of her house with a bundle of banknotes in her hand, waving as long as you could see her. Then she would slowly go back to her house, I imagine, to boil some potatoes; she would boil them around noon every day, so she must've done it that day as well. One year I came and nobody was there, the gate was closed, both houses were empty. I stayed at the teacher's house by the Orthodox Church, in the middle of the village; with plumbing and a running hot water. He had good wine, and his wife was a great cook. I spent two or three nights there. After that I never came back.

That old woman's home with its outhouse was my piece of this earth, my stronghold; the home of my anxieties and a temporary harbor. Because even when running from something, most likely from myself, I always had to find a place on solid ground though, as was always the case, I would later lose it. Nobody recognized me in this village by one of the Iza's tributaries, but I kept coming back and it was my place because I chose it myself. And now there was nothing, there was nobody, no foster family. I could finally travel around without purpose. I didn't need my barometer—this village, this woman, all of that which you had to take only one look at to see what has changed. I didn't care anymore anyway. My moorings had snapped and I kept on going.

Nothing Happens Here

Lithuania had a presence in our house as long as I can remember. Lithuania was a wolf skin hanging at my Nowicki grandparents' home, laid over the bed so that I could play or just rest on something soft. It had an air of danger with its glass eyes, wide-open jaws, exposed fangs. I remember I kept wondering if they had been lacquered, and one was cracked from its base all the way up. When my grandparents played with me they would scare me by saying it was still alive. My grandpa had it shot, out there where the wolves were and where you'd go to shoot them. I didn't know where, but I understood one thing—it was a long time ago. Wolf, man's best enemy, wolf the murderer, it deserved what it got and I didn't feel sorry for it. I admired the hunter for being able to hunt down his prey, just like in Karl May's novels, and later skin the dead animal. The pelt was steel-gray and I thought it was beautiful. And despite its jaws twisted in an angry grin, the wolf wasn't really dangerous because the bottom of the pelt was lined with some green fabric, sort of merry. This skin was my object of desire back then. I wonder where it is now, and if moths have eaten it.

The metal etching of Our Lady of the Gate of Dawn cast onto a piece of marble was from that same source—a source not of my past, but of Lithuania's. The stories too. They would play cards, have some tea, slowly, laughing. They would talk about things alien to me, about places from the past, far away. They would say "Well, in Michaliszki, ho ho, you could find some fine saffron milk caps, catch some good fish," just so they could start talking about how to get to Dziewieniszki, and then again onto something else, and on and on like that, immersed in themselves. I barely remember anything, mainly the backs of the chairs they sat on with secession-style flower prints because I'd sit behind them and stare. I remember the tea they sipped endlessly, the homemade honey, and the centrifuge standing in the corner. It was summer and it was used constantly. I remember challah baked in an electric baking pan. In *The Issa Valley* there are many words impossible to understand, lifeless. Miłosz describes unknown activities. Everything in that book is—except for Tomaszek, his fears and discoveries, except those of dying and madness—as if extracted from the woodshed, taken from an old dictionary. Miłosz's entire *entourage* looks like a meticulously reconstructed country cottage in a Vilnius museum. Not even a cottage anymore, more like a stage set. And so that's how their card games, grandma's electric baking pan, and challah turn into a set.

And they played cards, talking, slowly taking a piece of challah and a spoonful of honey. They would recall old neighbors. She, my grandma, had a Borderlands beauty: weather-beaten face, dark eyebrows, gray hair. From behind you could see her bun. He, my grandpa, was already massive and stocky back then. But I remember him vaguely and mainly from the time when he had already started the business of dying, when we would visit him at the hospital or when he came back home and kept moaning, half-conscious, with his face to the wall. He lay on the sofa that had a man-size divot in the middle (every year, he or my dad would stuff the sofa with sea grass; in the summer the bedroom smelled of hay). There was something Tartarish in Grandpa's face. They said that he used to be as strong as a bull when he was young, that he could climb a ladder with a sack of grain under one arm. My parents, my uncle, they would play cards with their own grandparents too because back then everybody played—it was a fad, now I remember. What else are you going to do in the evening in the countryside, if you already went for a walk by the Vistula River, sunbathed, and waited your turn in a grocery store line for a loaf of bread. You're done with garden chores and the family is all together. Nothing left but to play cards. But what they played, I never remember.

As an adult, I went to visit where they came from and where they never wanted to return. They waited anxiously for reports from those family members who had decided to take this one trip. And after hearing them out, they were still convinced of their convictions. They heard only bad news from them, "It's not the same," they'd say, "there're Soviets there now." So, in their place, I got on the bus—because that's how you travelled back then. I remember the smells of my journey rooted into the bus seats, food in plastic bags. I recall, and this might be only a hallucination after so many years, luggage inspections, piece by piece, at the border, them searching through my backpack and questions about everything, as if we were trying to sneak into paradise. This was back when the border was a solid object, covered with barbed wire. And then it was the city at dawn, losing my way despite the map and the streets, alleyways, walking up up up and loosing my breath, and then zooming down because the whole city is like that: up and then down. Vilnius—or rather, the Russian city of Vilnius with the old Polish "Wilno" blended into it—a fossil from a different era. I don't know what I remembered better: communal bathrooms in repurposed dormitories, digging out scraps of my Russian to communicate with the lunch hall monitor, or the city that was like a flower, but sentenced to rot and then saved at the last moment.

People who lived here in the past, or their descendants, come to visit. They boss others around, speaking Polish, certain that not much has changed. They walk the streets with books, their Baedekers guiding them around the non-existent city from the past. They hold close their Jerzy Remer guidebooks, published three quarters of a century ago, where only the marvels of architecture have been marked. They arrive with pocket maps where just a tiny bit of the city of Vilnius exists. They look as if they don't want to see it because they truly don't. They came to visit their memories and to see how poorly those memories are doing in the new world: their bright childhood pasts, now surrounded by darkness, by ugly places that have no place in their minds because they were built fifty years after their exile. They stare at the skyscrapers made of blue glass and they can't see that their own houses were poor. They look at Russian blocks of flats and can't see that their own lack in beauty as well.

Even though alien—that's true—they too possessed the ability to see the city in a less supernatural manner. The newlyweds Mr. and Mrs. Dostoyevsky stop by on their way to the casinos, to their promised fortune that will turn into ruin this time as well. Anna will note: "We arrived in Vilnius. The butler from the Hotel Hahna near Wiejska Street approached us immediately, seated us in his carriage and took to his establishment. At the hotel we were toured around, shown suites of all kinds, but all of them were filthy. Fyodor wanted to go and find a new place, but finally we found a suite that was decent and got settled. Service turned out to be rather unusual: you can ring for them all you want and they could not care less. And one more peculiarity: two of the staff were missing their left eye. Fyodor imagined it's because the impaired get paid less. And it probably was the case."

I push the Dostoyevskys aside, they don't like anything anyway and the world is a black ball, a septic tank with one golden nugget adrift—Russia. Vokiečių gatvė, that's where my aunt's family is, her yellow house. Now there's a new one there, but also yellow. Žaliasis tiltas—that's where, carried on the shoulders by my grandpa, my father could see the city's skyline. And where were they going?

Probably to the market, to Šnipiškės. "They named it all that way to spite us," is what the tourists say, tightly gripping their Remer's guidebooks, "as if there were no beautiful names for all those places, our names for all those streets and squares. Vokiečių gatvė sounds so alien, so idiotic and, after all, it's simply *ulica Nimiecka*—German Street. Žaliasis tiltas sounds so much worse than *Zielony Most*—Green Bridge—now decorated with Soviet sculptures slowly consumed by rust. Even the bridge itself is different, a successor to the old one. And finally, *Śnipiszki*, you can't say *Śnipiszki* anymore? Won't pass through your mouth? Why did you come here anyway, kike, what are you staring at? Are you happy none of it is ours anymore?"

It's different in the countryside. Roads are dusty and it's green. It seems flat, but if you take a closer look at the bushes, you'll notice they're filling up little valleys. If you take a closer look at the forest, you'll see it grows on a wavy, semi-flatland. Sand, rivers cutting into the soil: Neris—*Wilia*, Nemunas—*Niemen*, Nevėžis—*Niewiaża*. That's where all the tributaries meet, where they cut into the ground like a leather strap into skin. Then again, it's completely different in the winter. Snow calms everything. It covers everything, you can see only the villages, the rest is white and even and only the blackish-yellow water of the river stands out. You can only spot it in the bends, where the water breaks through the ice, escaping for a moment to the surface. Locals sit on the ice on metal boxes and fish through holes. "Why did you come here?" they ask, but without anger. It's the countryside, nothing much happens there, so they want to know.

One day, in the summer, we were driving through the back-road dust; this was before I got to see winter in Lithuania. We were driving and we kept getting lost again and again because the roads here are all the same. The sun was scorching. It happened before the visit to Joga, or maybe right after, near Mejszagoła. It's a small village, Joga. And, there won't be any Lithuanian names here because these are places from a different order, these names exist only in my own language. And it's not about Polish, but about an internal *tick-tock*. So, before Joga, or after, we stopped somewhere at a crossroads, uncertain. There were kids standing by the road, deeply tanned from the sun, with hay-blond hair and an evil eye from another century. But their clothes were from a thrift store, shirts with the Chicago Bulls logo peeling off, a trademark of the countryside. And only a "Ukraine" bicycle, too big for any of them, linked them to that current reality. Our conversation with them was dragging. Getting an answer was like pulling teeth, "Left? Right? Or are we going the wrong way?" And finally a big storm cloud came and a disc-shaped shadow appeared on the ground. We were in the sun, they were in the shade, and between us a border sharp as a razor.

Physical inventory from my travels. Sounds like the notes of a madman. So, photos of a bush and a bunch of trees in the middle of a field—that's the most important spot because there used to be a house between the trees and the bush. Not important for me, the house wasn't mine. My father lived in it with his parents. The house still exists and it stands somewhere else, precisely about half of it still stands. And inside is a woman, whose husband died or went somewhere, I can't recall now. Doesn't make a difference to me, anyway. I'm simply there with my father and he's visiting the museum of his past. She, the lady of the house my father knew as a child, is afraid, but offers us a cup of coffee anyway. It's the stench of old sugar in a can, trapped in humidity and lumpy. That same humidity feeds the mold on the wall. It's difficult to call this room a house, this wooden, almost-barrack filled with fear. She fears we're here not on a sentimental journey, but to take it all away from her. A different place, on a different day: two old men, one of them in a broken wheelchair, in front of a house with a columns. To reach the house you have to pass by a pile of huge concrete rings for drainage, make your way through the bushes, through the rubble of the fallen farm buildings. It used to be a kolkhoz, but a few years after it shut down it kind of disappeared off the face of the earth. And that wooden, mansion-like house, now roofed with asbestos tiles, is still standing, and those two old men sit in front of it. At least that's what they're doing in the picture I took; I don't know if they're still alive. They tried to save the building from utter ruin with pieces of linoleum and some old rags. There's an icehouse behind the main house, wooden doors that lead underground, but the view from there is of the fields because the house is on top of a hill.

Those fields I saw in the distance were like a flashback to the evenings card games, to my parents, grandparents, and my uncle sitting there with their backs facing me. I can see the floral patterns on the backs of their chairs, the play is slow, and the tea grows cold in their cups. All they talked about back then was catching crayfish at night, in bucketfuls, the fish so abundant. And now I'm standing behind the cottage with its thick, wooden columns. Where there are now fields there used to be fishing ponds, that's where they used to go catch the crayfish of their youth. They still catch them, on and on, and they'll keep on like that until the end. But now everything is flipped, twisted. Back where I had seen the holy bush that marked the sacred family house and the trees with a clearing beyond the house, there was now a homestead. Where there had been a forest, now there was a field. Where there had been nothing, now there was a hill with a machine ripping up gravel from the ground for construction. Everything is upside down, everything is shifted around, everybody's dead.

Back at that crossroads. Kids with hair bleached white by the sun stand in the middle of the road, beside them a forsaken bike. The cloud has arrived. They are in the shade, we are in the sun. Finally they give an answer, some clue, and we're back on the road. In the following order, or maybe not: furniture store, where room dividers and mirrors stand leaning against a wall. A lake, and around the lake are cars parked among the bushes because when these people see water nothing else matters and they go swim. They eat by the water and shed their thin, urban veils, leaving cities they came from behind. My father, I understand now, is one of them, one of the ones going into the lake to swim. Then, we stop by a restaurant, there's wind, and heat. We study maps and wind keeps ripping them out of our hands. The cemetery in the forest is different in yet another way, rustic. There are too many of those cemeteries. There's a grave to visit in every village, every city. You get all the names confused, the causes and effects intermingle. In the end we're drinking in Vilnius, we stagger back to the hotel. The next morning is heavy with a hangover.

Recently, in the outskirts of Kėdainiai, we faced the kind of winter that makes your knees crack and your face pucker. There was a roadside market; I look to see what they have. Frozen honey, "It's tasty, please buy it!" the lady at the stand urges me. There's one beetroot set out (the rest stay warm in the sacks in the back of a truck). There are other vegetables also on display, one of each: a carrot, a rutabaga, a potato, one bunch of parsley; and dried meat, smoked meat, pork fat. A woman wearing furs buys two slices of smoked bacon, thick as a finger. A farmer in overalls cuts it for her, his fingernails glistening with fatty dirt. They argue, she wants to buy less because it's expensive, he—unfazed—cuts it thick. And there are products from a different era, hemp ropes big as a man's arm, chains, overalls, leather belts who knows what for, old junk brought from someone's home with the hope of seducing somebody, not because it's pretty, but because it's cheap.

There's a bar in the basement of a house near by. There are cascades of artificial flowers, peddlers keep coming in, and you can see their breath in the cold air. A man slurps his sauerkraut soup while watching TV. His hands are stiff from the cold, he can't unwrap the spoon from the napkin, so he just balls it up clumsily. He has no time to wait for his hands to thaw. Women drop in to use the bathroom and take a shot. They sip it. There's cabbage, potatoes, and ground pork on the menu. All of that topped with a spoonful of sour cream. They know winter, and they know the best medicine for it.

I visit Šetenia, where Miłosz was born. In his prose these parts are heavily overgrown, barely traversable, and you have to wait for winter to finally settle to be able to travel by sleigh to the neighboring town. "But what do I care anyway," I can hear my angry self again. This urge to rummage through other people's memorabilia keeps sneaking up on me, the desire to visit places from other people's lives. I keep celebrating memory—only it's not mine. And now: several houses, and a man and his son fixing a car. Laundry has been hung out to dry, even though it's negative fifteen Celsius outside. It's hanging out because it's Sunday—the day of drying—and neither war nor weather will change that. There's nobody else except for these two by their car. All the dogs in the village look like they're from the same litter: short, stumpy bowed legs, with that typical village bark. They run across the fields, through the fresh snow, just to catch the outsider and show him who's boss. The Nevėžis River runs in the distance and ice has piled up on its banks. You can tell the river must've been wild under the ice. It takes only a few minutes to get to Krekenava via the asphalt road. And in Miłosz's writing, eons separate villages, deep forests and languages collapse. His world has hatred and belching swamps. There, you can hear the splash of boots in mud; in Miłosz's realm there's peeping on women of the village, and ecstasy felt in the herb garden. But now it's a little bit like everywhere else, reddish asphalt, clean and flat, and the vastness of snow. It's empty. The real place can't keep up with the memories. It just won't.

It was in the apartment where Grandpa Nowicki lay dying for so long that his body finally created a man-sized indent in bed. A year before his passing, he sat on that very bed talking to himself, broadcasting on his own wavelength, without paying attention to anything because he didn't care whether he had an audience. He kept repeating the names of places from the old country, to which he never went back. There was nothing to go back to. Whatever he had left there was long gone, and he smuggled only as much as he could fit in his head across the border. He'd sit on his bed, head heavily propped in his hands, elbows resting on his knees, and kept repeating his mantra: "There was the Nevėžis River and the Šešupė and Širvinta. And there was the Žižma River." That's what he said. I'm repeating it here word for word, just like my father repeated it to me. He also told me that he didn't cry after my grandpa died, but laughed because those names were beautiful, they whispered and swished, creaked like morning frost underfoot, thundered like water against the ice, and foretold the rustle of grasses and the coming of harvest.

And all those rivers were really there, they all exist. Let's take the Žižma for example. I find in *The Geographical Dictionary of the Kingdom of Poland and other Slavic Countries* among the left-bank tributaries of the Venta, a river in the Governorship of Kaunas and Courland. Its tributaries are as follows: the Avnova, Žižma, Virvytė, Wejszatis,

Šerkšnė, Varduva, and Lūšis—and I'm skipping creeks, although
their names are equally interesting. That's the first thing I read; I
find grandpa's full list and after that I blindly step into the pages
of the *Dictionary*, I drown head first in it because in that book of
non-existent language I find the words of my ancestors, their names,
their habitats. By accident I stumble upon an article about the parish
of Antonowo in Maryamposlki County. That completely unexciting
village of Antonowo composes the parish along with Armoliszki,
Bobroliszki, Borsukinie, Budwiecie-stare, Brantas, Czysta-buda, Czu-
jniszki villages. But there are also Egliniszki and Egłupie, Gajstry and
Girnupie, and Giwałtowo and Gobiniszki, Grzesie and Jodbaryszki.
That same parish also includes Kłampunie, Kojaćkiszki, and Koż-
liszki, and beyond them Krówieliszki and Kwiatkopusze. There are
Mołupie and Muryniszki, Nendrynie and Ożnogary, Plople and
Pocztaryszki. You'll find Podziszki, Pokieliszki, Przygrażyszki, and
Purwiniszki and Raczyliszki and Rudupie; you have Sanożyszki, big
and small, Skuczyszki, Smolany-piec. Finally, Szaliszki, Szalniszki,
Tartutyszki, Trakiszki-wielkie, Tymieńczyszki-małe, Wałajtyszki, and
Witkiszki. You could run out of breath. I read other lists full of names
sounding just as otherworldly and I can't escape them.

All those rivers mentioned before run through what my grandpa
considered "their" land because, as a young man, he used to be an
administrator of those estates and kept moving from one to the other.
And when he would be done with one job, he'd pack up all his tools
and move on to the next one. There have been a lot of estates, along
with the rivers, he supervised through the years, there were Gieżguny,
Jody, all the way to Michaliszki estate, which my father bought as his
own property. Those were the same Michaliszki where mail would
go first through Konwaliszki or Onżadowo, which the locals would
pronounce differently than I do. Among his rivers, my grandpa never
listed the one that was the most important to him—the Neris River—
or any of the bigger and well-known ones. He mentioned only those

that sounded like a wild love call, misfit rivers named in the their wicked dialects. He sat on his bed, his elbows propped firmly on his knees, and kept repeating the names, as if scared he would forget. Or, as if he had already forgotten that he had just listed them all, and he'd start over: "There was the Nevėžis River, there was the Šešupė and the Širvinta. And there was the Žižma River." I could keep reading that sentence out loud forever. My grandpa kept repeating it as if only then, on his deathbed, he realized that what he had once lost, he was bound to lose again, and soon.

At the house where the wolf skin used to reside, and where now there was nothing and nobody but bare walls, we would go outside as early in the morning as possible. So when I went to visit on my own many years later, I got up at dawn and started across the yard, even though I had no wish to do so. I passed the farm buildings, short and lined with swallows' nests, then went through an unkempt orchard right along the barn wall. The barn was next to an old apple tree that I remember smelled strongly in the summer. I would walk under it's branches heavy with apples, looking for the ripe ones. Now the tree was alien, in somebody else's hands, and I kept wondering whose. Next I passed by the forgery, or so it was called, although it was just a stockpile of old plows and engines under a leaky roof. No one ever forged or even fixed anything in there. Farther along there were pastures, now empty, and paths dividing them into enormous rectangles. You could barely figure out their shape, but whoever heard my grandpa lecture on the subject of Dutch drainage methods applied to these fields that comprised a depression, would forever see any melioration canals as crossing each other only at the right angles. The canals were lined with willows, trimmed once a year back in the day and now freely and strangely overgrown. Those who knew where to look could notice, and be amazed, by that perfect system, the ingenuity of which was imperceptible to an inexperienced eye.

The waters flowing into those canals looked like a piece of lace crocheted over the old swamps as if to claim a piece of land for farming. That's why the Dutch were brought in, that's how the windmills got here, and with them came this undeniable charm, which was later drowned by concrete and the poverty of collective farming, until its unnatural beauty disappeared almost entirely. Now, many years after our family visited, and feeling a little lost around these parts, I remember I should turn left somewhere to get back to the asphalt road. We wouldn't normally take the paths, their muddy ruts frozen rock-solid. Normally, we would cut through the pastures, helping each other over the barbed wire. Now, however, the pasture was surrounded by a decent electric fence because it was privately-owned land, and no longer in the hands of a mindless and ownerless institution, which is what the collective farms used to be. This new owner, who was universally hated by the locals because he preferred to buy modern machinery instead of hiring people, didn't want anyone on his soil. He didn't want alien boots on his grass, or rather, his field of incredibly tall burdock and other plants that didn't normally flourish here because in the past they had been mowed down by the cows.

This weird culture of growing burdock was just another attempt to forget the Dutch, to eradicate them from the history of Żuławy Wiślane. Now this culture stood in my way, blocking the view. I couldn't spot the only point of orientation I remembered, the last Dutch windmill in all of Żuławy. The fence guarding the weeds reminded me of brand new fences, still shiny, from the forest of Chantilly. The forest was divided into lots, and the shining fence stood as a symbol of the sanctity of private property. It also reminded me of similar fences along the border between Lithuania and Belarus. While other countries kept tearing down walls, here they were still building new ones. Hardware stores where finally supplied with the beloved merchandise of all border patrolmen: seemingly gentle, but incredibly resilient and strong steel-wire mesh. That's what is used to fence off a huge part of Lithuania, guarding it from being overrun by the Belarusians. Specifically the part of Lithuania my father was from. Although, maybe it was the other way around. Maybe it was Belarusian mesh. Property, land, my country, my weeds, all of it has been properly fenced off. And when I see how solid these walls are, I can't stop thinking about the old barbed wire, that fence against cows, not people.

I walked among the weeds all the way to the crossroads, where there used to be a narrow-gauge railway station. I wanted to experience that rhythm of old-timey trains, to sit on an old wooden bench, and hear the sound of ticket puncher. I was hoping to experience waiting under the station's roof in the middle of nowhere. But there was no roof, just some broken legs from the missing bench. Even the rusty railway tracks became a blurry image over the years and then disappeared completely, partly fading in the memory, and likely to the benefit of metal scrap collectors. I guess that's what I was expecting in the end.

From that station you would go to Nowy Dwór. Once in Nowy Dwór, you'd have to go from platform to platform to find the one with a train to Sztutowo, and then wait in an empty car that would gradually fill up and leave. It would fill up with workers, housewives coming back from grocery shopping, people from surrounding villages, and vacationers like myself. And I kept imagining how life must've been in those villages where there's nothing. I wondered how it must be to wait every day for a train by that one bench—a train that was usually late. I tried to imagine it, feel it, but I never succeeded.

I went to the National Museum of Ethnography and Natural History, only a few blocks away from the main intersection in Kishinev, a street named after Stephen III of Moldova, father of Bogdan III the Blind, also known as One-Eye, and a friend of Vlad the Impaler. There is a street named after him in every city around here; in Kishinev he also has a park, a high school, a police academy, and even a motorized infantry unit bearing his name. The museum is located in a Moorish style palace with a ticket booth next to the entrance. From the very first exhibition room I could feel the breath of one of the museum employees on my back, one of those ladies who walks behind you step by step. They could make the visitors' invisible leash a little longer, but I guess they don't know how.

I have a few favorite spots in this particular museum. I go straight for what I'm looking for. I pass all the taxidermied animals in their glass cases. They're kept that way so they don't collect dust. Then I pass by the birds in the bird rooms, where even a swan looks like a tempest of white feathers, protected from curious hands by a red sash. The local taxidermist isn't one of the world's finest, and I'm not sure if they didn't have glass panels big enough or if they wanted to demonstrate a bird marriage in crisis, but the drake is in its own case, separated, and staring at the duck through a double glass wall. Nobody turns the light on in the basement floor for me, but I keep leaning over a picture and staring at it: fine cattle in Kishinev city square, which, in the nineteenth century, was like Tiraspol's twin— wooden and muddy. Today it's different, blocks of flats up on the hill and blocks of flats down in the valley. The police patrol everywhere, but everybody's doing whatever they want anyway. In the pictures the roofs are broken, caved-in, smiling people wearing rags for clothes— after all, back then a visit from a photographer still meant something, but now nothing like that ever happens, unless there's a car accident. Weather-beaten faces with a dark smear of blush on their cheeks, framed by messy beards and with distinct noses, growing out in every direction almost like a big mushroom hat. I stare for too long. The security lady is now stuck to my back. Finally, something's happening. To her it's entertainment.

I go to the main floor, to the very last exhibition room. I glance over the placards: cross-section through the soil, explanations, half-life, empty cans of DDT. I came here to see an exhibit-cum-accusation, like a finger pointed at one's heart. Conjoined calves. There are two heads and eight legs on one body. The two front outer legs stand firm on the ground; the two front inside legs are up and squeezed between the two heads as if raised in some idiotic gesture of greeting. And my guard lady, new one for every room, drops her knitting and runs to turn on some extra light, remove any obstacles in my way. She grabs my hand and pulls me onto the exhibition stage, among the calves and other deformed freaks, so that I can take a closer look at that cabinet of wonders. She points to the cans of DDT in case I didn't understand the accusatory tone of the entire exhibit. She assumes a foreigner may not be familiar with the story of a chemical that kills weeds and deforms humans and animals. This entire museum is silent, a house of mute corpses beneath glass. But the worst of them all, a combination of circus and science, still seems very much alive—the conjoined calf twins making a grotesque salute that could be in the Moldovan coat of arms.

During his war peregrinations at the end of November 1942, Ernst Jünger arrived in Stavropol. On that date he notes: "Before noon I visited the municipal museum, established still before the times of the tsar and carrying mostly zoological exhibits. . . . My attention was caught by two pairs of two-headed animals—a goat and a calf. The goat's deformation brought to mind Janus's head. The calf, despite having two heads, boasted only three eyes, of which the third was placed on the forehead, as if in the image of Polyphemus. This particular combination had a certain aesthetic elegance: it seemed like an intelligent design, not so much zoological as mythological."

"So, the interest in collections balancing between circus, science, and pornography is not my vice exclusively," was how I kept cheering myself up in my tiny Swedish bed, waiting for the storm to pass, summing up all my travels, my utter contempt for all of them growing. "What I," was my thinking "say through photographs and stories, Jünger says through references to mythology. That's the difference between us. Conjoined animals, bearded women or men with tails, the tiniest of midgets, and people suffering from hypertrichosis, their faces or hands entirely covered with hair. Basically, no longer human beings, but objects displayed in circus tents—that's what fascinated Jünger, Sobieski's father, Pepys, and me, just like it has fascinated travelers and diarists of all eras. That, but also severed heads, mutilated bodies, dangerous psychopaths chained to their beds, or even regular crazies enjoying relative freedom.

I looked at those fused animals, about which Jünger wrote that they were more like neighbors in a chain gang rather than allies, and it's difficult not to agree. They've been sentenced to life in this crooked body. From afar, lying in my ill-fitting Gotland bed, too small for a normal-sized man, I begin to understand in a flash of epiphany that I'm just like those conjoined calves. I keep carrying with me the people I've been running from. I stumble and I run, but there is this giant polypore growing on me, an enormous fungus that cannot be removed. Or maybe it's the reverse, maybe I'm the one growing on it. I can see it now from the distance, from the darkness of a sleepless night. I'm not staring at the calves', but at my own conjoining. And it's about time to do something about it, to stop and take a closer look. It can't go on like this.

Countries that are on the outskirts of the world museum are just different. They still allow entertainment that was quietly banned everywhere else. These are not vast halls displaying half of the Parthenon, are not a bombastic Louvre; this is a Fort Knox of art with marble canvas instead of gold, and where people stop only at the command of the voice in their headphones. If they don't stop, after all, their trip was for nothing. Even smaller museums in the better parts of the world are still enormous, with halls full of obligatory canvases by the masters—but they're somehow boring. These Rubenses with a herd of little piglets, these oil canvases where half-women, half-pigs float in the air. What can I do about the fact that I can't handle Rubens? He hits me like the flu. I can't handle him like I can't handle many others. The museum becomes a place of obligation, of oppression. Here you have to nod politely before the paintings spanning acres, before the signatures, before the names. And these small, dusty collections on the fringes of civilization, in rarely visited cities, are less pampered and show things elsewhere yet unknown: a collection of ties, glasses, and Siamese twins. They are the essence of the country that brought them into existence, beginning to dig itself out of the mud of history.

There are quite a number of those museums, those collections full of other, groggier boredom, collections where I can't recognize a single name and where not even a single work of art catches your attention. I can't remember all of them; some were just an excuse to escape the city, to rest from walking. But a museum is not the best place to rest. I remember the National Museum of History of Moldova, also in Kishinev. It's a large building with a statue of the

Capitoline Wolf in front of the entrance so everyone knows that this country, this city, is no backwoods relative, but stems from the very epicenter of civilization. I went to see a forty-five by eleven-meter diorama depicting the Jassy-Kishinev Offensive, constructed by Nikolai Prisekin and Alexei Semonov. In the foreground, as is usually the case with battlefields, there are remnants of barbed wire entanglement, canons, shells—all of it original, collected off the battlefield. That's what the woman at the entrance assured me. It was a female attendant again, sitting in her chair, because there are women in museums everywhere. It's almost completely dark in the room because only the diorama is illuminated; the guard lady has to lean toward the hallway light coming through the slightly ajar door. It's a late work of art. Created in the 1990, but still entirely in the vein of social realism. It tells the story of the victorious struggle of a Red Army soldier. A year after its completion, Moldova announced its independence, and two years later separatist fights erupted. But that's a different story. This diorama that came too late and this entire museum that came too late, with its stucco rooms filled with exhibits from a different era, are somewhat exterritorial and outside of time. World War II rules here. Regardless, this war exhibit is just a Band-Aid for other infections. It's easier to show that which is marked by indifference. I was observing the diorama and I recalled my school field trip, years before, to Wrocław to see the *Racławice Panorama*. It was 1985 and the panorama almost worked like an oxygen mask for the suffocating audience. It's hard to believe, but people would go on a pilgrimage to see it. Just like they would go to get healed by those miracle makers, ones like Clive Harris, to whom I myself was once sent but without any results. Here, they come to see the diorama by the two Russian tinkers. They do it probably to forget that they can't always make ends meet, spend some time away from their neighborhood. You can find plenty of reasons.

I was travelling around Bukovina, the last remnant of an era in which the outside wall of a church was also a Holy Scripture. The winds and rains that haunt these parts are rough and have scoured off the paintings, leaving only something to be seen at the very top where the roof protected them. I stood in front of those churches, trying to decipher anything from that ancient science, but all I could see were pale outlines and nothing more. There were men and women in navy blue hassocks that they had rented from the nuns before entering the church, so they wouldn't offend God, this shy creature. His servants don't allow inappropriately dressed people, wearing T-shirts and cargo pants, to enter his temple. So now these people stand around in rented skirts and sheets, as if they jumped out of a barber's chair for a short break, dressed up freaks having to raise their heads in order to see from under their capes.

"And yet, my travels are more than wooden houses and boring, obscure collections," I caught myself thinking more than once. The journey turns the entire world into a museum. Every half-ruined church was becoming an exhibit, like that Evangelical Parish in Sibiu where, since the floor was gone, you had to walk on planks laid over a sea of sand. Not much inside that church recalled its past glory. There were several hymn books and some pews piled up, and a yard with overgrown trees. I stayed in the presbytery. When I arrived on the first day, late in the evening, I woke the pastor. He was scared and kept asking what I was looking for, how I knew about the possibility to stay there overnight. He was calcified in the fear of a different era and hadn't yet resurfaced from it. And I thought about my host as I lay in a room prepared by the German Society for Assistance, staring at a large metal key that looked like it belong to a different age, impractical and heavy but, because of that, impossible to lose. Now he was allowed to do anything. He could preach whatever he wanted in his temple. He was freed from his daily chores by young, smiling Germans looking at the world with a sense of love and guilt. Except he couldn't preach anything anymore, didn't want to. I'm not sure, anyway, what was stronger in him—the simple feeling of being discouraged or the feeling of being already dead inside. I kept visiting his temple, but he never came to it himself, he didn't have the strength. We would eat breakfast together and he would smile pleasantly and remain silent, staring at the edge of the table and his own hand clenched tight around its edge. There was a feeling about the town of Sibiu, or Hermannstadt, as if it had been abandoned, though on the other hand it was happy and full of life.

Elderly people from a homeless shelter were sitting together in one of the churches, because the shelter itself was right next-door. They sat in their pajamas in the few chairs that had been set out. Those people were the temple. Between these walls there was no divine pomposity left. The church had a worn-down dirt floor instead of a real floor, and wheezing old men with their filterless cigarettes. Where were they supposed to go for a smoke if not there. Where to sit if not on those chairs with woven seats; seats identical to those in the churches of France, or Germany, but with holes from devout sitting. Where they were supposed to go for a smoke? To the Brukenthal National Museum, the pride of the city? Their place was right there, among trash, on top of rubble. And the Brukenthal Museum, the pride of Sibiu, is worth visiting. They have a *Crucifixion* by Antonello de Messina—one of three, and probably the weakest. But its vista is mesmerizing despite all else, despite not being as clean or as audaciously aflame like its Antwerp counterpart. Despite the fact the bodies don't hang as spasmodically as in Antwerp. The version in Brukenthal is full of cracks and bumps, and that's what makes it moving. It evokes emotion as a testimony to the history of that city, that country, all those countries. It's a coincidental map of destruction that burned out my pastor, even though he still came for breakfast at the same time, smiled, and even read the scripture. He was burnt out like millions of others just like him.

The story of Lviv's own painting, entitled *The Payment of Dues*, is also complicated. It changed owners and locations several times. Even its authorship was contested. The first entry into the collection ledger stated: Geraldo della Notte, or Gerard (or Gerrit) van Honthorst. Finally, somebody spotted a signature with "La Tour" and parts of a date, but it's impossible to decipher it now. Georges de La Tour, son of a baker, *peintre ordinaire du roi*, born in Vic-sur-Seille and died in Lunéville in Lorraine. The period during which the painting was made was also debated. Some pointed to the beginning and some to the middle of the artist's career. It's not a big painting, one meter by one meter and a half, horizontal. It depicts a night scene: six people, a table, money, papers, a dagger, a ledger, all by candlelight

My path to finding that painting was a complicated one as well. It begins in the Louvre, where I stood for the first time in front of a different painting of La Tour's—*The Cheat With the Ace of Diamonds*—one of those incredibly designed and executed flashes of painterly virtuosity, the brilliance of colors moving from gold to gold through dark and yellow ochre, silver, olive, cinnabar, and black. The background of that painting is black like the curtains in a theater, creating a black box. And just like in the theater it reinforces all the other colors, lights, and the suspect card game and the spectrum of facial expressions. On the right is a young nobleman, beautifully dressed and entirely immersed in the game. There are two women in the center. One is sitting and playing, the other is standing, ready to pour more wine. On the left is the cheat, pulling cards out from under his belt behind his back, including the ace of diamonds, which will win all the gold from a noble shmuck. A simple story. The cheat and the standing woman turn their eyes to me, the viewer. The woman with the cards watches the cheat. Only the nobleman being cheated has his eyes down. He, poor soul, believes it's just a game of cards.

I once again go over what I saw when I went to the Lviv National Gallery for the first time: cracked paneling, water stains, and damp patches on the walls and ceilings. Paintings were hanging under the most certain sign of hopelessness ever invented by our civilization— flickering fluorescent light. I found La Tour's painting by accident; it wasn't as much a painting as it was a black, cracked, and convex rectangle barely recognizable at that point. I couldn't leave. La Tour's nocturne was covered with an extra layer of patina. Beyond the painter's history and my encounter with his work, there was a story of painting's own tribulations. It went through a lot, tortured on many occasions, until it finally cracked under the weight of its darkened varnish and was ready to fall off the canvas. I saw the painting under that dark net, I observed the chaos of looks between depicted figures that reveal not only the violent character of that painting style but also, once again, its well thought out structure. The La Tour in the Lviv National Gallery perfectly resembles the history of the city that stores it. In the corner of that room with dirty-green walls and water stains was a painting worth travelling for. The closest window, in the next room, looked out onto the museum's yard—a garden, more specifically—and was wide open. There was a broken-down truck parked permanently among the wild apple trees, and a heap of coal sprinkled with lime rose nearby. Even local museums felt as if sick with gangrene, a disease corrupting them from within, inducing fear in visitors, rude in the way they welcomed you.

That's how museums in my part of the world are—full of damaged pieces, secondary and weaker works, sketches or paintings done by students from a master's workshop, but stubbornly attributed to the great master. "The museums aren't the most interesting things," I thought to myself while in my narrow bed in the Gotland town of Visby. It's with great pride that the town's museum exhibits skeletons excavated from the ancient graves. In my parts the living dead are the most interesting things—those old men sitting out of illness and boredom in old churches. Or, in a different country, the entire city of Skopje is the center of interest, curating the memory of its own demise and a failed attempt at rebirth, the time shown on the clock tower frozen at the hour of the 1963 earthquake that erased bridges and old and new houses alike. Even now, half a century later, the city is still half in ruins. On the one hand, there are major investments, huge public service buildings from the 1960s and 1970s—and next to them are empty lots with unrealized plans. Four fifths of the city were demolished, and even after so long it's still easy to spot that destruction.

The path across those countries is a trail of museums that pass out protective felt slippers for you to put over your shoes before entering. And nobody knows why you have to do it anymore, since word got out that the Renaissance floors were laid by the boys from a nearby village and they could redo them at any time. In those countries, in those museums, you'll always encounter some kind of obstacle, a little humiliation, so that there's no way you'd feel like royalty. In Budapest, the walls burn with heat and it's hard to breath inside. The women guarding the halls fan themselves with newspapers, but it still looks like they're about to pass out. In Bucharest you have to wear felt slippers, and once you've glided through all the rooms it turns out the visit was for nothing: there's maybe one sculpture by Brâncuși that makes the ticket price worth it. I wandered around the museum with hopes for something to happen, but nothing ever did.

No epiphany. There was only this empty palace, as if for a tyrant, full of objects that left me indifferent. So, instead of wasting my time in more museums, I walked around the parks of Bucharest; instead of paying attention to art I ate meat and drank beer in public gardens, or lay in bed in my room, wasting time. I walked around orthodox churches that had mysteriously escaped destruction, and I tried to buy train tickets to a different city. But mostly, however, I observed people, the inhabitants of the train station, its parasites, hanging out in McDonalds, on benches, everywhere they could. I rode the subway back and forth to see the suburbs. It was useless, but I did it anyway, and spent my time in tiny bars drinking coffee with too much sugar, or Ursus beer. I watched the streets throb heavily with activity. Next to a block of flats, a man had chained some coffins to a sycamore tree. It was a showcase of his handiwork. Dacia cars with flat tires gradually sunk into the asphalt between the buildings. The dogs chained to the entrances of stairwells could smell a stranger in their sleep, and when I passed by you could hear their barks echo off the concrete. I thought everyone was watching me because I was invading their lives and they knew it. That city, these cities—they were like one big museum. "Museum" became a term with a shifting meaning and concerned the entire space, people, their customs, their scents, faces, even vistas. And I, wearing my felt slippers, glided through their streets convinced it would stay like that forever. Those museums weren't more beautiful, or more interesting than the grand museums of the world. They were different.

I remember that a few years after that trip full of sleepy boredom, after sightseeing blocks of flats identical to those everywhere else, I saw—for the first time—bales of hay wrapped in blue plastic in the fields of Banat. Up to that point there were only haystacks blackening under the open skies. That's when I understood the era of the museum was slowly coming to an end. Something else has already happened—simply life, same as anywhere else. An era of new cars,

fast Internet, the latest cell phones, credit cards, and young leftist art-
ists has begun. And me, even though I've been observing the symptoms of that change for a long time, I missed all of it happen. That's
how I feel about it, anyway.

I'm awake when I travel, but am in fact closer to the borderlands of a dream. A kind of movement, a whirling or simple dance, sometimes sneaks into that dreamy journey. Just like that time in Moldova on the road ahead of a some collapsed bridge, where people started dancing with their hands up in the air, clapping, surrounded by a cloud of dust. Or this other time in a bar named "Gnome" in Transnistria, a country that doesn't really exist, which is why no one should be buying flowers at the market there, or think about owning a better car. In general, it shouldn't be possible to have a normal life there since normal lives have been banned, not to mention dancing, which, after all, isn't needed to sustain life. And yet, I was sitting in a bar in Tiraspol and the bartender wouldn't come over to wipe the table even though it was grimy. She was too resigned. I was sitting there watching how, in a tiny square of space free from tables and chairs, a young girl—unquestionably a family member because there were no other clients inside—swayed to the music of her own misery. She balanced on the edge of being and non-being. A young and beautiful nymphet, the embodiment of melancholia, a sad-drunk angel, and, like all the girls around here, in a skirt too short, heels ridiculously too high, and Band-Aids on her heels. It was almost one in the morning and she kept swaying, gently crossing her arms over her chest as if she was cold. She danced like that for nobody because there were only few of us in the bar: her mother the bartender, me, and some people she called Aunt and Uncle. They stared at the TV screen, listening to reports about how good things are and how much better they'll get in the future. They stared through the bar's windows at the streets, which were still visible even at night. But they didn't *see* anything, even the girl dancing with her most faithful partner—sadness.

It was in Lviv that I first realized that people dance not out of some social obligation, but for pure pleasure. I was walking down Horodocka Street, somewhere between Odessa and Vovchok Streets. They had different names before the war, but it didn't really interest me. I was there to get drunk on life, not to evaluate and control. It was early evening, but it was already completely dark because the city couldn't afford the electricity. When it gets dark in Lviv it's a little scary because the potholes in the street are so deep it's a miracle if you make it across—otherwise you find yourself brooding knee deep in asphalt, or polished basalt cobblestones. I saw it in a bar, one of those places where they serve cutlets and fried fish for breakfast starting at six in the morning; the vibe was mellow. Men in striped shirts and creased trousers sat with their women, drinking sparkling wine and Georgian brandy. "Those goddamn knockoffs," these men would say, "No shame. Everything is fake." And then one of the guys pulls his girl up from the chair and his friend, not wanting to stay behind, grabs his as well and both women, like Siamese twins, smooth out their skirts and surrender their bodies. Couples started whirling awkwardly. I stood only a couple steps away, but hidden in the darkness of the street and invisible from the inside. I was in a different world, watching them glow, turn—an eternal peeping Tom from a different world. I observed the two couples framed by the entrance, a few stairs above street level. I stood surrounded by the noise of a tram passing in the dark, that very noise being the warning for people who couldn't see it. I can see all of that but I have no idea what kind of music was playing that night.

Years later I saw a couple similarly lost in themselves, as if the entire world was left behind an imaginary boundary line of darkness. They were in a bar, the name of which I can't recall—I'm not certain it even had a name. It was in Kishinev, next to the main market and by the stonemason's workshop. On the fence outside the workshop was a slab of stone portraying the face of a man, maybe around sixty; the slab was cracked in the middle from top to bottom. An advertisement of sorts. Local graves, which are typical for this part of the world, usually consist of a black gravestone with a white etching—a perfectly accurate portrait of the deceased with all the necessary details: golden chains, rings, and, if need be, guns so that everybody will know whether or not the deceased was rich. So they can know if he was a man of deed or some lousy paper pusher, the kind you can find in Gogol and Chekhov, only contemporary.

And yet there is a bar next to the stone mason's shop. It's hard to notice during the day because it disappears among the other storefronts. I remember I went to that strip to buy some spices—at the time we lived in Kishinev and had to organize something resembling a home for ourselves, and I remember all the sausages and all the spices smelled damp, the counter ladies were rude in that peculiar Russian way, and I left with nothing. Behind one of the grocery stores there was a mechanic's workshop, but when it closed in the evening the customers would start making themselves comfortable around the half-disassembled, half-painted cars. A plump woman in a red dress would serve, and the cloth of her dress was so tight you could even read the tag on her panties. She walked around with a blue plastic pitcher of wine. Nobody cared that it was filthy, or that it wasn't really made to serve wine. So we drank wine from one of the mechanic's uncle's winery as the owner himself sat there counting money; in real life, as he claimed, he was a poet, an artist. He would hand out pictures that showed him reciting or writing poetry, always with his sad drooping mustache and a ponytail; always in the embrace of the woman in the red dress. In the entryway to the locale, though it wasn't much of a locale anyway, was a pathetic bathroom on the left and something like a train-station ticket booth on the right, a glass counter and some shelves with beer . . . So, at the counter stood a man with an open shirt, playing a synthesizer, and singing. Of course, he had a golden chain around his neck. In front of the bar was a woman dancing with her two-year-old child. The child laughed and she laughed too, fatigued but still young. She whirled like a dervish that night and she was happy. Her man slumped off the bench and she was soon to follow, but for now she held on and her and her child's laughter echoed around the place. Others danced in all different manners. I was kidnapped by a fat bartender lady: a tray in one hand, me in the other one, two or three spins, and she let go of me because she had to go behind the counter to grab a couple more bottles.

A few moves, a few steps and I was left on the side again. Journeys are just like that, you spend several moments together and then you're on your way somewhere else with a feeling of longing to stay just a moment longer, just enough for one more spin. I saw people dancing in Kosovo as well. We stopped in a village one time, a place that had nothing except for a bus depot the size of an airport, and completely empty. Weeds grew from between the concrete slabs that paved the depot's area. I saw all of that and I knew, I didn't suspect but I knew, with absolute certainty, that all of it would turn into dust one day. It would disappear just like the rest of the country—that's how it looked. The bus station was enormous, but not a single bus was stationed there. There was a phone booth at its perimeter, but the telephone was ripped off. There was also a shopping center, but the kind you'd find in a small town—not the kind we're used to. It was like a two-story concrete box divided into smaller cubicles: a copy shop, a barber, and a tanning salon. There was a flowerpot in the stairwell and a sports bookie's office on the first floor with a fluorescent light and papers all over the floor. There were also boutiques with clothing, but not from our parts of the world. Rumbling echoed through the corridors and from one of the spaces emerged a group of high school kids. They were gasping, smoking, and kissing. They rested for a moment and then disappeared behind another door. I opened it—it was completely dark inside. Light fought to get through the black coverings on the windows. It smelled of sweat and cold smoke that was being reheated. The room was filled with a packed, swaying crowd. In the middle there was something else, something that organized the crowd around it. There, in the middle, was a spinning circle of people, and within that circle was another circle, spinning in the opposite direction, and then a third circle inside that composed of only three people, spinning again in the opposite direction. It looked like a huge sex party. Hormones were evaporating into the air and dripping to the floor with sweat. Girls had their glistening shoulders exposed, and the boys were in an exited stupor, resting leaned against the walls. This small room on the first floor of a small-town shopping center, between an internet café and a barber, was a mass orgy in the darkness, humid, full of peculiar smells, and in the atmosphere of mystery. But those people forming the circles, young men and women, all equally ready for action, touched each other through white handkerchiefs. And if somebody didn't have a tissue, they would use a paper napkin. "It's not the right time of day," I thought, "they should come here at night." But they just kept spinning and spinning without paying attention to anything else, without alcohol, soda, or water. It lasted until the clock struck a certain hour—I don't know which—and suddenly they all just disappeared. Time is irrelevant when you're traveling. Someone opened the door and they were all gone. They boarded buses in front of the building and went back to their villages. No one came into the mechanic's shop bar after that. The smell of teenage sweat was all that was left.

The most difficult part to understand was the fierceness with which they spun. It looked like something completely natural, a determination of people who don't need great art. They didn't take any classes, didn't practice tango in pubs and bars like people in my own town, who gather after dark and dance close to perfection, but resent each other for every misstep. There are fights over false moves like over poor card game play in my family, always painfully commented. The art of their dancing, those young students from an agriculture vocation high school in a small town in Kosovo, was natural and alive. They dance whenever the opportunity presents itself. Of course, there are better and worse dancers among them because strength, speed, and natural talent all matter. But they dance regardless of age, in groups, and I've seen this happen in other villages as well. There is always music at the center. There are two or three guys around a giant drum, giant because the rhythm has to be strong and pronounced. The drum is always accompanied by a tired and dented brass section that's on its last legs. They go from village to village, from dance to dance. But why would anyone replace the brass instruments when the players themselves are all in their eighties? There will be no second life, and the instruments they already have designated for the first one will do. They play loudly, and if it's coming along nicely, every now and then, one of the dancers will come along and drop a banknote to show his approval, and that he can afford it. That's important too. And so they keep on playing and the banknotes keep falling out of their stuffed pockets, from behind their belts. Men and women keep rewarding them as if they were not elderly musicians, but girls pole dancing. They reward them for beauty and bravado, and generously too. People dance divided into several circles, which sometimes connect. They interlock their arms and dance to one side, left leg following the right, kick, step, and repeat. They're celebrating Đurđevdan, also known as Ederlezi. It's been raining all day, but they just keep exchanging glances, pairing up, and dancing.

I could get out at each train station like that. I sleep all day long and at night I stare at the road beyond the window. I count mileposts, or the stations we pass without stopping. I get out whenever I have to and I see people dancing, whirling. They have nothing better to do, or maybe that's their only idea of fun. I feel as if I'm standing motionless in one place and they are the ones on a journey. That's one of the numbing effects of travel. Not only does the concept of time become confused, but both countries and space seem homogenous. It feels as if I were a giant statue of Buddha and the entire world was spinning around me. As if I was truly one of my own clan; a clan eternally sitting in one place. I am calcified, and the world is spinning.

It's been like that since I can remember. In the dark corners of Tangier I encountered male couples, blasé queers sitting around without hope for a sober romance. Sitting all day, slowly sipping their drinks. They waited for the night to come to start dancing. Dusk was the universal hour of shamelessness. As if a curfew had been lifted. At that point, alcohol would take over even in bars with official licences. A few glasses of wine from Meknes, always in complete darkness, and that was enough. Elderly homosexuals held each other gently and danced without music, only to the rhythm of the news of the world because the bar had a TV set. In a bar for the hetero drunks everyone beelined for the only woman there: a dame in her sixties wearing a seductive outfit. They would buy her wine she didn't drink; the bartender would give her half of the drink money and the men would take her to the dance floor. She stood there, like a sleepwalker, stepping in place while they swayed. Maybe they hoped for something and maybe they didn't. They repeated the ancient gestures, the necessary gestures, for their imaginations to come true. Bars buzzed and boiled, and drinking and desire were always kindling for dancing and whirling. Officially frowned upon, desire was separated from the prudish streets by a mere curtain, yet visible and obvious to everyone. I remember, years before, it was like that in the bistros along Saint-Denis in Paris, which were dominated by glassy-eyed blacks, drunk every night. They'd drink every day, and dancing was an added and free pleasure. Wherever I go, motionless, I see people longing for fun. I see dancing stages set up in parks in Ukraine's fallen cities, and I see people dancing in the winter to the sounds of music played through giant megaphones. I see people from Kolkata ready to win the cricket cup, people dancing with a tinfoil goblet imitation all night long.

"That's what I travel for," I kept telling myself. I have never seen girls dancing lazily, as if drugged with sadness, or a mating dance with white handkerchiefs like the one I witnessed on the first floor of a shopping center. I've never seen whirling so full of life in a bistro on some dark street, with music overpowered by screeching of a tram. I have never seen anything like that before. That's why I travel. I need to travel in order to see.

Nothing happens here. We've been driving since dusk and for several hours now. There's nothing interesting along the way, only empty villages. We hit a dog in the morning. It just ran out in front of the car. We drive for hours thinking what went wrong, then we curse the dog for lunging out into the road. We see bars in the villages, but most of them are closed. After all, who's going to visit them anyway? They don't have money. If someone decides to splurge, they usually buy a golden lion on a concrete post to put by their front gate, sometimes even before the house is finished. Finally, we find a bar that is open. It's called Rendezvous; the tables are covered with plastic, red-and-white checkered tablecloths scattered with cigarette burns. The holes are lined up next to each other at the very edge of the cloth. That's because when people want to free their hands they lay their cigarettes at the edge of the table and forget about them, immersed in discussion. The entire surface is speckled with tiny holes from cigarettes dropped or forgotten. Now, the only clients are a grandma with her grandson, sitting at an empty table. They haven't ordered anything, but the bartender lets them stay. They're neighbors after all. They stare silently at a black and white TV, also silent. A lion hunts for a gazelle somewhere in Africa. It's incredible how much room for speculation there is when there's no commentary.

There's a plastic, gold-colored clock above the bar. It's around 9 P.M., but the clock shows 3 P.M. and runs backward.

We are driving through a forest in the mountains. I recall other forests just like it around the Srebrna Kopa in the Czech Republic. I used to go there, too, always in that indeterminate moment between late autumn and early spring, when it's easy to get a lot of wind, the trees are still bare, and people are bundled up. But right now I'm in Serbia, close to Bor. We're driving between mining complexes, through a forest filled with smoke from wood being burnt on the side of the road to produce charcoal. And it's been thirty, maybe thirty-five years since I went to the Czech Republic.

It's unknown where boredom comes from. It catches you at the train station when your connection is delayed, or in a hotel along with a high fever and a weird swelling of your limbs. Long hours, but not really meaningful. It's worse when they turn into days. I fill them with trifles. Your companions meticulously consume their meals, elegantly wiping up the remaining sauce with bread. You can watch the spectacle carefully once your outrage over their lack of manners finally passes. A naked beggar sweeps the street with a broom made of twigs and sticks his arm out. His doing it naked to show everyone: "I'm a maggot, my name is Job." There's no real activity, but there's always this minimal something, these micro-movements. Merchants carry out their rituals; you can see from your hostel room if anything outside has changed, or you can try to scare away boredom with a newspaper. It doesn't go so easily with a book. Books don't usually work on a trip, they don't move you one way or the other. They don't concern the here and the now.

There are books that can derail you, lull you, and then you wake up at the wrong stop, hours too far. The best books, and I'm speaking only for myself, are the ones in foreign languages. They keep you tense just by virtue of their sheer linguistic barrier, by need of a more attentive reading. I've seen people with the Bible or the *Communist Manifesto*, but the most commonly read book is a Lonely Planet guide.

You can buy them everywhere, usually slightly used. When you're leaving a place it's good to leave the guidebook behind you, it would be a dead weight anyway.

Each era has its own guidebooks, the echoes of which can be found in literature. Petrarch claims in his letters that he crossed the Ardennes Forest alone. He writes: "It was known to me through writings of other authors, but looked dark and menacing." It's a kind of proof that this first modern tourist who traveled—as observed by the astonished Hungarian writer Sándor Márai—for the sheer pleasure of wandering and looking through the guidebooks available to him at the time. But there is another motive to Petrarch's journeys: a need for a moral lesson and transformation of travel into literature. Márai continues his short history of travel literature: "Numerous traces of it remain in naïve, kind letters written while traveling, up until the end of Renaissance. These were the times when the goal of an escapade was not to change one's location, and the goal of a letter written from the road was not to become literature. Behind all of these stood the desire for experience. That's what disappeared from traveling when people started moving around for practical reasons, and went searching for new worlds or because of strong feelings felt for somebody else. From that point on, the goal of a traveler was no longer to learn about Rome, but to learn about himself. Later on, at the end of the eighteenth century, travel turned into an elegant sport for intellectuals. Then the steam locomotive appeared, and after that Lindbergh, followed by a booking agent waiving a large poster and yelling 'Around the world in thirty days!'"

There were others who came after Lindbergh; Márai lived to see the Concorde take off and experience times of truly fast travel. But he didn't want to last in those particular times, and took his own life.

A guidebook can be useful. I use one to calm myself down, usually on my way to metropolises on other continents because they seem so clear and transparent on the pages of a book. Nothing in there signals endless, narrow alleyways, a spider web of streets impossible to tame, and medina quarters still not fully explored. I read about the monuments; that's just my way, I need to know a little bit. I read a novel or a memoir based in that place. I try to compliment the various Baedekers with other books found on the spot, often published on lower quality paper. And there are books you take with you to kill time.

There's only one novel that has accompanied me throughout the years on almost every extended trip. It's George Perec's *Life A User's Manual.* Ever since I read that book for the first time, back in the day, it has stayed with me. I have two editions of it. One with a canvas cover, perfect to be read at home, and one pocket edition, lighter and much more handy. It's a couple hundred pages of a walk through the corridors of human termitary. I like to remind myself that the termitary is the creation of a protein computer, Perec's brain, a hothead with wild hair, a madman with a seaman's beard and a charming smile. It's charming until you learn he had rotten teeth, yellow like a mammoth's tusk, from smoking Gitanes cigarettes. I don't think Gitanes took away his charm, although the corroded smile maybe a little bit. Under this crazy hair, under the cat sitting forever on his shoulder (there is a picture of him with the cat like that), Perce is a cold-hearted analyst, an engineer of the worlds, and one of those who either becomes one of the greats or ends up at the hospital of the Holy Ghost for observation, then treatment or maybe off to Kulparkowo for good. I take all of Perec's attributes with me on the road and I think about his teeth more than I probably should. I think about his imperfect smile. Maybe if he had a better smile he would've written worse? I carry his book in French because that's how I protect my own French speaking skills, the last bastion of my weirdness. I hide it away, as if in some fancy little jewelry box: lay there my love, my intimate language understood by nobody, *lingua franca* of olden days, slowly dying away. But there are books by Perec,

I notice it only now, that I've read only in Polish, but I'm okay with that. *Life* is the only Perec novel, I believe, that is worth being dragged on a long trip, when there is a lot of emptiness to be filled, numerous layovers. It's worth taking on passages counted in days, not hours, or when there is a sickness that confines you to a hotel bed, striking you with fever and dehydration, and you pray for all of this to end one way or another.

Perec came to me and stayed with me, just like that, a permanent piece of equipment often stored in my camera bag, which is my most private luggage. At the end he's usually rugged and torn at the edges.

When people write about Perec it's usually about all the obstacles he created for himself and then had to overcome. It's enough to take a look at the manuscript of *Life a User's Manual*, to see a list of those obstacles, points, and mandatory words. It's not a thin copybook, but a thick volume hard for outsiders to understand. The plots of life go according to their own paths and pace in this novel and the difficulties have been overcome, which is why it's hard to notice them. These difficulties were a necessity, helpful obstacles. And so, whenever people talk about Perec, it's always about how hard it was for him to write and how peculiar it was for such lightness to come out of such struggle. I'm convinced he couldn't do it any other way. He wrote about it himself, the hardship was necessary. He outlined mandatory checkpoints, signposts along his ski route, and it was all he could do to follow them. He couldn't go straight, but had to slalom his way down the mountain. One of his admirers, Italo Calvino, wrote in his *Six Memos for the Next Millennium* that he knew only a few of Perec's constraints, but there were many more than Perec admitted.

Suddenly you see, all within one second, into a Parisian townhouse on 11 Simon-Crubellier Street, as if the entire façade was removed to reveal everything within, the interior, the rooms, the people. It feels as if, in a sudden flash of light, you see all their stories. It doesn't happen slowly, by meticulously reproducing chains of events, but rapidly, in a single glance. That's Perec. He's not obvious; an artificial design from start to finish. And it's that artificiality that should transpire through every seam. But there are no seams. And so the journey across the landscape of inhabitants' frozen lives, which are exposed like a brain during trepanation, takes the path of a knight on a chessboard. I follow the knight, mindlessly and without paying attention to the fact that it lands in every square only once, and that it skips one of the squares entirely, even though it doesn't have to. And that's a flaw inscribed into the perfect structure of that journey, a distortion that makes it even more beautiful. I move like a chessboard knight. I sit around provincial train stations, airports made of glass. I sit for hours on the train, separated from the rest of the world by a language bar-rier. I find myself inside an artificial world woven out of ideas, and if I'm a little distracted while I read (that's how most people read, after all) I don't stand a chance. Perec substitutes himself against what is real. If you were to add the commonly known fact that he was fasci-nated by mathematical riddles all his life, and that he wrote *A Void*, a three-hundred-page long novel, about the disappearance of the most common letter in the French language, the vowel "e," without which this language seems impossible and as a result deprived him of two thirds of the French vocabulary, then the image he creates becomes clearer. Perec's was a beautiful, but perverse mind. He was doomed, or so it seemed, but whenever he approached failure he would always come out victorious.

I always wanted to grab him by the sleeve, learn about more than is written down throughout his literary games; games that, nobody knows how, turn into great literature like water into wine. I knew very little, only as much as anybody else: that he died of cancer, probably because of those Gitanes cigarettes, and that his parents were from here, from Poland. They were Icek and Cyrla Peretz of the Szule-wicz family. They left for France before the war. His father died after volunteering in the army. His mother, by contrast, never volunteered anywhere. The war came for her. Cyrla was sent to Auschwitz and never made it out.

Perec's own life, the one without a user's manual, the life that grew wild and escaped mathematical laws, was spent visiting psychoanalysts—taking drugs—the contemporary equivalent of Bedlam chains. He lived in several different places, including Poland, I know about it from friends. He came and was different than in the pictures. He wasn't so radiant, so burdened with a cat on his shoulder, not so Egyptian. He looked more like a bum, rather tired with his different lives. It wasn't a trip to find his roots, but rather a penance in the form of a pilgrimage to the place of hollowness and disappearance. And so I was jealous of friends who got to meet him and did nothing to keep the memory of him for me because back then I didn't understand that, actually, they had. They told me part of the story.

Another moment of beauty in Perec is his endless calculations, lists of objects, people, facts, and occurrences that stemmed from each other. Lists of consecutive owners of certain objects filling out spaces that, in the end, disperse like smoke over a meadow because, as the author claimed himself, they had never existed, were neither beautiful nor ugly. They just weren't at all. There's no romantic plot in *Life*, only chains of events, one next to the other, that captivate the reader, and enforce their own rhythm into my head—a rhythm far more powerful than the clamor of a train. The powerful rhythm of that novel, its wit, and ironic smile behind the hidden mistake—that one skipped square . . . When there's a row of rotten teeth behind the wall of lips, how much more real does the image look? How much more trustworthy life becomes when cancer corrupts it from within. The characters are shrouded in irony, and that's why you perceive them as so real, this bunch of crazies, Bartlebooth and his servants, like Winckler. And all of that in order to bring a story as vast as the universe to a close—because between its beginning and its end is an entire world, packed in with its creation, painting lessons, trips

attested by the number stickers on trunks. There are puzzles com-
pleted and ruined from being brought back to their initial form—an
empty sheet of paper and a thin board. There were people, later they
were gone, and we can't say anything about them. That was the ideal
according to Bartlebooth. Perec, with his dying man's smile, testifies
to something different because he tells us everything about his people.

If I were to count all the trips I probably spent with Perec, it would
add up to many months. One time in Arles, in the south of France,
we were in a café on a market day—the crowd flowed before our
eyes, overloaded with seafood, cheeses, and local wines. We were sitting, sipping coffee, then picon or some other muddy aperitif of the
south that tastes of anise. Suddenly one of my friends nonchalantly
said that maybe we should stay longer so that we could meet Perec's
widow. So we sat by the boulevard des Lices in Bar du Marché; time
went by and we were getting progressively more and more drunk.
The widow was nowhere to be seen and never showed up in the end.
I don't regret it, and I even feel silly for waiting for her on that day.
What I really waited for that day, as Grandma would say, I haven't
got the slightest clue.

I would've never learned about the sedan chairs on the streets of Dresden if not for the memoir of composer and orchestra conductor Karol Kurpiński. There are more operas, churches, choirs, organs, chamber music, Italian singers traveling from city to city, their throats ruined to no surprise after performing twice or even three times a day, more dances, ballets, operettas, meetings with music publishers and composers according to this slightly unreliable-seeming journal of his 1823 journey through Europe than there is actual life outside of music. Oftentimes Kurpiński doesn't report anything of note, but sometimes, accidentally, he will mention a thing or two and that's how, *en passant*, he directed my attention to this unexpected mode of transportation employed in Dresden. "What a preposterous idea," I thought to myself, "to get around a city in a sedan chair in the middle of Europe and not see anything immoral about it." Although, on the other hand, it's like riding in a rickshaw pulled by a man, somewhere in Asia. That still happens today. But in Asia, of course, it's commonly accepted. A Western Man on vacation pardons himself because, after all, he's far away from home and people there do the same if they can't afford a car. But a sedan chair carried by men—because we're not talking about a basterna carried by mules— in Dresden in the nineteenth century is something different.

Kurpiński isn't the only one who leads me through countries full of facts that are not entirely comfortable. When I read in King Sobieski's father's journal that some Frenchman, wild with hatred and surrounded by other wild Frenchmen, ate pieces of Ravaillac in his scrambled eggs, I don't think about the mental limitations and innate brutality of those people. When I read passages by the London chronicler Ackroyd, about how pieces of convicts' bodies were in high demand and how some pregnant woman took a dead man's hand and placed it on her stomach because a hanged man's hand was supposed to bring health to the baby, I think about all the official methods of applying death that produced these human bits and pieces. It all happened by order of the court, not by revenge under the cloak of the night, and not by a robbery gone awry. It all happened in broad daylight, on a square, in order to show what happens to men who break the law. And for a little bit of entertainment, too. Gallows were designated for the lower classes, common criminals. Their bodies would hang in the city or along the road. Those who were born to a higher social class deserved a more dignified death, by sword or ax, which reminds me of the medieval custom, beautiful but extinct, something locked in stone and frozen in a tale just barely comprehensible to us today. It doesn't bring to mind times that are in the past, but almost around the corner of our memories. From that second, more dignified way of bringing about death, by sword or ax (not always foolproof because the blade could slip and the whole procedure would have to be repeated), came an ingenious idea by doctor Guillotine, and later so eagerly put into practice by the French Revolution. He commenced a democratic process of decapitating all enemy heads, regardless of class and with mechanical precision.

The beginning of the guillotine's industry and its marvelous period of gaining momentum, when heads kept rolling into wicker baskets, are generally well known. The conversation about its end is sparse. And for me, the end of its story seems far more interesting. In France, the guillotine ended its career not too long ago—in 1977 and to the misery of the last general executioner for the state, and to the former and longtime assistant to the general executioner, who was fired after two executions he performed out of his own initiative. Only twelve years earlier, communist Germany decided to stop decapitations because Germans, not only in the communist East, liked rolling heads too. Jünger noted in the forties: "mainly horse butchers applied for the job. Those who still carried out executions by ax felt a kind of artistic superiority toward guillotine operators. They had a sense of a service tailored to each individual customer."

During the first execution under the rule of Kniébol "the executioner, who took off his tail-coat for the occasion, reported for duty wearing a shirt and a tilted top hat. He was wielding a bloody ax in his left hand; his right was raised in a 'German salute.'"

Kniébol stood for Hitler. That's how Jünger nicknamed him in his memoir.

Kurpiński is extremely helpful as a tour guide around that gone world; a world assumed to be similar to ours out of laziness. Without him, I also wouldn't know about *lonlokaj*. He doesn't even explain the word, just like my family never explained words they brought to me. *Lonlokaj* is a servant for hire to travelers who also acts as a tour guide. That's what I learned from the footnote. *Lonlokaj*—a beautiful word hidden in times when travelers needed servants. It's an almost extinct category because barely anybody needs servants anymore, or human tour guides for that matter. Today's traveler prefers a guidebook, or to look around online. A human tour guide is usually a pain, his jokes a little stale. That's why, on my journey through Europe in the first quarter of the nineteenth century, I choose to rely on a book, on Kurpiński, and observe with a half-smile from a distance of almost two centuries how he runs like a madman between the theaters and opera houses of Europe to compare performances with those staged in Warsaw. But I also notice moments when he manages to observe a little something more, paintings, sculptures, women. He sees so clearly sometimes that he momentarily becomes tempted to stray from the path of virtue. He's ready to sleep with a beautiful French girl, even though according to him they remain deaf to the sighs of men who are not backed by a coin or two. He doesn't consider any other reason for rejection. And so he remains faithful despite himself. He complains that his pocket is too empty for infidelity, just so that in the end he can ask his wife to type out the manuscript. Kurpiński crosses Germany—and it's a country completely different from the one I know. He travels through France, also different of course, and through Switzerland. He gets stuck in Italy for a long time, naturally because of the opera. In Rome there is a break in his records, no more descriptions or cries for his beloved dog and wife. Kurpiński barely finds time to list all the places he went to and all the things he saw, and sometimes he fails to do even that.

I read his memoir and Kurpiński becomes my *lonlokaj*. I search for guides like him because when my own clan wanted to teach me about the world, my ears were plugged with ear-wax and my eyes were sewed shut. Ever since I can remember, my family bored me. They would recreate an entire hagiography, a story of our holy clan, a monolithic being centuries old without a single crack on its surface. They would project their vision of this beautiful creature, morally dominating over the rest of the world. Even if it was simply based on virtue of where we came from. After all, we came from those better parts, and only those born there could compare themselves to our family.

The sky turned dark and it was raining almost vertically. There were just two of us, me and some black guy, under the roof of a waiting area. He took out his suitcase from a locker and set up shop on the table next to the closed café. He had some chips, toasted bread, and some hot dogs. He was making supper for himself. After about an hour, the hallway was packed because the ferry was leaving soon, but he kept on methodically stuffing his face, kept on composing nicely squared sandwiches while surrounded by the crowd. I was trying to dry my umbrella and my shoes. Everything was wet and heavy.

At that time of the year ferries as huge as the Ararat Mountains leave from Nynäshamn—almost empty. The captain kept announcing through the speakers that we had over a hundred cars on board, even though it could fit five hundred, and that there were three hundred twenty-six passengers, even though it could take five times more. The ferry left the dock, and the invasion of the bar commenced. Then eating, anything to kill time, those three and a half hours of travel in the dark. Finally, after midnight, the island—Gotland.

It was the end of the tourist season. Only on the weekends could small groups be spotted wandering around with a map of town in their hands, so they could see everything there is to be seen in the sole town on the entire island. They were out to see the ruins of churches, defense walls, and wooden cottages. I would often watch from behind my desk how they approached our house on the hill, a house with the view of the city, of the rooftops smeared with sunlight, and of the sea. I could hear a tour guide announce: "And behind me, ladies and gentlemen, is a famous center for writers." And all eyes would look into our windows.

I would meet my housemates on the promenade. They would be throwing rocks into the water or coming back from somewhere by bicycle. I would meet them at the store and we would exchange laconic greetings. Sometimes they'd be gone for an entire day, which meant they were working, locked up in their rooms. Only the Greek guy could be spotted day and night because he had a room on the main floor, facing the street. He would translate Greek poetry and cookbooks interchangeably, smoke Azeri cigarettes and drink wine. Sometimes he would wave to me from behind his desk to come in, have a cigarette and a drink. We would arrange to meet in the kitchen in the evening.

I don't know why I had such Balzacian ideas about writers, that they always work hard until they drop, are always chased by deadlines, but when the job is done—craziness ensues. They drink, eat, and party until dawn. I went into the kitchen on my first night there, quietly, to take a look around, figure out what's up. Three stoves. Three fridges. Several coffee machines. There were a lot of cookbooks in the corner because everyone cooked for themselves. There was a great celebration of gluttony ahead of us, a chance to try Swedish, Finnish, American, Belarusian, Indian, and German cuisines, I don't remember all the other countries people were from.

In the evenings we would sit together around a scratched table in the kitchen. C. would drop by, a Swede from Finland, mumbling something to himself. He would grab the biggest frying pan, and the other pans would drop to the floor and scatter. Everyone would go silent. C. would then grab olive oil, a quarter of a kilo of bacon, eggs—six if he bought a smaller box and eight if he got the bigger one. He would make himself scrambled eggs and bacon with vicious intensity. It would stick to the bottom of the pan because this center for writers had only cast iron pans. And so he would try to get all of it off the bottom with a wooden spoon, cursing in five languages. He wore an army jacket. He was short and this jacket was supposed to make him look more serious. In the end he would sit down with the frying pan at the table, still silent and still wearing the jacket. He'd devour his scrambled eggs, bite into his bread greedily and as fast as possible. He would soon disappear, with his pockets filled with beer bottles. The table would come back to life. "I mean, it's rude," the American would say, "I don't know how to interpret that" she would add. "Someone should tell him," and she would go back to eating her avocado salad.

"You have to kill time somehow," C. would later tell me, when his angry days of scrambled eggs on bacon were gone. When calm, he would eat oatmeal, talk about benign subjects, and drink his beer with everybody else. He used to say that oatmeal is good for everything, that it's almost like a medicine. "Five minutes!" he would scream from the stove back at the table, giving me instructions to last a lifetime. "You're supposed to cook it for five minutes and stir in one direction, just like I do! That's how my father taught me and he was right, even though he was a rotten alcoholic." (And I would just mumble back that I don't like oatmeal.)

S. from Belarus, whom we called "Rusky" to make things easier, secretly hated the Swede, his fits of anger, even his eating habits. I would see Rusky making himself powdered soup, half a packet for dinner, and then hatefully glaring at C. over his barely dissolved bowl of soup. After a week he discovered canned beans in tomato sauce at the store. He would eat half of the can, and directly from the can too, to make the whole process quicker. One Saturday, he fired up two cutlets, one for Saturday and one for Sunday, and he ate them with *köttbullars*, meatballs he bought at the supermarket. And then he finally spoke from above his meal of meat. He explained that he spent all day in his room because he was writing a novel with a fountain pen, which was the only way to produce true high literature. It was going to be a lampoon on modern-day Belarus. He was hoping to finish the volume on Grodno, one hundred fifty essays. It was a big volume because the city deserved big things.

C., the one with scrambled eggs on rage, calmly groomed his literary work—a seed, as he liked to call it. Sometimes he got mad and turned to devouring bacon because he didn't know if the seed would survive. He ate out of frustration and insecurity. Every morning he added a couple dozen words, four or five lines, he had it all figured out, precisely, and the group of efficient writers laughed every time he admitted to it. They would drink wine out of a box, eat chips, and ask: "How many? Four, five pages? Well, not too much, not too much." And he would respond: "Me, ladies and gentleman, I'm not as talented as you are, I make up for it with persistance." (Only on the rage days would he write page upon page, from early morning and late into the night, pissed off and with faith in his powers; the next morning he would cross everything out and be back to eating oatmeal).

Everyone laughed at Rusky, too. It was hard not to laugh at the fountain pen and his little eastern tics, like when he would eat chocolate and wash it down with wine because chocolate on its own was too bitter for him. And the rest of us, in fits of class, would abandon beer for the sake of boxed wine and, encouraged by said wine, say things like: "This Rusky, he's weird, right?" And so Rusky would be silent days on end. He was afraid of people because he lacked the language. He also lacked trust toward foreign foods. He didn't drink because it was too expensive. F., a rising author, felt bad for him. He was working on his debut, an expose on Sweden seen through the world of advertising. That's what he said. He also only ate ready-made meals, but was disapproving of Rusky's food, of course. F. would buy the more expensive meatballs, or soups that came not powered, but in a box, decent ones that would say "Italian Soup" or "Spanish Soup" on the front. It all came from the same Swedish food factory. He would also buy a block of Danish cheese. "It's excellent," he would exclaim, "and lasts for a long time."

There was another C., a German woman with a Polish-sounding last name. She spent entire days in the forests. And the forests of Gotland are peculiar, midget sized. That's because there's bedrock right beneath the grass. And black sheep graze on that grass, and it all looks like a dark fairytale. C. would sit among the trees with her laptop. She was writing a play about the Holocaust, a drama for kindergarteners. The house and the town were audaciously beautiful, so she would go into the forest because it was weird there, a little hostile, and she could better get into the mood. She would come back in the evenings and eat the most regular foods: potatoes, sausage, onions, mushrooms (there were mushrooms in those forests), and a lot of beer. She ate just like she would eat at home, in the Mecklenburg countryside. She would gladly join us at the table, especially if P. was there, also German, and who was writing a novel for adolescent girls and ate the same things as C. P. had started writing a book at one point, hoping it would become great literature. But his publisher told him it wouldn't sell. "It would be better," the publisher had said, "to redo it. It'll resonate with the teenagers." P. took his advice.

One and only K. didn't see anything, didn't stare into anybody's plate or business, and remained transparent himself. His presence was announced by the dry crack of his door resounding twice a day, at lunch and dinner. K. was just starting on his latest book, he couldn't remember himself which number it was, his thirteenth or fifteenth, and so he was focused and in a different world. On the first day he brought back a huge bag of frozen food from the co-op to last him the entire stay. Each box contained two black trays, and each tray

197

had three sections: potatoes, meat, and vegetables. He also had boxed soups. I don't think he paid attention to their flavors. He reminded me of B., a Hungarian translator of Proust, whom I met one time in France in a similar house. Like him, she divided every day into portions of frozen food because she didn't want to waste time. She ate spam for breakfast and Carrefour's frozen foods for dinner. Other than that, she took her nourishment from Proust. She tried to convince everyone that one of the volumes of his works needed to be retranslated, even though none of us could speak Hungarian and it was hard to confirm or oppose her views. And in the moments of darkness, after she had little wine, she would tell us how she was alone, living in a block of flats with trash piling up beneath her windows. That's how her country was and that's why she was hiding in Proust.

The Finnish guy ate robotically in front of his computer. He was blind to the world outside and deaf to the sounds coming from the kitchen. The Greeks were cooking German food and were ready to fight about it and Z., another Finnish guy who wrote in English, would talk about himself in an Indian accent and cook pasta. His Indian girlfriend would bring condiments to the table. "One thing I miss sometimes when I'm in India," Z. who had lived there for the past twenty years would tell us, "is our European food. Of course, I love Indian food regardless." He would say that and examine every strand of pasta. At the same time he would ask A.: "I cooked it for twenty minutes, you think that's enough?" And A.—the Indian woman—would set ketchup and mustard on the table and tell him "Cook it some more, you never know." That was how they ate, some overcooked pasta with ketchup and mustard. "Where I'm from in India," A. would state, although there was no sign of India in her voice, "we don't have pasta like this." "But," Z. would add, "this particular one is a little tasteless. I don't know why."

Leon would come back to the island in those days. We would pick up wine in Systembolaget and then go to the co-op to get some food. Leon would tell me his life stories as we walked the aisles of the store, tell me about his arrests, interments, and his Swedish adventures. We bought potatoes and onions, tomatoes, salad, some herring. We would get some liverwurst and butter—all you need for good living. He would try to seduce a girl at the fish stand, would give me a meaningful wink and ask her some stupid questions, just so she would keep talking. And Leon would listen, enchanted, because she spoke with an islander's accent, differently than others. She talked about salmon, whether or not a piece was too lean, or maybe he'd prefer a different piece, more from the middle, and Leon would hesitate. Maybe he would prefer the other one, or maybe not, and she would start talking again. And so we talked about food wherever we went. I was curious what people ate there, and Leon was simply hungry and wanted to listen to people. We would sit over a plate of *surströmming*, lean Baltic herring, not like those fat ones from the Atlantic, and significantly smaller too. We would pair it with mashed potatoes. Questions would start back at the house. "Are you frying herring? The canned kind? What's that smell? Nutmeg with potatoes?" So Leon and I would ask if they'd like some. "If that's no trouble," they'd be coy. And they ate and were surprised, thinking it must be some Ukrainian dish, Eastern for sure.

C., the guy who ate the rage-scrambled eggs and oatmeal and would bang the frying pan around on bad days, was in a phase of starting his rants with Plato and ending them with Marx. He'd eat our *surströmming* and say "Ah, you see, my dear friends . . ." and he'd go on mumbling. He liked food, but he resented himself for that weakness, so he had to take penance in the form of a lecture. Even the Indian woman tried some herring because she wanted to be European, she was frustrated by this Mother India of hers. Only the cheese was beyond her limits because to people from India, cheese is simply rotten food. Rusky would disappear immediately when people gathered, or when Leon would start his concert stories, or when the drinking, smoking, and shouting really began. It always went the same way. The Greeks would be the first to pull out their cigarettes, and the rest of our bunch—these meatballs, frozen foods, and boxed soups—would shyly take out their own shameful smokes, tucked away somewhere secretly. They would reach out for food so alien to them and for their reserves of cheap wine. They tried to forget quickly that *nulla dies sine linea* and that there's work waiting for them in their rooms. That in the morning it will all start over again.

"Miserable is the writer's plate," I thought to myself while we were getting wild and the stories started to flow, "half empty and chipped at the edges." But it's not because they're poor. They skimp on time and have no curiosity left. They were like my dead aunts, or their husbands—uneducated people who made sure their flowerbeds had perfect lines, their fences newly painted, and their cucumbers watered. They were people who never travelled because they were afraid of trains, of everything, terrified at the prospect of leaving because they knew burglars would come as soon as they're gone. They preferred their apartments over the rest of the world, although I have to say in their defense that they had some good reasons. And so my companions on the island tended only to the flowerbeds of their literature. They were so different from their ancestors, their Balzacs and Pepyses. As if they weren't from a different era, but from a different world.

In Chantilly, France we saw that parts of the forest were fenced in. Just like in Poland people would fence in a private property or an old communist State Agricultural Farm. Back then, nobody thought of fencing in forests because forests were nobody's property. We were walking around Chantilly and there were women dressed just like the mythical Amazons in the movie, running by us up and down the path. We were wearing some flashy clothes from a store that we were impressed by back then. We probably looked like a bunch of fragile glasshouse flowers and a little out of place, too. We would walk from one fence to the next, disgusted with the stiffness of the wire that made the forest seem far too domesticated, almost agricultural. Finally, we'd had enough. And on top of that there were horses. Only later did I learn they train them in that forest. How was I supposed to know that? We had to trek through the mud to escape the horses, in our new designer outfits straight from the store, bought at a nice discount. They were so heavily marked down even we could buy them, as could other poor citizens of Paris, often of African descent. We ran into the bushes to save our fancy clothes, even if they were a little tacky.

We were from the outside, from behind real barriers. We watched those delicate fences and with an air of border connoisseurs, especially borders impossible to cross, we would laugh at those fences in the middle of the forest put up by people fearing someone will take their wild berries, or take a leak. Poland's rotten forests have been open since forever, and "stealing" from the forest never counted as stealing. The forest belongs to nobody, there were no designated gateways and you could always just walk. As long as you kept it reasonable. As long as you didn't shoot a deer, or didn't take out foxes by the dozen, or cut down Christmas trees to fill up an the entire wagon. One tree is fine; one for yourself will do, but trees for trade was too much. There was freedom to our forests and we were able to compare them only here in Chantilly. During the summer holidays when I was a child we would go through the forest, taking a longer route, to stop by the lake where my grandpa used to oversee his little huts. We would go there to take a swim, and there was nothing much there, only the forest, dirt, and some hills. And on our way back we would always find some berries or mushrooms. We would find parasol mushrooms alongside the trail, so we were set for dinner. Or there'd be an abundance of saffron milk caps that would be our meal for the day. We would lay down on the thick blanket of berries, all smeared and dirty, watching the sky, the jays flying around with their parrot-like feathers flying, or we'd stop at the little bridge to stare into the water and watch pond skaters or water measurers, I can't remember which. That was how we, little maggots in bright YSL outfits, understood the forest and its freedom back in those days.

I don't think we talked about Fritz Karl Watel, also known as François Vatel, back then. But he was the person responsible for a famous three-day banquet that took place in that forest. A partial failure of the celebration was the cause of his subsequent suicide on April 24th, 1671, on the second morning of the party. But despite the king's expressed grief, as mentioned in a letter to the daughter of one Mrs. Sévigné, "the next day's dinner was very good and the desert was served. After supper there were walks, games, and hunting. The smell of daffodils was everywhere. Everything was splendid . . ." We saw the castle from outside, from afar. But it was enough to pay for the trip out there from Paris. The entry fee was too much, so we were left with the forest and a lot of walking despite all the inconveniences. It felt much more familiar, even though it was lined by fences left and right. We were walking among the trees, we were different than when we left Poland for the first time, crossing the border by bus, but still not like what we were supposed to become upon our return: accustomed to fences that establish obvious boundaries. The fence spoke about private property rights and that was it. But we were still dreaming about the forests of Ardennes, the unchartered woods, freedom, and Chantilly, but without those fences or a highway passing right through it. We were on a paved road that turned left, making a grand arch, behind the bus station. We were walking and I remember thinking: "Ozimska Street, the beauty of cobblestones shining in the sun." I was thinking about the widest, most amazing streets covered with setts that I knew. I used to remember a lot of them because, back then, a lot of streets used to be like that. Not anymore. The old stone has died. And back there in Chantilly there was an amazing curve of the road, shiny and long, and at its end was a castle with an enormous library that I never saw because I was cheap, and preferred to go for a walk in the park and in the forest. That was free at least. I preferred to go for coffee in a nearby bistro. And castles? "Castles," I thought, "I've seen a lot of castles in my life already."

Mene, Mene, Tekel, Upharsin

I was lying in my Swedish bed, a short and narrow one, and around me the sea was roaring as if the ferries were about to snap free from their moorings and tip onto their sides; as if rushed by the waves, they were going to enter the roadstead, sail off into open water, and then sink.

Now I think about this, while sitting on my enormous bed, also made in Sweden, looking like a pirate. Currently one-eyed, with a swollen face and stiches in my head, having been beaten up by life and those stories that I keep ripping out from inside of me with such difficulty. And the floor around me rocks like an ocean. It is in this bed of mine, in St. Wojciech's boat, and in its safe harbor—that's where I found shelter and where I preach.

I sailed away from my harbor, snapped from my moorings, and left my homes behind me, because when I leave them I establish new, temporary kingdoms, and that's the truth I discover with greater confidence, even though when I began my story I had no clue. I go in circles among the swarms of my people, of my places. It's easier for me that way. I'm like those Turks in exile, racing through Europe and through the world; Turks who, no matter where they live and what documents they carry, remain Turks, and Germany will remain their European homeland forever. And it was Germany that brought them here first, and who cares if it was only meant for a little while. They acted like the *Gastarbeiters* of all nations of all times before, like the Italians in America, or the Chinese and the Puerto Ricans. They did what the Portuguese did, or the Poles, the Ukrainians, the Greeks, the Croats, the Bosnians, and the Albanians. They did what so many before them have done—they simply stayed. They took what was offered—a low paying job. They toiled through steam rooms and factories, sending home the little they earned; money that turned into fortunes back home. They saved everything they could, living in rotten conditions, but when the time of their official stay ended, they didn't take the opportunity to go back. They didn't listen to threats, calm at first and later much more forceful, both explicit and insinuated. They simply disappeared or stopped communicating with the world. I travel like they did and my home, all of my homes, both current and past, are with me. I travel, like a snail with multiple shells; soft flesh and on top: tumor after tumor after tumor.

During that Gotland night, I was like one of those difficult cases from the Holy Ghost hospital, like one of those finally sent to Kulparkowo without a chance for salvation, or one of those tragic catatonics who fell in too deep for anyone to spot them from the surface. Boring nightmares torment me just like they tormented the others. I look inside my head, but I see very little. In the dark hole where I find myself with ghosts from Kulparkowo I can hear only moans, reminders of murders and lashings, exiles and misfortunes. This is my family's history, and I've kept in me against all odds. If it has any bright moments, then they shine through from a distant past, from a long time ago and from far away, from something that didn't exist for ages and is unknown to me. I go and I carry bright and dark moments, assembled like cobblestones, *salki* filled wall to wall, *nyże* full of long-forgotten staples, attics filled to the brim with a questionable wealth of lumber. At nights, and particularly during that very night in Gotland, everything came back—that which was long forgotten recalled itself, people, their smells, the clinking of a teaspoon in a cup, conversations, rather mute lips engaged in speech; mute because the sound evaporated a long time ago. Only the sense of words remained like dried up sediment. There are shreds scattered all over my *salki*, scraps of my escapes and travels; I don't know myself what to call them. But neither the beginning nor the end survived, neither the cause nor effect. My entire family lives in there. Who cares if a few people are missing, if their portraits are incomplete, if sometimes a head is unaccounted for, or a body. Their grievances and longings exist and constituted their essence. Every atom in their bodies was saturated with sorrow.

I remember against all odds. After all, I didn't listen. I didn't pay attention when they told stories. And yet, it all comes back to me slowly, there are voices coming from inside, whispers and hoots, tips from ghosts and from the living, and I see terrible images, even though it's not right, even though I haven't seen them before—the holy history of my clan.

And I see clearly that I myself, just like my nutty aunt, dreamt what will happen to her in her life. I dreamt her future, long before the terrible killings in Gaje, I dreamt of the men in her life, her father, husband, son, about Bandera's people, and about one anonymous man, whose identity was not yet revealed at the time she told her dream to my father's microphone. She repeated it just like she had many times before, and after that too, to anyone who'd listen, or not; to those who had no will to listen, in her own house and when visiting others, on trains, public transportation, at the market and at work, and, finally, on the streets—grabbing people, tugging at their sleeves, saying "I had a prophetic dream." She would recount her dream and I wouldn't listen until it finally got to me years later, and it became mine because I'm the only one who can keep telling it.

I am kept hostage in my own head. They should tie me up and feed me opiates, let some blood, place some leeches on me so they, too, could have their share before falling off. The exact same leeches

I observed with curiosity and disgust in the jars lined on the window-sill at my, so-called, legless aunt. Although back then she still had her leg; she lost it later because of those leeches. My aunt raised the killers of her leg on her own windowsill, made an effort to keep them hardy, kept them in clean water until they got hungry and were ready for the task. Her befriended nurses kept bringing more jars. Leeches, I would learn later on, were classified in *Systema Naturae* by Carl Linnaeus, who at one time also visited Gotland and the neighboring island of Fårö, and just like me had some unfinished business with the local sea. He writes that, before they got to shore, "the waves were like furies and the ship was tossed around between the roaring chops. My fellow travelers got seasick. Our hearts were filled with despair." That's it for Linnaeus. Supposedly he was a sea coward and was terrified of water. But he reached Gotland in the end, and almost everything went according to his plan, except he didn't find argil for porcelain production, which was his primary task. When he docked at the harbor of my Gotland city, the only one on the island, he found it destroyed by the Danish. I, however, was leaving it in order, even though I didn't find what I was looking for in Gotland either.

My aunt applied the leeches to her leg herself, until the infection forced its amputation. And yet, despite the fact she became a shut-in after that, she was one of the few family members who had left at one point, who moved around, though I don't know when. She wanted to leave behind everything, of that I'm sure. Her albums were full of pictures cut in half. In the pictures: her and the abyss next to her, her half is slightly uneven and the cut too close to hide the fact that someone is missing. There had been someone, and later I even learned what he looked like; the man who was a speck of glue on cardboard under the fragment of a picture in her albums. The memory of him was reduced to ashes in the kitchen stove: a lover boy with a thin mustache who kept messing with the heads of the women in my family. The type of guy you'd meet at a café, wearing a fedora and with a cigarette always nestled between his fingers. She cut him out of her albums just like he cut her out of his life. She left because she had nothing to lose here. She lived in Canada and worked in a stocking factory. Already then the leg industry was giving her a hard time and zero happiness, although she never took it as a warning. She had no dreams; maybe her nights were empty, and maybe that's how the first jar of *Hirudo medicinalis* showed up on her windowsill, only to take her leg later on.

Her room was filled with memorabilia. Her entire past was there; the best part of it hung across from the door, on the best walls, to remind her who she used to be—a traveler in a Canadian paradise, even though she spent all those years in a factory. There was a trunk from the M/S Batory cruise liner standing by the wall, a companion and a witness to her journey and her return; a steel box painted brown, a true transoceanic piece of luggage most definitely not designed to be carried around on one's own. During travels back in those days there still wasn't a need for luggage you could carry. When the Canadian branch of my family—people completely unknown to me—came to visit my grandparents, these people dressed in a peculiar way and acting strange, their luggage was the same. They had these huge, bulky, square valises filling the house instantly and almost spilling outside into the garden. My aunt spent the latter part of life in this room with its souvenirs from a failed attempt to escape; a room with a tiny kitchenette behind a little curtain, with fading pictures of movie stars, and a trunk from an ocean liner. At first, she used to walk around the apartment with great difficulty and pain, and she became unbearable to be around. After the surgery, her personality soured more with each week. She scared people away with her madness, with her looks. And then, suddenly and unexpectedly, she got better and started jumping around like a one-legged kangaroo, though still with difficulty. She was a terrifying old being, with her hair and thoughts in shambles. It was scary, visiting her for her name day; a name day at a legless aunt's with a perfect cake, because in terms of cake baking she was unparalleled.

All of these old aunts and quiet uncles have crowded me since forever; they've been on the road with me at all times. That was the wild bunch I carried with me at all times. When I was lying in my Gotland bed and thinking about my travels, my entire family, and wishing I could fall asleep just for a little while they were there with me. I had by my side a calm uncle with one leg and his equally quiet wife—Aunt Emma—as well as their son, who had died suddenly. I had the company of my legless aunt, patched with leeches for good health, even though leech-therapy didn't end well for her. Also by my side were Uncle Dudek and Aunt Walercia, who used to live by the train station. He had a smaller frame and was forever old, and had a big bald head and the sad face of an accountant, and whenever he heard a train whistle go off he would take out his pocket watch and check if it were on time. He knew the train schedules by heart. In his basement he kept a shovel or, in his old tongue, a *ryskal*, brought for *back there*, their paradise to which the gates have been shut forever. He kept it for when they would go back—back home. They lie with me, and their dead children, shot and buried in the orchard, lie with us all as well, and keep wriggling like I do too. I won't even mention my four grandparents, or my grandmother's sister, Aunt Gardian, who one day stopped being Ukrainian and never mentioned it again. They are all here and I'm with them, even though I don't want to be. I grow restless in bed and they start shifting as well, they hide their heads under the pillow and I hide mine too. Where they go, I go, and it's becoming unbearable.

In this cramped bed on the island of Gotland, I recalled a day when I went back to Ternopil, the city listed in my mother's identification documents as her place of birth. I was driving through Berezovytsia again; again I set foot in Gaje. These were their places, not mine, but I felt something of an obligation to go back, except that we were always rushing off to the next destination. Soon after passing the city limits I realized I didn't remember anything from that first trip. Besides, everything changes here, just like it does in the rest of the world, in the old republics and satellite countries. It used to be gray here; my memories are built on color tones, I can't remember a single color, and the only sign of anyone tending to the surroundings was the women who would be going out in the morning, carrying brooms made of birch twigs and buckets of water, which they would sprinkle over the road, going slowly left, right, left, even though the road was lined with dried mud. After few minutes, everything they had managed to swipe away was back on the road again. And yet, Castle Street, Russian Street, Shevchenko Street—these I recognized immediately, probably because of the heightened memory of that first trip abroad, because of that expectation for everything to be different. And everything was different, even though my aunt's house stood surrounded by a garden just like ours, and there were apple trees, chives, carrots—it was all the same. My aunt would send me to bring some in, "go by the fence" she'd say, "you'll find it there," and whatever I'd been sent to get was there, identical to our yard. Again I found myself in Ternopil, a city I didn't want to go back to because it wasn't mine and I had nothing to do with it. And anyway, I didn't want to seek out places that had changed, and that don't fit the memories of, well, others. "What now?" I triumphed over my own stupidity, "You laughed at them, at your own clan, that they didn't want to come here, that they spent their lives on their asses, as if they were bolted down. You laughed at their fears, and now you're repeating all their gestures." These were sermons I kept preaching at myself until I reached the city and the point of no return.

The city has a lake and a park. I remember the lake. There is an amphitheater in the park, and deep inside that park is a pool hall—a small box made of metal sheets and with two pool tables, a little furnace, and a heap of coal. A woman wearing *valenki* was managing the business, dressed warmly because, despite the summer, you could feel winter breathing from inside. She kept staring at newlywed couples from her door. They were wandering around the park that day, a dozen or so couples, two every half hour, as if they were coming off a conveyor belt. They came from the direction of downtown, took pictures with trees in the background, in the grass, and then would go to the harbor and catch a ferry with a photographer in tow. I too watched them walk around, as if they were advancing to another level in one and the same board game, because you know that in the end they'll reach the same goal—get married—and half a year later she'll leave for work or he'll start drinking heavily. The wedding venue was on the other side of the street, but there was a limousine parked at the park gates anyway. At the top of the stairs was a weeding cake waiting, and it was crowned with a figurine of the newlyweds made of sugar, a pale representation of the actual couple—this combination of a meringue-like wedding dress and the snake skin quality of a suit because here, for a celebration, they like to dress with class.

I don't know why I stopped there. I roamed around in alleyways at first and then in the city streets. I don't know why I followed the young couple that kept looking over their shoulders nervously before running away. Everything here is unfulfilled, it's all different than it was supposed to be because I imagined, or rather hoped, that it would be a kind of continuation, that something would happen, that those buried will come back to life; that the uncles who drowned themselves in alcohol and the aunts scattered all over the world would assemble for a single moment. But nothing happened, as usual, like everywhere, as in this city and every other city in the world.

I was lying in my Gotland bed thinking about the journeys that led me nowhere, and I'm not sure that they were supposed to lead me somewhere; at least not to where they took me, not to those places. I was expecting some conclusions, results, some knowledge, anything, but certainly not for the travels themselves to be the outcome. I didn't expect aching legs and corns on my feet to be it. I go on a pilgrimage with their burden on my back, and get nothing in return. I go around carrying their fear, in their name, even though nobody asked me to. On the contrary, they always begged me to stay, but I didn't. I hear the wind when it blows, I smell the ozone when thunder strikes but no celestial being appears before me, everything is small and earthly. There's no transcendence in it whatsoever.

I woke up and sat up in a bed as uncomfortable as the Swedish one, covered with mosquito netting through which barely anything was visible. A river of sand and mud was flowing through my room, my feet were immersed in slush, and ants trailed directly over my bed, as if the net was non-existent. They simply walked over me, some over my arm, others over my thighs; my skin itched. When I was falling asleep the room had been dry and relatively clean, maybe with exception of my bed sheets. Now it was a swamp, and the ants saved themselves on me like on Noah's Ark. I had slept through a hurricane.

Once I saw a picture taken in this town, a fishing settlement outside a major city. Back then I thought that the photograph was brilliant, but I'm not sure I'd stand by that claim now. And yet I went there, though I don't know why—I guess to prove to myself that, just like the author of the photograph, I could accomplish something there. It also was a winter trip; except winters there are different than ours. I followed a faint trace, I was lead by a single photograph and I landed on an island-bed and became an island for ants. I stayed in that village, although I didn't know why. I froze, slightly passive. I can't recall all of what I did there, only some of the activities. I ate my breakfast on the beach. I watched fishermen summon good weather, making circles in the sand, butchering a chicken and throwing its head into the ocean. (How many decapitated heads have there been already across my travels). A dog would run after the head and jump into the water. For hours I watched people dragging their canoes; how they mounted the paddles and pushed into the sea. In the end, I helped them because they couldn't do it on their own. I watched how they squatted and shat on the beach. Water carried in and took away everything there. I did nothing. I wandered day after day hoping something would come out of this, but nothing ever did; absolutely nothing.

riving a car is like a journey on a boat going downriver. It's me—St. Wojciech—I go down that river to encounter what's inevitable, to encounter a wild tribe that believes something different than I do and buries its dead differently than my people do. I sail in my car like on a boat among barrows, sepulchers, among other languages of which I know only scraps of words for the gas station: "please," "thank you." I understand the prices on the shelves in local supermarkets. I understand words like bread, wine, fish, and olive oil. I need them the most, so I learn them the fastest. Villages and cities keep zooming by—quick frames—there's no time to take a closer look. It's the same thing on the train, and that's why I prefer cars. I don't drive, though, so I can look around as much as I want and can always say "stop." Unexpected images fly by. There are no such views in my country. The night escapades of drunks, who end up sleeping in the middle of the road, might be the worst thing of it all. There is the fear that, in the end, someone will cross your path, just like that dog we hit in Serbia, and his or her skull will crack on the asphalt with a splat; that someone will end up just like the two bodies in my former city, lying next to each other, ripped open and dripping their fluids. I flow down the road, wherever the current will take me, and there are girls standing on the shoulders in outfits too light for that time of the year because, yes, they are a dream, a trap set for those craving a break from the monotony. They stand in the forests, or by the gas stations, glimmering from afar—but stiff up close and with dead eyes.

All of my people brought bad aura with them—a tragic *miasma*. They engrain it into their children and grandchildren, shared it with their friends. And they do that with an earnest smile on their faces. "And why would you go there?" my grandma would ask, surprised. Later she would ask questions about what it's like out there because she wanted to know, she was curious; mostly to confirm her own fears and justify them for the nth time. They kept sitting in their gardens, cucumber tentacles kept spreading in abundance, the pear tree heavy with fruit; only a cherry tree had to be cut down because it dried up. They sat on benches outside their homes, or on their post-German garden chairs under a plum tree, and everything around them was theirs, forever, until the end of the world. And they continued being amazed by anyone who, like me, would go on a journey in a boat, but forget journey's purpose once on the road. They would inquire politely, demand information, but interpreted it on their own—as treason and a loss.

And so I sailed in my boat, and foreign tribes kept swarming on the shores, busy with themselves. "Why are you going there, huh?" those who occupy my head kept asking, speaking with an accent I hear only when I travel to Lviv. "Why? Why? Why?" But did they know, on their death beds, what the bleached-red of the roofs in Pristina, with their minaret towers shooting up from between them, look like? They never went to Trepçë, didn't drive on a mountain road along the river and through the tunnel. Gray blocks of flats everywhere, people on welfare, someone throwing garbage directly into the river. "There are great riches here, plenty of gold," the locals used to say, truly believing that was the reality, "Mountains made of pure gold." But my people couldn't hear that either.

My family, following the example of a certain homegrown historian specializing in misfortune, would gladly list three hundred sixty ways in which the Polish population has been tormented and murdered; all of them observed by the aforementioned historian during the Volhynia massacre. They would recite them quietly at first, then raise their voices and "one, hammering a long and thick nail into the skull; two, scalping; three, being hit over the head with an ax handle." It would be still pretty quiet at this point, but soon after they would speak up, my grandfather in a growl because he was deaf, my grandmother melodically, but rather flat, even though she could muster silver notes with her voice if she wanted. "Thirteen, piercing the inner ear with a long, sharp wire, all the way to the other side and out through the other ear; seventeen, slitting the throat and pulling the tongue out through the opening." Until they almost lost their voices, but they'd keep going because nothing mattered more than memory. "Fifty-one, inserting a red-hot steel rod into a woman's vagina; fifty-two, inserting pine cones into a woman's vagina, the narrow end first; fifty-three, inserting a sharp, wooden dowel into a woman's vagina and pushing it through, all the way up and out through the throat; fifty-four, ripping open a woman's body with a pair of garden shears, from her vagina up to her throat, and leaving all the entrails exposed; fifty-five, hanging the victims by their entrails;

fifty-six, inserting a glass bottle into a woman's vagina and breaking it; fifty-seven, inserting a glass bottle into the anus and breaking it."

That's how they would sing around evening—him, dressed in pajamas, her in a nightgown—their mantras on memory. "Ninety-one, mounting a child on a wooden spike"—their rosaries of pain, and I wouldn't listen to them usually because I'd be busy with much more important stuff, and why would I listen anyway? "Three hundred fifty-five, taking one's life with twenty two or more blows of a knife; three hundred fifty-nine, nailing one's hands to one's doorstep; three hundred sixty, crushing a child under a wheel," and *da capo, da capo*. I didn't listen because I didn't know how to listen. Just like my neighbors got rid of Witek the imbecile, in the same way they sent away their deformed dogs for an eternal retreat to the mud of the countryside, I sent my family away—and only now I'm trying to rebuild it on my own, crooked and lopsided. It's too late to change it, so that's merely my written elegy.

I try to recall the strong Witek; Witek the imbecile who, all tensed, with his veins popping out on his neck, tried to lift the back of his parents car. And then he disappeared one day, together with his retardation, and his regular sized head, though obviously a dysfunctional one. His weak mind was his greatest strength; it was the source of his power because he lived entirely in his mind. When he was afraid of something, he would run. When somebody threatened him, he would lift them up and hold them in the air. When he was happy about something, he was happy with his entire body, he'd laugh and shake and salivate. And then, one day, he just got shipped away; it was sort of inevitable. Our neighbors were the kind of people who moved to our city just recently. They came with some assets and some clout and weren't like others who took jobs dedicated for the newcomers, poorly paid gigs for the internal *gastarbeiters*. They were uneducated directors who were given their positions for reasons other than their exceptional skills. They earned them through unthinkable humiliations, hundreds of vodka shots, by distilling moonshine so they could save on store-bought alcohol. They were true people of the countryside, resourceful and cheap, and they could do everything themselves. The bred pigs in their basement and were astonished by neighbors who couldn't stand the smell. They were genuinely upset when, after castration, one of the pigs would be healing poorly and fading, so it had to be butchered, which, by the way, they also did on their own because they didn't want to pay the vet and the butcher. Or they were doctors from the countryside, already after being promoted for the first time, having moved to the city with more success yet to come. They wanted success as quickly as possible. They desired it more than anything, like anyone else, and it was no sin. So, their retarded children and crooked dogs would be sent back to the countryside "to get some fresh air," as they'd put it, for fresh milk straight from the cow. As if the fresh air and blue skies could help those poor mutts in any way, as if sending Witek somewhere else, far from people's stares, would solve the problem forever, and erase him from existence. They did that, acting as if they wanted their chained mutts to squeeze every possible ounce of happiness from life, as if they cared about their fates at all. Their dogs were always loud and their children were forbidden to be around them because a dog was like an electric fence, working twenty-four-seven, dangerous and almost entirely cost-free.

But times have changed and they've gotten rid of their defense systems, though reluctantly—a bad dog meant good security. But they'd get rid of them and buy purebreds instead. They had to do this because purebreds brought prestige in an urban environment. They assumed that sending their shameful children and beasts to the villages, to boarding schools with a permanent residency, was equivalent to sweeping the sidewalk in front of your house—so that luck wouldn't trip on its way in. The dogs howled under the open sky, ugly and mixed just like before, but at least no worse than the rest in the neighborhood, nor more dangerous. There, where the dogs ended up, nobody cared about their looks or pedigree. The neighbors didn't complain about dogs barking all night, or that they'd attack you and bite your ankles. After getting rid of these failed creatures, nobody made any more remarks to the newcomers about beating up the animals, or children, to which they used to respond with "fuck off" because it was their dog, or their child. The city was not a place for those animals. Even dogs' names condemned the owners in the eyes of proper city dwellers, making them the butt of a joke. So dogs were all kicked out, along with Witek the imbecile as he was called and never took any offence because he couldn't understand. His parents called him other names lacking affection, when he'd come back home in the evening all dirty; "you dumbass" they'd say, "you big dummy," and he was huge, he was a giant who grew up with a head to small to make room for the alphabet. It was obvious he was created by his parents to be ridiculed. Witek left, I don't know where and I'll never know, but it's not like anyone cared anyway and, to be honest, I never thought about it twice either. In the beginning they'd bring him back every now and then, in that car of theirs he'd tried to lift by its bumper so that he could show them he was alive, that he was healthy, that they can't get rid of him entirely. And he was getting bigger with every visit, at first crying and sniveling from happiness at seeing his old tormentors, and then one day he disappeared for good. It was as if water had closed above his head, like it does above a stone dropped into a lake.

11/16/78

"**D**ear Children and Gc and Ggc—"

This is how the letter found in a broken cupboard begins. Gc stands for grandchildren. I'm among the great grandchildren to whom this chaotic story about a life coming to an end, this letter arrived too late from the valley of death, is also addressed. Only now, thirty odd years after being sent, I can read it consciously and very carefully, just like the five holiday cards sent between 1958 and 1976. It takes great concentration to read them because my great grandpa didn't use any punctuation, and had issues with orthography and language in general. He knew Polish mostly from hearing it, which is how I reconstruct it now, and he passed maybe two, maybe four grades in school. At home they spoke Ukrainian. I'm not saying that to excuse him because he doesn't need to be excused. He lived through his life somehow, even though it wasn't easy. But the explanation is in order to understand where this stream of half-intelligible sentences came from. I preserved the following text as it was in the original. I can't show the letters themselves. They appear childlike, slow, and in their own way meticulous. But it was a senile hand writing them and so it's hard to decipher sometimes. Holiday cards are fairly easy, but this letter is much harder. I've been working on it for a long time and there are still spots left blank.

Dear granddaughter tank you very much for the letter
Alot you have written and it is good
Its worthwhile reading this columns as always
Im sick and so time of mine and life I live on
[here unintelligible] meet I can eat ground everything
As log as its soft all of that gives me
Hernia and no option is left but procedures
[here, he most likely says there is no other solution than the operation]
But I scared 85 years will pass
17/7 next year and my life for me
Brings nojoy because what I feel always
Pain –

And in 1958, around Easter, he wrote about that pain that accompanied him at all times: "Allpains me, such is my Life," and for Christmas it was much like that as well, "Sick I fallen, allpains me but what is there todo." In 1976 he confirms his suffering once again. And so, from his eternal pain, my great grandfather Skowroński, a widower after my great grandma was killed in Gaje, the only one of his family who escaped, God knows why, moves without a comma or a full stop directly to the story of his life; his post-war life that we knew nothing about. It seems he wanted to write it down, or maybe someone asked him to:

. . . I came to England it was 48 I was
in Germany in gulag then to America to
Kanada but for youth I waited in 48 England
Older [?] goto England I was 54yo
Worked on the farm 1y 1 year in kitchen
In Scotland from scotland I goto England here
I worked in textile in bakery in gasworks

Last I worked 5y in textile and
On wages becuse here you can work
65 years unless youre good then factory
Keeps you me they didnt want to let

I can put some meat on those bones, a little bit of everyday flesh, a piece of a single day and the usual hardships. He described them in his Easter card from 1976 and, somewhat strangely, everything seems to fit. On the one hand it's an endless wandering from country to country, from continent to continent, but on the other hand it's a life identical to that in other places where the rest of the family lived:

Dear Children and Gc and Ggc
Tank you for letters for pictures
Dont worry I dont write alot
To you but what will I
Write I'm alone have nothing
To write I reach my day
What is left I think is to die
That is all I dont interest
Myself in anything because there no need
Yesterday I was in the garden I planted
Potatoes broad beans and onion but here
Its cold a lot of wind when it
Gets warmer than I will sow spinach peas
Carrots if grow cabbage
Califlower beet roots lettuce
This interest me this is my
Everything I had letter from uncle
Wasyl so I dont write to nobody
Only to you I write and I think to

Help you because I have noone else
My head is [?] stomach
Will not stop such is my life

This is the end of the card. In the letter, on the other hand, the only letter that survived—that preserved his life's history—my great grandfather tells the story of how he retired and how he went to the hospital, but I can understand very little beyond its general sense. My grandma is long gone and can't read it for me. She was the one who knew all his letters and could put them together, and then distill some sense. *Mene, Mene, Tekel, Upharsin* she would say, although everyone saw in it only convoluted nonsense and she, like Daniel, kept explaining what those words meant. That's why my family was shocked, but also had their spirits raised because, even though the stories were full of sadness and written in a foreign language, our great grandfather lived in England, a dreamland, and, one way or another, it couldn't be that bad for him. The clothes that he'd send us sometimes, the clothes that were later repurposed into something more appropriate for us to wear, were the proof.

Later on in the letter there is a detailed list of all the financial misdeeds of different people, of different financial miseries, and, finally, my great grandfather writes:

. . . such fake peoples how many of mine [things]
Been lost on people they took all from my
Apartment kitchen bed sofa 2 dressers table
Knives forks kettle glass flask
25p lost all is lost I was here 7m
Not even but I suffer and dont say a thing
People I saw only fake
I live here for 13p becasue she lowered
[he meant that his landlady, his worst enemy, lowered his rent]

I payed 14p so it leaves 8p almost
[of his retirement]
I buy tobaco for 3p and some fruit somewhere
I buy busfare for 2 weeks bottle of vodka for 4f
I wash my underwear myself sometimes to 11
I have tv here sometimes I watch to 11 I go to sleep

And then follow more complaints about health and descriptions I'll keep for myself because I have no desire to share them. Finally, I read these words and I feel as if I hear my own grandparents speaking:

. . . I dont live just for myself
For you becasue I dont have no life no happiness

And right after that, there follows a general reflection about life. My great grandfather reports that fate was harsh not only to him. On the contrary, it was actually generous to him in a peculiar sort of way. It wasn't only the poverty and desolation, not only the "ruthlessness" of the surroundings, but also the madness that feasted on the minds of others:

And when I look at how many people gone mad or
They took life themselves Jarymowicz she 4y
Younger 10y he rests in the ground too
Lost his mind how much trouble I had before I
Always talked to him let God Father bless
I sent 11/14 70p to Sławka child
20p and rest divide between your children and grandchildren
. . . now I wait for you to write for those
Stockings and about the visit if I live for
Another [year] we [see] how is health / I end now

All the best to Kopiec Family to
All Friends and God Bless all
The best

When I lost my Roamer watch on the train in Romania, a gift from my great grandfather, I lost the only physical link between him and me. Now all I have is this letter and five holiday cards, his self-portrait as an old man. Not too many words, one longer letter—the only trace. It's worse than when I had nothing. Maybe in his other letters things weren't so glum, but in those cards—every sentence is misery. Although, I comfort myself, at least I have something left, so let it be. It's a written testimony where the history of life blends with the glass ampoules stolen from his kitchen, the cruelty of his surroundings, with him saving every penny to send back to the family. There are more questions than answers, but it seems that's how it has to be. Not a single word about his suspected visit to Cuba, which everyone knew about, though I don't know how they knew and I'll never learn. And one last thing: out of his life, which ended long ago—the life of a defeated man—came a blessing for my own. God Bless.

Wojciech Nowicki is a Polish essayist, journalist, critic, photographer, and even writes a culinary column. He is also the co-founder of the Imago Mundi Foundation devoted to promoting photography. *Salki* is his first book to be translated into English.

Jan Pytalski is a graduate of the American Studies Center at the University of Warsaw, and has an MA in Literary Translation from the University of Rochester.

**OPEN
LETTER**

Inga Ābele (Latvia)
  High Tide
Naja Marie Aidt (Denmark)
  Rock, Paper, Scissors
Esther Allen et al. (ed.) (World)
  *The Man Between: Michael Henry
  Heim & a Life in Translation*
Bae Suah (South Korea)
  A Greater Music
Svetislav Basara (Serbia)
  The Cyclist Conspiracy
Can Xue (China)
  Frontier
  Vertical Motion
Lúcio Cardoso (Brazil)
  Chronicle of the Murdered House
Sergio Chejfec (Argentina)
  The Dark
  My Two Worlds
  The Planets
Eduardo Chirinos (Peru)
  The Smoke of Distant Fires
Marguerite Duras (France)
  Abahn Sabana David
  L'Amour
  The Sailor from Gibraltar
Mathias Énard (France)
  Street of Thieves
  Zone
Macedonio Fernández (Argentina)
  The Museum of Eterna's Novel
Rubem Fonseca (Brazil)
  The Taker & Other Stories
Juan Gelman (Argentina)
  Dark Times Filled with Light
Georgi Gospodinov (Bulgaria)
  The Physics of Sorrow
Arnon Grunberg (Netherlands)
  Tirza

Hubert Haddad (France)
  *Rochester Knockings:
  A Novel of the Fox Sisters*
Gail Hareven (Israel)
  Lies, First Person
Angel Igov (Bulgaria)
  A Short Tale of Shame
Ilya Ilf & Evgeny Petrov (Russia)
  The Golden Calf
Zachary Karabashliev (Bulgaria)
  18% Gray
Jan Kjærstad (Norway)
  The Conqueror
  The Discoverer
Josefine Klougart (Denmark)
  One of Us Is Sleeping
Carlos Labbé (Chile)
  Loquela
  Navidad & Matanza
Jakov Lind (Austria)
  Ergo
  Landscape in Concrete
Andreas Maier (Germany)
  Klausen
Lucio Mariani (Italy)
  Traces of Time
Amanda Michalopoulou (Greece)
  Why I Killed My Best Friend
Valerie Miles (World)
  *A Thousand Forests in One Acorn:
  An Anthology of Spanish-
  Language Fiction*
Iben Mondrup (Denmark)
  Justine
Quim Monzó (Catalonia)
  Gasoline
  Guadalajara
  A Thousand Morons

**OPEN
LETTER**